COTTAGE BY THE SEA

Center Point
Large Print

Also by Robin Jones Gunn and available from Center Point Large Print:

Under a Maui Moon
Canary Island Song

**This Large Print Book carries the
Seal of Approval of N.A.V.H.**

COTTAGE BY THE SEA

ROBIN JONES GUNN

CENTER POINT LARGE PRINT
THORNDIKE, MAINE

12/12
center
point
LP
Gun

This Center Point Large Print edition
is published in the year 2012 by arrangement with
Howard Books, a division of Simon & Schuster, Inc.

This book is a work of fiction. Names, characters, places,
and incidents either are products of the author's imagination
or are used fictitiously. Any resemblance to actual events or
locales or persons, living or dead, is entirely coincidental.

Unless specified otherwise, all Scripture quotations are from
THE HOLY BIBLE, NEW INTERNATIONAL VERSION®,
NIV® Copyright © 1973, 1978, 1984, 2011 by Biblica,
Inc.™ Used by permission. All rights reserved worldwide.
Scripture quotations marked NKJV are taken from the New
King James Version. Copyright © 1979, 1980, 1982 by
Thomas Nelson, Inc. Used by permission. All rights reserved.

The text of this Large Print edition is unabridged.
In other aspects, this book may vary from the original
edition. Printed in the United States of America on
permanent paper. Set in 16-point Times New Roman type.

ISBN: 978-1-61173-544-4

Library of Congress Cataloging-in-Publication Data

Gunn, Robin Jones, 1955–
Cottage by the sea / Robin Jones Gunn.
pages ; cm.
ISBN 978-1-61173-544-4 (library binding : alk. paper)
1. Large type books. I. Title.
PS3557.U4866C68 2012b
813′.54—dc23

2012010332

For my dad, who taught in the Irvine School District from 1959 to 1989. And for my mom, who lovingly and faithfully cared for him at home for five and a half years after he suffered a stroke in 1996 that paralyzed his right side and took his speech. I can't wait to see you again in heaven, Daddy.

I will give you the treasures of darkness, riches in secret places, so that you may know that I am the LORD, the God of Israel, who calls you by name.

—ISAIAH 45:3 NKJV

COTTAGE BY THE SEA

1

May you always have work for your hands to do.
May your pockets hold always a coin or two.
May the sun shine bright on your windowpane.
May the rainbow be certain to follow each rain.
May the hand of a friend always be near you.
And may God fill your heart with
gladness to cheer you.

Erin Bryce pulled up her russet-colored hair in a clip and followed her husband out to the driveway of their Southern California, ranch-style home. For as many years as she could remember this had been their Monday morning routine. She would give him a kiss, and he would respond with an affectionate pat on her narrow backside. Mike would then put on his sunglasses and drive off to work in Irvine while Erin went for a brisk walk around the lake that centered their neighborhood like a well-set opal.

This Monday, however, instead of walking shoes Erin's feet flaunted their new kitten-heeled sandals. In place of her workout clothes she wore her favorite floral sundress with a matching spring green sweater that turned her eyes the shade of clover.

"Big day for you," Mike said as he climbed into his car.

"Yes. Yes, it is."

"You and Sharlene have waited a long time for this."

"Yes, we have." Erin leaned over and gave Mike another kiss.

"Go get 'em, Tiger." His grin infused her with just the right amount of confidence to quell the flutters in her stomach.

"Love you."

"Love you, too."

Erin waved as Mike drove off, and then she turned to face her own front door. Drawing back her shoulders, as her mother had always told her to do, Erin strode forward. She liked the sound of her heels clicking on the front walkway. She liked even more that the moment she stepped inside she would be at work. No more morning commute. Her new home office was now open for business.

I should find some ribbon and loop it across the entry. That way, when Sharlene arrives, we can have a ribbon-cutting ceremony.

Erin went on a quick search through the box of gift wrap in the hall closet. The best she came up with was a few feet of red-and-gold-plaid ribbon left over from Christmas. Not exactly what she had in mind. Before she managed to stuff the box of gift wrap and bows back into the closet, the cell phone she had left on her new desk in the front bedroom rang. Her heart did a little jig.

This is it! Our first call! I wish Sharlene were here for this.

Erin hurried to the bedroom that had been transformed into her new home office and picked up the call on the third ring. "Good morning. The Happiest Day, this is Erin."

A booming female voice came through the line. "Do you have patio umbrellas?"

Erin pulled the phone away from her ear and switched it to speaker. "Ah, well, we work with a number of companies that can provide canopies."

"Canopies? No. I'm looking for an umbrella. A patio umbrella."

"Actually, most of the wedding locations in the area recommend canopies as a better solution—"

"Wedding locations? Who said anything about a wedding? I'm trying to find an umbrella for my dog."

"For your dog?"

"You know, for when he's outside." The voice on the other end paused a moment and then asked, "This is Patio Galaxy, isn't it?"

Erin lowered herself into the desk chair. "No, this is not Patio Galaxy. This is The Happiest Day. We assist with wedding planning."

"Well, that's not what I'm looking for." The

confused caller paused. "Unless . . . do you also have one of those services that matches folks up with their soul mate?"

"No, we don't offer that sort of service."

The doorbell rang just as the disgruntled woman hung up.

Erin hurried back to the front door and opened it to see her business partner up to her chin with a stack of boxes. Petite Sharlene wore her jet-black hair short and feathery around her face. She always reminded Erin of a ruffled bird, ready to flit off somewhere. Sharlene had somehow managed to balance two grande lattes on the very top box.

"Quick! Grab the coffee." Sharlene looked up at Erin over the top of her stylish blue-and-green-rimmed glasses. "The one on the right is yours."

Erin took both lattes and with her foot kept the door open for Sharlene.

"Guess what we have?" Sharlene sang out, as she made a beeline for the office.

"I hope it's our brochures."

"You guessed it. But these are not just our brochures, Erin. These are our beee-u-ti-ful brochures. Look!"

Erin put the lattes on the desk and took one of the trifold brochures from the top box. "Oh, nice! Yes. This is exactly what we wanted. I love how you changed it and put the gazebo in the right corner. Very nice." She unfolded the brochure and scanned all the text she had labored over for days. With each line she read, Erin bobbed her head. "Perfect. Just what we wanted."

"I'm thrilled with how they turned out." Sharlene placed the boxes of brochures in the corner, stacking them neatly against the wall. "Did you stay up till midnight to see our website go live?"

"No. I checked it when I woke up this morning. It looks great, too."

"I found a few glitches on the floral page. Two of the links didn't click through. I already let Jim know. Everything else loaded beautifully." Sharlene took a seat in the chair beside the desk and reached for her latte. "You know what this means, don't you? We are official, Erin. This is it! We are open for business!"

Erin picked up her latte and took the chair at the desk. "I tried to find a ribbon to drape across the front door before you got here."

"Why?"

"So we could have a ribbon-cutting ceremony."

Sharlene laughed. "How about a toast instead? Here's to us and to all our hard work. May The Happiest Day be wildly successful."

"Yes and amen." Erin lifted her latte, and the two friends toasted with a dull *fwap* of their waxed cardboard cups. Before taking a sip Erin added, "Wait. I have a blessing for us. I found this verse in my mom's diary." Erin reached for a tattered journal on the corner of the desk and removed the bookmark she had placed in it two days ago. "This is what my mom wrote on February 24, 1988."

"February 24? That was just a couple of days ago."

"I know. That's why I marked it so I'd remember to read it to you. 'May the favor of the Lord our God rest upon us; establish the work of our hands for us—yes, establish the work of our hands. Psalm 90:17.' "

"It's our very own blessing."

"Exactly. That's what I thought." Erin lifted her coffee cup and repeated, " 'May the favor of the Lord our God rest upon us' and 'establish the work of our hands.' "

"Hear, hear! Cheers to that." Sharlene took a quick sip. "Your mom would have been proud of you, of us, wouldn't she? She would think what we're doing is a good thing."

Erin smiled. "Yes. Absolutely. My mother would have been very proud of us. She also would have loved being a part of what we're doing. I was missing her this morning when I was making breakfast. She always used to use a heart-shaped cookie cutter on our toast or pancakes on mornings that were special days like our birthdays. I was wishing I had a cookie cutter this morning to make some heart-shaped toast to celebrate."

"Why didn't you use a knife? You could have cut out a heart in your toast with a knife."

"I suppose. It wouldn't be the same, though."

Sharlene gave Erin a sympathetic gaze. "I'm sorry you lost your mom when you did. She left this earth too soon, that's for sure. I wish I could have met her."

"I wish you could have met her, too."

The two women sipped their coffees for a moment in quiet contemplation. Their first heart-to-heart conversation had taken place over lattes two and a half years ago. That meeting also was punctuated with comfortable moments of silence; something they both knew was unusual in a friendship, especially with someone you had just met.

Their meeting happened while the two of them were sitting in neighboring chairs at a hair salon. An offhand comment led them to discover they were both working in the bridal industry and knew a lot of the same people. They had even heard of each other, but their paths hadn't crossed. Sharlene supervised the alterations side of the dry-cleaning business she and her husband owned. Their Corona del Mar location had become known as the best place for quick, expert alterations for wedding gowns and bridesmaids' dresses. The chain of four dry-cleaning stores had earned the reputation of being the best place to take a gown for cleaning and proper boxing after the big day.

Erin, who worked as an assistant wedding

coordinator at a hotel in Newport Beach, had often sent brides to Sharlene for both alterations and storage of their gowns.

After chatting with ease during their hair appointment, Erin and Sharlene spontaneously decided to go next door to Café Kate. That wasn't something Erin normally would do, but the charm of their friendship had become clear in the salon. They were two old friends who just hadn't met yet. And they needed each other.

Erin knew she had closed up parts of her life for almost a year since the death of her mother. She had lost her closest confidant and gentlest friend. Having a mom like that, who also happened to live close by, meant Erin had never invested a lot of time developing close friendships with other women. She hadn't realized what a gap that would make in her adult life until her mother was gone.

Sharlene arrived like a gust of fresh spring air, and Erin eagerly opened up the windows of her heart to let the friendship come in. Sharlene told Erin that she had been too busy for too many years to take time to cultivate a friendship. Now that her daughters were out of the house, she, too, was ready to embrace the next season of her life. She just didn't realize how much she needed a close friend to join her on the journey.

These were the poignant topics they shared the first time they sipped coffee at Café Kate. They left feeling energized and made plans to meet again the next week. The fourth time they gathered Sharlene asked the question that changed the future for both of them. "Have you ever thought about starting your own business? Something in the bridal industry?"

"Yes," Erin replied without hesitation. "Have you?"

Sharlene's dark eyes glowed like polished obsidian. She started her next sentence with "As a matter of fact," and right then and there the vision for The Happiest Day was born.

Two and half years later, here they were, sitting in Erin's home office, sipping vanilla lattes on the morning of their grand opening. The dream had become a reality, and the friendship remained strong.

"Oh, I almost forgot to tell you," Erin said. "We had our first call right before you got here."

"Really? And?"

"The woman thought we were Patio Galaxy. She was looking for an umbrella."

"Why did she think we were Patio Galaxy?"

"I have no idea."

Sharlene frowned. "That's a bad sign. My grandmother would have said it's a bad omen, and then she would have spit at something."

"Please don't spit in our new office."

"Okay. Fine. I'll wait until I go outside for the rest of the brochure boxes in my car. Check to see if our new business phone number is close to the number for Patio Galaxy."

Erin did a quick search online and pointed to the computer screen. "Yup. Their number ends with an eight, and we're a nine."

Sharlene hopped up to view the computer screen. "Are you kidding me?"

"It's too late to change it. We just had our number printed on our cards and all the brochures."

"I can't believe this."

Erin rounded her shoulders back. "It could be worse. We could be one number off from the IRS or traffic court and have people screaming at us when we answer with 'The Happiest Day.'"

Sharlene laughed. "You are ever the sunshine girl, aren't you, Erin? Nothing ever gets you down."

Erin knew that wasn't true. She had had plenty of dark seasons. This just didn't happen to be one of them. This was a springtime season in her life, and she intended to enjoy every buttercup moment.

With an overly cheerful lilt in her voice, Erin playfully said, "Maybe we could find a way to cross-promote to future callers from Patio Galaxy. What do you think? If they call asking about ropes for hammocks, we could ask if they're thinking about tying the knot."

Sharlene groaned.

"Or how about if someone calls about wind chimes? We'll ask if they're hearing wedding bells."

"You can stop any time now." Sharlene stood and headed for the door. "I'm going to bring in the rest of the brochures."

"Ooo! Wait!" Erin called out. "I have an idea. A good idea."

"I'm sure you do." Sharlene didn't wait to hear what Erin had to say.

Picking up the phone, Erin called Patio Galaxy and asked to speak to the senior manager. After explaining who she was and how their company connected brides with all the services necessary to create "the happiest day," she asked, "I'm wondering if you rent patio furniture. You see, we have a number of outdoor wedding locations that are ideal for a staged seating area at the reception."

"Are you referring to our open-air living room furniture? We have a line of luxury padded couches and chairs."

"Yes, that's exactly what I'm interested in. We would send couples to you to rent whatever groupings you offer. And I think we also would have couples interested in renting outdoor lighting such as tiki torches or hanging lanterns."

The manager paused on the other end of the phone before saying, "We've not done this before. We're not a rental service. But, you know, it's not a bad idea. Let me talk to the powers-that-be and get back to you."

Erin gave him her contact information and was wearing a satisfied grin when Sharlene returned.

"What did I miss?"

"A possible new agreement in the works with . . ." Erin leisurely rolled out the rest of the sentence. "Patio Galaxy."

"Are you kidding me? Just now? You called them?"

Erin started to give Sharlene the update, but the phone rang before she finished. The two friends paused and both stared at the phone as it played its "Here Comes the Bride" ring tone.

"You get it this time," Erin said.

"No, you. It might be Patio Galaxy calling you back."

"Or it could be someone else looking for Patio Galaxy."

"Just answer it! Put it on speaker."

Erin cleared her throat and pushed the button. "Good morning. The Happiest Day, this is Erin."

A woman's voice said, "Hi. I wanted to see if you have any openings."

Erin and Sharlene exchanged apprehensive glances. Sharlene whispered, "Openings for a job?"

"For what sort of openings were you looking?" Erin asked.

"I wanted to see if you had openings for new clients."

Sharlene made a victory clench with her fist and mouthed the word "Yes!"

"Absolutely. We have openings for new clients. When is your wedding date?"

"I'm getting married in May. I saw on your website that you recommend a lead time of nine months, but my fiancé is in the military, and he's being deployed the first of June. We want to get married before he leaves."

Erin placed her hand over her heart, touched by the tenderness in the young woman's voice. "We would be honored to help you to make arrangements for your happiest day."

Sharlene sat in the chair and leaned in closer.

"I understand the way this works is I meet with you and tell you what we have in mind for our wedding, and then you put together a list of the best location and florist and all that."

"Exactly. Think of us as your personal shopper," Erin said.

"My fiancé said you're like a broker."

Sharlene made an exaggerated frown.

"I suppose that's another way of viewing what we do. However, you don't pay us anything. Our commission comes from the businesses you decide to use as a result of our recommendation. The best part for you is that many of our partner merchants have offered exclusive discounts to our clients."

Sharlene gave Erin another affirming nod.

Those selling points were the ones they had rehearsed at a recent small business workshop. After practicing client phone calls with each other, they were now actually talking to a "live one."

"I saw that on your website, too. I know you're going to save me hundreds of hours because I'm not good at organizing things. Is there any chance you're available to meet this morning?"

Erin looked at Sharlene, who was nodding vigorously. "Sure. This morning would be fine. Did you see the list of suggested meeting locations on the website?"

"Yes. Could we meet at Café Kate? It's only a few miles from my apartment. And are you available to meet there around ten? I know this is last minute."

"Ten o'clock would be fine." Erin was trying to keep sounding professional. It was challenging because Sharlene had jumped up and now had her hands on Erin's shoulders and was shaking her back and forth with glee over their first official appointment.

"I'm easy to spot," Erin said. "My picture is on the website. I'm the tall one with the red hair."

"I have blond hair, and I'll be wearing a jeans jacket."

"Okay, ten o'clock at Café Kate. See you then." Erin pressed the End button on the phone and turned to Sharlene with an exultant smile and both arms victoriously lifted in the air. "We are in business!"

"Yes, we are! Come on! Happy dance."

Erin stood, and together they did a wiggly, gleeful jig that ended in a hug. Erin always felt awkward hugging Sharlene because of their height difference. She didn't feel too tall around Sharlene in everyday interactions. When they sat together, they always seemed to be eye to eye. But at moments like this Erin realized how much she towered over her demure business partner. Sharlene commented on her stature often, saying, "It's my Sicilian genes. I may be short but watch out! I have just enough Gypsy blood in me to be dangerous."

"Where's your new briefcase?" Sharlene headed over to the assembly table that ran the length of the wall. Everything needed to put together a personalized presentation portfolio was neatly organized in boxes under the table and in the closet.

Erin went to the closet and pulled out her "briefcase," a fabulous, designer shoulder bag crafted of soft, buttery caramel leather with a front kangaroo pouch and shiny gold buckles. Sharlene had come across the beautiful bag months ago on a clearance table at an outlet mall. She declared it to be their official briefcase since it would make them look classy when they showed up at meetings.

This was the little stunner's maiden voyage.

"Make sure you have extra business cards with you. And here—extra brochures. You have the Getting to Know You forms in there along with the contract. Can you think of anything else you'll need?"

"No, that should do it."

"Okay, then. Off you go. Time to make history with our first client." Sharlene paused. "What's her name?"

Erin froze. Her eyes widened. "I don't know."

"Are you kidding me? How did we miss that? Here." Sharlene pulled one of the sticky notes from the dispenser on the desk's corner. "I'm putting this note by the phone. ALWAYS ASK THEIR NAME."

"Good idea. And hand me the phone, will you? I want to copy down her phone number."

"Right. Good. Phone numbers. We should know this stuff. These are basics. Basics!"

"It's okay. Don't worry. We'll work out all the glitches, Shar."

"I'm not worried." Her expression said otherwise.

Erin glanced at her watch. If she left now, she would be early. But early was good. She was too excited to stay in the office. Just as she was about to exit the door to the garage, her home phone rang.

"Do you want me to get that?" Sharlene called out.

"Yes, could you? Thanks! Take a message for me, or if it's one of my sons, tell him to call my cell." Erin pushed the garage door button on the wall, opened her car door, and tossed the new briefcase onto the passenger's seat.

Erin was just about to slip into the driver's seat when Sharlene yanked open the kitchen door and came toward Erin with the phone next to her ear and an unpleasant expression on her face. She still was speaking to whoever was on the line. "Yes, can you hold on just a minute? I'm sorry. Just one second."

"Who is it?" Erin asked.

Covering the mouthpiece Sharlene whispered, "It's Delores. She thought I was you. Erin, I'm so, so sorry."

Erin felt her skin bristle. Her father's new wife was the last person she wanted to speak to right now. She wished she hadn't told Sharlene to pick up the call; it could have rolled over into voice mail.

Erin reached for the phone and took note of Sharlene's shaken expression. It seemed strange for Sharlene to wear such a scowl since she had never met Delores or even spoken with her. But the abrasive woman did have that sort of souring-in-the-stomach effect on people.

"Delores?"

"Erin? Where did you go? I thought the signal dropped. Did you hear what I said?"

"No, I'm sorry. What did you say?"

"Your father has had a stroke."

Every molecule in Erin's being seemed to come to a screeching halt.

2

May God grant you many years to live,
For sure he must be knowing.
The earth has angels all too few,
And heaven is overflowing.

Erin caught her breath. "What happened, Delores? Is he okay?"

"Here. He wants to talk to you. Jack? It's Erin. She wants to talk to you."

"Hello?"

The familiar voice filled Erin's ear, sounding the same as always—a little gruff, a little sad. Erin released the air in her tightened chest. "Hey, Dad. Hi. How are you? Are you okay?"

"Fine. Fine, fine. How are you?" His words came out abrupt but with a slight slur.

"I'm good. But what about you? Delores said you had a stroke. Are you feeling better?"

"Yes!" He yelled into the phone so loud that Erin jumped.

"Okay. Well, that's good. Can you tell me what happened?"

"It . . . I'm . . . it . . . the . . . aaa . . ."

"Dad?"

No reply.

"Dad?"

"What?" He shouted his response, and that frightened her even more.

"Dad, are you sure you're okay? You're not making sense."

"Fine. Fine."

"Dad, let me talk to Delores."

"Why?"

"I want to ask her a few things."

"You hate her!"

Erin blinked and tried to form a sentence. She knew in her gut that something was really wrong. Her father had always been direct, but in the year and a half since he had married Delores, none of them had spoken the raw truth about how Erin and Delores viewed each other.

Erin tried to control her tone, but her voice wobbled. "No, Dad, I don't hate Delores. I just need to talk to her for a minute."

Sharlene stepped closer and placed her hand on Erin's arm in a gesture of concern. Sharlene was the only friend to whom Erin had confided her feelings about her seventy-year-old father marrying a fifty-three-year-old woman he had known for only two months. To everyone other than Sharlene and Mike, Erin had defended her father's decision, saying that perhaps Delores was just the person to bring back the sparkle that had faded from his baby blues since Erin's mother had died.

Erin didn't have the chance to watch for that returning sparkle because only a few days after her father surprised them all with the announcement that he had gotten married, he made a second stunning announcement. He and Delores were moving to a seaside cottage in a small coastal town in Oregon. Erin hadn't seen her father since his abrupt move eighteen months ago and had talked to him only a handful of times.

"Erin? You wanted to talk to me?" Delores's voice sounded as gruff as her father's had.

"What are the doctors telling you? Is he okay? He doesn't sound coherent."

"He hasn't seen a doctor yet. They're backed up at the clinic. I told the admitting nurse that I think he's had a stroke."

"You're at a clinic?"

"Jack wanted to come here. It's a twenty-four-hour emergency clinic."

Erin rubbed the back of her neck and paced the small space between the door into the kitchen and her car. "Delores, don't you think he should be looked at by a doctor at a hospital and not just at a clinic?"

"That's not what your father wants." Delores's words were firm. "He told me to bring him here."

"But, Delores, he doesn't seem to be communicating clearly. It sounds like he needs to be seen by a doctor at an emergency room."

"I wasn't calling to get your advice, Erin. I called because your father wanted to talk to you."

Erin reeled at Delores's snappy response. It took Erin only a moment to reply with equal verve. "He needs to get to a hospital. You need to take him to the hospital now."

"He doesn't want to go to a hospital, do you, Jack?"

Erin couldn't hear any reply from her father in the background. Her heart was pounding wildly. "Delores?" Erin paused. What she was about to say made her feel sick to her stomach. "I'm coming up there."

"Why would you do that? There's no need for you to come."

"I think there is a need. I'll come as soon as I can. Please tell my dad that I'm coming to see him."

Delores didn't reply.

"Delores?"

"You don't need to come, Erin. Are you trying to pressure me to take him to the hospital? Is that it? Is that why you think you need to come? Because I'm telling you right now the doctor at the hospital will say the same thing the doctor here is going to say. Your father has had a stroke, and he needs to go home and rest."

Erin wanted to scream. She switched the phone to her other ear and with firm, authoritative words she said, "Delores, please take my father to the hospital. Now."

Delores paused. "All right. Fine. I'm telling you now, it's not going to make any difference. There's nothing they can do for him."

"Please call me as soon as you have any news from the hospital. You have my cell phone number, don't you?"

"I have no idea."

Erin gave Delores her cell number as well as Mike's cell and asked her again to please call as soon as they had any further information.

When Erin hung up, her hands were shaking. Sharlene stood close by and asked, "You okay?"

"How can that woman be so uncaring? I don't understand. My father sounded completely off balance, Shar. He is not okay." Erin felt tears pool in her eyes. "I told her I was going up there. I don't know what to do."

Sharlene stretched her arm around Erin's middle and gave her a comforting hug. "Why don't you call Mike and let him know what's going on? I'll go to meet with our client. If you need to be with your dad, then that's what you should do. I can take care of everything here. Don't worry about any of the business details. Your dad is your priority right now."

A surge of anger replaced the stunned concern

Erin had felt during the call. She narrowed her eyes and felt her jaw clench. "I just don't understand why she didn't take him to the hospital right away. He never should have left Irvine. This is his home. If this had happened while he was here, he would be in much better shape right now."

"Your father is a strong man," Sharlene said. "If anyone can pull through this, he can."

"You're right, he is a strong man. Strong and determined. My father left Ireland when he was seventeen years old and put himself through college. He was the first teacher in the Irvine school district. Did I ever tell you that? This whole area was nothing but bean fields and strawberry fields when he and my mom moved here. The Irvine Ranch had one tiny school for all the farmworkers' children, and my father was their teacher."

"I never knew that." Sharlene held open the kitchen door.

Erin walked back inside, her thoughts racing furiously. "My father taught for the Irvine school district for forty-seven years. Do you know anyone anywhere who has done that? Been a teacher for forty-seven years? And when he retired, there was nothing. No thank-you. No letter of appreciation. And look at Irvine now. Half a century after the bean fields, it's nothing but rows of houses as far as you can see."

Erin stopped by the kitchen counter. She felt her face burning as a molten topic overflowed from her erupting heart. "When my father left Irvine, he told me that after my mom died, there was nothing here for him anymore." A tumble of tears choked her words. "Nothing here for him. Nothing at all. That's what he said."

Erin lowered her voice and added the final, painful truth. "But the thing is, I'm still here. And I'm not nothing."

She let the tears fall. There it was: the soul wound that hadn't healed in the eighteen months since his departure. Her father chose to marry a woman who was nothing like Erin's mom, and then he moved a thousand miles away, preferring Delores's company over the familiarity and proximity of Mike and Erin.

Sharlene reached for a paper towel next to the kitchen sink and offered it to Erin for her tumble of tears.

"I can't believe I'm saying all this."

"It's okay. It's better to get it all out now."

"Shar, we promised we would take care of him. Mike and I promised that to my mother. So how are we supposed to do that when he's so far away and his *wife* won't even take him to the hospital?" Erin dabbed away her tears with a rounded edge of the rough paper towel and answered her own question. "I guess this is how we do it. I get on an airplane and go to him in Oregon."

"You're right. That's what you should do."

Erin blew her nose and drew in a wobbly breath. Gathering her thoughts, she said, "I need to call Mike."

"Are you sure you're okay?" Sharlene asked.

"I will be. Are you okay with meeting our client at Café Kate?"

"Yes, of course." Sharlene gave Erin a side hug. "Call me if you need anything. I'll be back in a little while."

Over the next few hours Erin managed to book a four o'clock flight, pack a bag, and leave her supportive husband a love note on his bedroom pillow. Mike had immediately agreed with her assessment when she had called him. Even if her father was okay, which Mike said he doubted, he thought Erin should be there to help to decide if further steps needed to be taken.

Sharlene returned with a great report of her meeting with their first client and offered to drive Erin to the airport so Mike wouldn't have to leave work to take her. By two thirty Sharlene and Erin were headed for John Wayne Airport. A light rain splattered against the windshield.

"Did you pack warm clothes?"

"Yes. I'm sure I overpacked. I don't know how long I'll be there. I hope only a few days. Call me if you need anything, anything at all."

"I will. But don't worry. I'm sure everything will be fine here."

"This is the worst possible time for this to happen."

"I know."

Even though Erin understood that her reasoning was out of whack, she felt angry that the long-awaited day of the opening of their business had been hijacked by this emergency. She hated that she was thinking such a thing. It wasn't her dad's fault. Yet as much as she tried to adjust her feelings, her attempts to summon up gracious thoughts weren't working. The anger she felt lingered through the check-in process and through security. She headed to her boarding gate with jaw-set determination.

Just as Erin's flight boarded, her cell phone rang. It was Delores. She sounded much more amiable than she had that morning.

"We're still at the hospital. You wanted me to call you as soon as I had an update. They ran some tests. Your father had an ischemic stroke."

Erin wasn't sure what that meant.

"The doctor said this could be an isolated incident or a prelude to more of the same. They weren't able to see any more blood clots, but that doesn't mean others aren't hiding. The doctor did tell me that the best time to run the test is within three hours after the first symptom appears. He said it was good that we came in when we did. You were right about that, Erin."

Delores's small accolade acted like a tiny pin that poked a hole in the inflated anger Erin had been carrying with her. She could feel the fury dissipate with a hiss. "How is he feeling?"

"Better. He said he's better and not to worry about him."

"Delores, did you get my message? I called earlier and . . ."

"Yes, I listened to your message."

"So you know that I'm coming up there."

"Yes."

"I'll rent a car, and I made reservations at a hotel near the hospital."

"You can cancel the hotel. Just stay at our place."

"Are you sure?" Erin tried to evaluate Delores's spurt of hospitality.

"Of course you can stay with us. Unless you would rather not."

"No, that's fine. Thanks for the invitation. Did they give you an idea of how long my dad would stay at the hospital?"

"The doctor is sending Jack home now. He put him on blood thinner and told him to go home and get some rest. I have a list of symptoms to watch for. Bad headaches, shortness of breath—"

"Delores, sorry to interrupt you, but my flight is boarding."

"Do you know how to get to our place?"

"Yes, I've got it."

"I'll leave the floodlight on above the garage, so that should help you find us. Just remember it's a gravel road from the highway to our place, so slow down as soon as you make the turn."

"Okay. I'll see you later tonight." Erin found her seat, stowed her carry-on, and closed her eyes, hoping her seat companion wasn't in a chatty mood.

She couldn't quite figure out what to make of Delores's responses. Was it fear that had made Delores so abrupt and aggressive in her earlier phone call? The news about Erin's dad wasn't good. He had experienced a stroke. But maybe all he needed was the medications the doctor had started him on. Maybe that would be enough to resolve the problems he had encountered.

Erin wondered if she had been too hasty in deciding to go to Oregon. No one had asked her to come. There wasn't anything she could do. She really needed to be home, working with Sharlene.

The slow-burning, teeth-clenching anger she had felt earlier returned and seemed to be sitting on her lap in the narrow airplane seat. Earlier all the anger was focused on Delores and her father for marrying Delores and moving so far away. This time she didn't know who to be mad at. Delores was as much at the mercy of her father's condition as Erin was. She knew her father had the right to choose to live his life the way he wanted, and if he chose to marry Delores and move to Oregon, that was his decision. Erin shouldn't disapprove of his behavior when what he wanted was to live his life this way. When it came to her anger over his having a stroke, Erin knew he obviously had no control over the rogue blood clots that had made their way to his brain stem.

Why am I so angry?

For a moment, Erin wanted to blame Mike for her angst. He could have talked her out of going. He could have told her to wait for the medical update. But he didn't. He urged her to go right away.

In the end, Erin chose to blame herself. She was the one who had given way to her emotions. She had taken on the role of mother. Now that her own mother was gone, more than once Erin had fallen into trying to fix everything for everybody. She couldn't fix this, not a stroke.

As the plane lifted off the runway, Erin remembered something her mother had written in her journal.

It's not always about what I think it's about. The older I get, the more convinced I am that God has a hidden objective tucked into every disagreeable situation I encounter. If only I would collect those sparkling gems of truth while I'm in the midst of each difficult relationship or experience, I'd leave this earth a wise and spiritually wealthy woman.

Erin reclined her seat. She felt lighter. That was often the way she felt when she drew a cool sip from the fount of her mother's journals. The words her mother left behind were words from her heart, and they still touched Erin deeply.

Faith O'Riley had indeed left this earth a wise and spiritually wealthy woman. Erin could only hope the same would be said of her. Oh, how she wished her mother were here now.

3

May you have warm words on a cold evening,
A full moon on a dark night,
And the road downhill all the way to your door.

As the plane landed in Portland, Erin wondered if she should call Delores to let her know where she was. Opting to get on the road before she called again, she picked up her suitcase at baggage claim and followed the signs to the car rental shuttle.

The air felt icy and damp when Erin exited the shuttle at the rental lot and made her way down the row of cars to space B-15, where she found her red compact. The trunk was nice and roomy, and the car had only 1,783 miles on it, so the new-car scent lingered.

As soon as Erin entered her destination into the GPS on the dashboard, hail pinged across her windshield. She wanted to retrace her steps to the airport shuttle and take the first flight home to her comfortable surroundings in sunny California.

For the first five or so miles, the traffic inched

along as the hail turned to slush and came at her small car on great gusts of wild wind. Erin couldn't believe anyone would want to live in a place like this. The fog closed in around her as she headed south, and the traffic systematically siphoned off at each subsequent off-ramp.

She pulled out her cell phone, dialed Mike's number, set the phone on speaker, and placed it on the dashboard.

"I was just about to call you," Mike said when he answered. "How was the flight?"

"Fine. No problems. The weather is horrible here, though. Hail and sleet. It's freezing. I'm so glad I brought my old ski jacket. This is really terrible weather for driving."

"Do you need to stay there in Portland for the night?"

"No, I'm okay. I'm going to take it nice and slow."

"I don't want to distract you while you're driving. Why don't you call me back when it's easier for you to talk?"

Erin agreed and continued down the freeway past towering evergreens whose tops were now obscured by the brooding gray clouds. She fiddled with the radio dial and listened to classical music for nearly an hour as she tried to think through what she would say and do once she was with her dad and Delores. During the flight, her feelings of wishing she hadn't come slowly gave way to a quieting of her soul. Like her mother, she wanted to find the hidden agenda God most likely had tucked into this trip. Secretly, she hoped the gem she was supposed to search for had nothing to do with Delores. She hoped the treasure would be in her reconnecting with her dad. More than anything, she prayed he would be okay.

For a long stretch, the view on either side of the freeway was of open fields partially obscured under a blanket of fog. By the time she turned off the freeway and headed west for the coast, she felt it was safe enough to put her phone on speaker and call Mike back.

"How's the traffic?" His familiar voice filled the car and instantly gave her a sense of comfort.

"No more traffic now. I'm out in the country."

"How much farther do you have to drive?"

"According to this GPS system, the distance to my destination is sixty-two miles."

"That's farther than I thought."

"Me too. It'll probably take me at least two more hours to get there since I'm driving so slowly. I've never driven in weather like this."

"Should I let you go so you can concentrate on the road?"

"No, don't go. I can use the company. I'm not distracted. Just talk to me. How was your day?"

Mike gave her a rundown of his less-than-exciting day full of meetings and phone calls at Pure Sight, a company in Irvine that manufactured contact lens solution. For the past seven years Mike had been an associate VP in the Research and Development Department. He told her about the strawberry cheesecake they had in the lunch-room that day for one of the employees' birthdays and chatted about other random office news.

Erin drove through what was now a fine mist and peered out at hills heavy with timber. She tried to describe the surroundings to Mike just as the fog broke in the west and allowed the last streaks of silvery winter light to illuminate the world around her.

"You should see this, Mike. It's like Narnia. I'm driving through the forest primeval, and the light is hitting the trees just right. Every branch looks as if it has been decorated with strings of crystal beads. It's extraordinary."

"I'd like to see that part of the country someday."

"This is really beautiful."

Within a few minutes the last trace of sunlight was gone and so was the glittery ice that clung to the branches. "It's dark now," Erin told Mike. "All the enchantment is gone."

"I'm glad you got to enjoy it while it was still light. I hope you don't have too far to go in the dark. Are you going to stop for some dinner?"

"No, I'm not hungry. What about you? Have you had dinner yet? I don't think we have much in the refrigerator."

They talked another ten minutes before signing off with their usual "Love you."

"Love you, too."

Erin drove on through the darkness, thinking about how great things were between Mike and her. She loved him more than ever.

Their relationship hadn't always been like this. Nearly fifteen years ago Mike had gone into a lingering depression after the sudden death of his twin brother followed by being laid off. For at least three years Mike struggled uphill every day to work through the losses. Many days Erin felt like a single mom, as she raised their three sons without hands-on support from Mike. He found a new job, but that one lasted only five months, and then he was laid off, which dipped him into an even deeper depression.

Erin's closest girlfriend back in that season of life had watched her go through the tough time day after day, month after month, and finally spoke her mind. "You should leave him. He's not going to change. You're doing everything for him and for the boys. It's like you're a single mom to four children."

Erin found it easy to let her friend feel sorry for her. She spent more than one lonely night con-templating her friend's advice, which unfolded along the lines of "I'm not saying divorce him right away. You could just move out and file for a separation. At least that way Mike will know he has to shake off this depression and take responsibility if he wants to see the boys. And if he wants you back, let him fight for you."

Erin knew Mike had no fight left in his bones. But she also found she had little life left in her spirit. She wanted someone to take care of her for a change.

In a brave move, Erin put aside her pride and went to her mother, seeking some heart-healing advice. She and her mom had always gotten along well. But they weren't confidants during Erin's early married years. Because of a variety of normal tiffs most mothers and daughters have over how to keep a house or raise children, Erin had pulled back from sharing anything with her mother more personal than the everyday surface topics.

When Erin went to her mother with all the broken pieces of her marriage, she didn't hold back. She confided the depth of her exhaustion in her seemingly hopeless, loveless relationship with Mike. Then she admitted that she had been contemplating a separation. Her justification was that it would give them space to work through the difficult time.

Her mother's poignant words returned as Erin drove through the dark night on her way to the wild Oregon coast. "There are no shortcuts in committed love. This is your path. No matter how long or lonely it may be right now, to experience the fullness of love, you must go the distance. Only the strongest and bravest stay on the path. And you, my darling girl, have been given everything you need to be among the strongest and bravest."

That defining conversation marked the moment that Erin and her mother bonded as two women who breathed in the same mercy every morning and prayed under the same canopy of peace every evening. Erin's mother became her best friend as well as her faithful prayer partner.

Now that Erin and Mike were in such a strong season of closeness and contentment, she found it hard to remember exactly how Mike had emerged from his dark season. She knew the prayers had had a powerful effect. Perhaps part of their effect had been in changing her heart and her view of Mike and their marriage. *Grace* became a whispered byword that kept her calm and steady when she normally would want to accuse or go into inner isolation.

She vividly remembered the afternoon when it became clear something had changed. Mike was driving all of them to the beach for a family outing. She looked over at his profile and could tell that something was different. All three boys were buckled up safely in the backseat, and for the moment, they weren't fighting. Their dog, Bo, was curled up contentedly next to the ice chest and beach towels. It was a Norman Rockwell sort of moment of family bliss.

What Erin noticed next was that the sadness lines, which had been etching their way deeper into Mike's forehead each day, were no longer there. The corners of his mouth were turned up. He looked over at Erin, gave her a grin, and focused back on the road with his chin lifted. It was as if Mike had remembered who he was and where he was going. And now all five of them were going there together.

From that day forward their relationship wove itself back together. Mike found a good job and immersed himself in their sons' lives just as their eldest was starting junior high. Erin restructured her days. She found her pace, a sweeter, calmer pace. She pursued her passion and obtained a job as a wedding coordinator at a resort hotel in Newport Beach. By the time their three sons had galloped through high school and had moved out of the house, Erin and Mike found themselves entwined in a love deeper than either would have thought possible.

Everything Erin's mother had told her was coming true. Erin was experiencing the reward of committed love and was so grateful she had stayed on the path.

Now she was on a new path. Or, more specifically, a road. A literal winding road through the woods to the Oregon coast. This was another difficult path she would not have chosen on her own. Her father needed her to extend an added measure of grace eighteen months ago when he had made the decisions that brought him to this place. And now he needed even more grace.

Erin put her thoughts on pause. She passed a road sign indicating the distance to Moss Cove. Her GPS told her that she had only eight miles to go. Erin pressed Delores's name on the lit screen of her phone. She waited for three rings before her call was answered.

"Hi, Delores. I thought I would let you know I'm almost there."

"Okay. Well, we're here waiting. I left the light on above the garage, as I told you. Remember, it's a gravel driveway, and it comes up pretty quickly. It's a sharp turn off the highway."

Even with Delores's warning, when Erin hit the steep gravel road twenty minutes later, she knew she was going too fast. The road was narrow and led down into a protected cove below the main road. The tires spun the tiny rocks up against the side windows as she drove toward a strong light at the end of the private road. She had no idea what else was around her because all that could be seen was a cleared turnaround area ahead to the left and a narrow garage door under the bright, blue-tinted light. As soon as she stopped the car, Erin felt her heart pounding.

She wished she hadn't come. She wished her father hadn't had a stroke. She wished Mike were with her. Most of all she wished it would be her mother's face that greeted her at the door of this cottage by the sea in the darkness of the night.

Unlatching her seat belt, Erin reached for her purse just as a tapping sounded on the closed passenger's window. When Erin looked up, she felt an involuntary twitch as she saw Delores's oval face peering into the car. Delores was neither smiling nor frowning. A chilling blue shadow from the light above the garage highlighted her broad nose and plump lips. A knit cap covered her short, dark hair.

"Hi!" Erin waved and tried to give a convincing smile. She told her apprehensions to go away.

You did the right thing in coming. It's a good thing you're here. Don't overreact. Be calm. You have everything you need to be among the strongest and bravest daughters.

4

May your troubles be less
And your blessings be more
And nothing but happiness
Come through your door.

Opening her car door, Erin was met by a shockingly cold wind. The air carried the ocean's salty scent. Not in a refreshing, cooling, dash-of-salt way, which is how she felt the coastal breeze in Southern California. The wind here was heavy with the brine of feisty, churned-up winter waves. Erin's hands and nose instantly felt cold.

"I'll take your suitcase," Delores called out over the whipping wind. "Is it in the trunk?"

"No, it's right here. I can get it." Erin pulled the single bag from out of the warm car's backseat and couldn't believe how cold she felt. Cold and damp.

"Your father has been waiting. He's glad you came."

Erin took Delores's greeting as an olive branch of peace. While Delores hadn't greeted her with a hug or any other welcoming expression aside from coming outside in her slippers and fleece robe, she had started Erin's visit with something positive. Her father was glad she came. All earlier tense messages from Delores were put aside. This was a good start.

Erin returned the greeting by saying "Thanks for being so understanding about my coming on short notice. I appreciate your letting me stay here." Erin trotted quickly to catch up to Delores, who was tromping ahead through the gravel to a wooden deck. "So, how are you doing, Delores?"

"I've been better," Delores called over her shoulder. "Watch your step."

With the bright light from the garage now behind her, Erin found it difficult to see the two steps up onto the wooden deck. The deck appeared new, but the front door looked like something from a hundred-year-old fairy tale cottage, complete with an arched top and a beveled pane of glass in the shape of a half circle at eye level.

Delores called out as she opened the door, "You were right, Jack. That was her car. She's here."

Erin entered and found she was in the kitchen. She quickly shut the door, keeping the icy breezes outside. Then she took a quick look around and was amazed at what she saw. The cottage was adorable. The kitchen looked as if it were an Irish cottage set for a movie, complete with a big, black potbelly stove in between the kitchen and the adjoining living room. To the right a tidy table for two sat under a window that had been dressed up with green print curtains tied with a bow in the center. The cupboards had yellow daisy knobs. On the blue-tiled counter sat an espresso maker, blender, toaster, and basket neatly filled with fresh fruit.

The cuteness surprised Erin. If Delores had done the decorating, this certainly wasn't reflective of the personality she exuded.

"Your kitchen is charming," Erin said.

"What are you doing in there?" Her dad's voice rumbled from around the corner in the other room. It carried its usual gruff tenor but seemed a bit wobbly. "Did you come to see me or the kitchen?"

Erin was stunned that his speech was so clear and cohesive. After the way he had sounded on the phone that morning, she half expected him still to be unable to form a complete sentence. She didn't know enough about the effects of a stroke to know if all the symptoms went away after the initial danger passed.

Entering the moment as if nothing had happened to prompt her visit, Erin playfully said, "Well, hello to you, too, Dad. I thought you would give me a chance to at least get all the way in the door before you barked at me."

"That wasn't barking. You want barking? I'll

give you barking. Why did it take you so long to come see us? We've lived here a year and a half, you know."

She left her suitcase and purse in the kitchen and made her way into the next room where she saw her father. He was in a recliner with a puffy blanket over him and a beanie cap on his head. Erin made a beeline for him and snuggled right up, kissing his scruffy cheek. As she pulled back, she smiled broadly.

"I'm here now, aren't I? Isn't that good enough for you?"

"Never good enough, you know that. I always want more. So what did you bring me?" His right eyelid drooped a bit, and his skin was more sallow than it had ever been in the Southern California climate. Other than that, he looked just as he had always looked, her dear old dad. His thick hair had turned white many years ago. Fringes of the snowy strands stuck out under the stocking cap. His high cheekbones seemed to rise with his smile when he looked at her. This wasn't the strong, familiar image she had expected to see.

"What did I bring you? I brought pictures of Joel from his latest basketball game and a whole lot of advice. Which do you want first?"

He gave her a crooked grin. "You can keep your rotten advice. I've had enough of that lately."

"You look good, Dad. How are you feeling?"

"Fine." He spoke the word quickly, as if he were irritated that she had asked. That's when she realized he hadn't gotten out of the chair to greet her when she arrived. It wasn't normal for her father to stay seated and let people come to him.

"Were you able to get some good rest today? Isn't that what the doctor ordered?"

"That's all I've been getting since we came back from the hospital." He shot a sideways glance at Delores, who had positioned herself on the sofa with her arms crossed.

"That's good. Rest is what you need right now." Erin tucked the blanket in around her father as if that were what she had come to do—make him more comfortable. The scenario was awkward and unfamiliar. Her father never was sick. He wasn't a man who wanted to be coddled. Ever. Yet he didn't protest Erin's caring gestures.

"They have me doped up with all these drugs. I don't like it one bit."

Erin smiled at him. He caught her generous grin and smiled back. Erin's eye went to the framed calligraphy on the wall behind his recliner. She recognized it as the gift she had done by hand and given to her father for Christmas when she was fifteen. The printed letters were uneven in a few spots, and there were some spacing blips.

"I can't believe you still have that." It pleased Erin that he had hung her gift in such a prominent place.

" 'Course we do."

Erin silently skim-read the lines she had care-fully copied long ago.

An Irish Prayer

May God give you
For every storm, a rainbow,
For every tear, a smile,
For every care, a promise,
And a blessing in each trial.
For every problem life sends,
A faithful friend to share,
For every sigh, a sweet song,
And an answer for each prayer.

"Did you have any trouble getting here?" Delores pulled Erin away from her reminiscing moment.

"No. It took longer than I thought it would, though. The weather definitely slowed me down."

"We've had a lot of ice this winter," her dad said.

"Well," Delores said, rustling in her seat, "things here are not at all the same as they are in California, are they? The icy roads this morning certainly made it difficult for us to get to the hospital. Interesting, isn't it, how a person doesn't have a full understanding of another person's life or circumstances unless they are in the situation themselves."

Erin took note of Delores's pointed comment. "You're right. And I'd like to apologize, Delores. I probably came across pretty intense on the phone this morning about getting Dad to the hospital. I don't have a full picture of what you two are up against here with weather conditions and limited medical facilities."

"No, you don't." Delores's voice softened slightly. "You've not been here, so you don't know what it's like. But you were worried about your father."

"Yes, I was."

"You can put your worries to rest," her dad said. "I'm fine, as you can see. There's plenty of spit and vinegar left in me."

Erin smiled at him, trying to give the appearance that she believed his words. It seemed, though, as if a chilling sea mist floated in the air among the three of them, trying to obscure the truth that not one of them believed their worries about his health could be sent sailing.

"So, what do you think of our place?" he asked, changing the topic with ease.

"It's really nice," Erin said. "You've fixed it up adorably."

"Show her the pictures, Delores. Where's the book? Show her what we've done."

Delores went to a built-in bookshelf to the right

of the big picture window that took up most of the front wall of the living room. She motioned with a nod of her head that Erin should take the open seat next to her on the sofa.

Erin took off her coat and laid it over the couch's arm. Before sitting down she gazed out the large window. Outside everything was too dark for her to make out any specifics, but Erin was pretty sure she would be greeted in the morning with a sumptuous view of the vast Pacific Ocean as it rushed to meet the wild and rugged cliffs. Even with all the windows closed up nice and tight, the low, rhythmic bellowing of the salty waves could be heard in the not-too-far distance. Erin knew at once why her father wanted to live here. She knew this was his dream. Southern California had been Erin's mother's dream. This untamed place was her father's dream.

Delores handed Erin the photo album. "We tried to keep a record of the renovations." The album was covered with blue-and-white-checked gingham, and across the front in hand appliquéd letters it read "Hidden Cottage."

"That's a nice name," Erin said, repeating the words. "Hidden Cottage."

"That's what this place was called when we bought it," her dad said. "It was hidden, all right. Hidden by overgrown shrubs. Show her, Delores."

Delores opened to the first page of the scrapbook. Erin studied the large photo of a neglected cabin with several shutters, each hanging on by a single, rusted hinge.

"This is what it looked like when you bought it?"

"Yup." Her father held back none of his obvious pride over the transformation. "This is what your mother and I . . . I mean, what Delores and I . . . have been doing for the past eighteen months."

Erin turned the page and was impressed. When she saw the original, neglected condition of the kitchen and living room and how it had been transformed, all she could say was "Wow! You two have been busy. This is amazing."

"It was bad, all right. That's why we bought the place for a song." Her dad pulled off the blanket and pressed his legs down on the recliner's footrest so that the chair returned to an upright position. "Come on, I'll show you the rest of our mansion, and then you can compare it to the photos. It's better if you see it all first."

"Dad, are you sure you're supposed to be up like this?"

"Of course I'm supposed to be up." His tone was indignant.

Delores immediately backed him up. "The doctor told him to resume normal, moderate activity."

Erin had a pretty good idea that the renovations her dad had undertaken over the past eighteen months had been neither "normal" nor "moderate" activity.

"I'll start with showing you the bedroom we added on. It's this way." Jack led Erin to the halfway opened door adjacent to the living room. He pushed it open. She could feel his gaze on her, ready and waiting for her exclamations of amazement.

She didn't need to pretend she was impressed. The seashore theme of the immaculate room was definitely "ooh-able." Delores had exceptional taste, and a keen eye for combining colors. Never would Erin have expected this hidden talent tucked away in abrupt, efficient Delores.

"Not bad, is it?" her dad said.

"It's wonderful. Really beautiful."

"Do you like it? Honestly, I want you to tell your old dad the truth. What do you think of the place?"

"It's beautiful."

Delores was right behind her so Erin added, "You're an artist, Delores. You and my dad have transformed this place."

Erin couldn't tell if Delores was smiling since, unfortunately, her smile and smirk were awfully close.

The three of them headed up the narrow stairs located to the left of the bedroom door. Upstairs was a dormer-style bedroom. In the compact space Erin recognized an old dresser topped with an amber-toned lamp that set off a soft glow when

Delores flipped the light switch. A twin bed and a wicker rocking chair completed the furniture that fit in the small but lovely room.

Erin sang another round of praises for Delores and quietly slipped her hand into her dad's. She gave him two quick squeezes. That had always been her mom's secret code for saying "Love you." Three squeezes back meant "Love you, too." Erin had passed on the secret squeezes to Mike and their three sons. Those four men in her life had always responded with three squeezes. Erin waited to feel the three squeezes back from the first important man in her life.

Instead of squeezes from her dad's large and calloused hand, all she felt was his releasing himself from her grip.

In that moment, Erin felt as if the floor had dropped out from under her. Her father had raised her to be tough enough to take a hit in the face from a football or to keep running even after she had rubbed a blister on her heel. She had always worked hard to gain his golden approval. On a few occasions she had known he was proud of her. But what she had worked even harder to receive was his fatherly affection. All she needed was three squeezes, and she would know without a doubt that she mattered to him.

Yet even now her father could not or would not give her the one thing for which her little-girl heart longed.

5

May the raindrops fall lightly on your brow.
May the soft winds freshen your spirit.
May the sunshine brighten your heart.
May the burdens of the day
rest lightly upon you.
And may God enfold you
in the mantle of his love.

The next morning, before the first light had crept into her small upstairs room, Erin was awakened by the roar of the winter storm raging outside. Tiny beads of hail pelted the dormer window, as if a Romeo were trying to gain the attention of his Juliet.

The churning blast of the waves seemed to have turned up in volume since Erin first arrived, and the fierce wind now roused her from under the down comforter. She put her bare feet on the braided rug and took four steps across the floor to pull up the shade to take a look outside. She could see nothing but a few rounded shrubs and her rental car parked under the still glowing light above the garage. In the light she noticed the streaking pellets of ice as the wind pushed them toward the east at an angle.

Beyond the immediate perimeter of the cottage the rest of the world remained shrouded in darkness. She could hear all the sounds rocking that outer world, but here inside this steady fortress she was safe. Her father had made this tiny castle of his nice and safe, and Delores had made it pretty.

Erin thought of the Hidden Cottage scrapbook. Last night her father had sat beside her on the couch and gone over every before and after photo with detailed explanations. He was proud of the work he and Delores had done. Erin also got the impression he was proud of Delores for documenting the process step-by-step and putting it together in such a beautiful book.

Erin's mom never quite got around to creating scrapbooks. Faith O'Riley loved people, and she loved God. Those two distinctions permeated her life, and one could see by the way she ran her home and her life that she put people before projects. Therefore, Erin's mom left many little projects unfinished when she went to heaven. Erin had appropriated a number of her mom's treasures, such as her diary. But Erin safely could assume that many photos and mementos of her childhood were still in boxes. Most likely they were packed away in one of the orderly storage bins she saw stacked up when she'd been given the tour of the garage last night.

Erin hopped back into the twin bed and rubbed her cold feet together, trying to warm them. The wind seemed determined to play its shrillest notes, forcing them in through the tiniest spaces around the window frame.

A memory came to Erin, turning her lips up in a soft grin. When she was in the fourth grade, she took up playing the flute. Every afternoon her mother made Erin practice. She discovered that if she waited until her father came home, around four thirty, and if she inserted just the right amount of extra-shrill notes in the middle of each piece, her father would open her bedroom door and excuse her from practicing anymore.

Erin continued to play the flute all through high school and improved to the point her mom could make requests, and Erin could pick out the tune and play it accurately after a few tries. She did duets with her mom at the piano. Their favorite duet was "Für Elise," and Erin had decided when she was eighteen that if she ever had a daughter she would name her Elise Faith.

She felt wistful, curled under the blankets listening to the winter wind and missing a daughter she'd never borne. In truth, it was her mother she missed and knew she would miss every day for the rest of her life.

While Erin had been curled up under the comforter, the daylight had slowly brightened her room the way a dimmer on a lamp gradually increases the amount of light and reveals previously unrecognizable details. The pale winter light that now filled the room prompted a return visit to the window. This time she could feel the tiny stream of chilled air as it whistled in through an opening in the left corner of the window frame.

I'll have to tell Dad. He'll want to know about that so he can fix it.

The view outside caught Erin by surprise. It was dismal and gray, as she suspected, yet the scope opened up before her was unexpectedly majestic. The cliff on which the cottage was built extended another fifty yards beyond the front of the house and then appeared to drop off dramatically over a cliff formed from black rock. Beyond the cliff was the ocean. Nothing but pale gray water churned to a froth of whitecapped breakers that bashed against the rocks with such force they sent their spray into the air like a bursting geyser.

To the right Erin could make out what looked like a large area of tide pools where the coastline took a dip inland, giving an even greater impression that the land on which the cottage stood was alone on an isolated cleft of impenetrable rock.

Pulling on her warmest apparel, Erin tiptoed down the stairs, trying not to make too much noise. The old wood floor groaned, giving away her escape route. She could hear low voices murmuring as she passed the closed door of her dad and Delores's downstairs bedroom. Since the only bathroom in the cottage was next to their room and accessible through a second door off the kitchen, Erin tried again to accomplish her morning routine as quietly as possible but without much success. Every sound seemed to echo through the house.

When she stepped back into the kitchen, Delores was there to greet her, still dressed in her robe and slippers as she had been when she had greeted Erin at the car last night. She wore a knit cap, just as she had the night before, with all her hair tucked under the edges. This cap had a crocheted flower affixed to the side. Erin noticed how clear and unflawed Delores's pale complexion was. There was something Old World and elemental about her fair skin and dark-eyed appearance that gave off the aura that she thrived in the cold.

Erin had to wonder if the same appeal her father had for this place that reminded him of Ireland applied to his wife as well. Did Delores remind him of the Irish women he had admired for their brawn and capabilities when he was young? She remembered the one trip she had made to Ireland with her parents when she was only six. Her brother wasn't born yet, and Erin was sick part of the trip so she didn't have many memories, and the ones she did have weren't magical at all.

She did remember saying to her elderly grandmother that she was very cold. Her grandmother had said, "Best cure for a chill is a broom." Then, handing Erin a broom, she indicated that doing a brisk job of sweeping the floor would warm her right up. As a matter of fact, the kitchen of that Irish cottage couldn't have been much larger than this one. Only, when she was six it seemed enormous.

Delores opened a cupboard door and said to Erin, "If you would like coffee or tea, you can find whatever you need in the cupboard there behind you. We have a little milk, and there's some half-and-half in the refrigerator."

"Okay. Thank you. I hope I didn't wake you."

"It's too small of a house not to be woken." The statement bore just enough indignation to make Erin squirm.

"Sorry. I'll try to be quieter."

Delores turned the faucet on the kitchen sink to stop a slow drip and returned to the bedroom.

I get the feeling that it isn't just me that Delores doesn't like. I don't think she likes anything. So why does she like my dad?

A short time later, with a cup of tea warming her hands, Erin sat on the couch in the living room with her stocking feet tucked under her to keep them warm. The expanded picture window was providing her with an unlimited view of the ocean with all its muted shades of blue and gray. The storm had stopped. The wind seemed to be subsiding. The raucous waves, however, still were vehemently crashing against the rocks. It was like watching the *1812 Overture* being played on instruments improvised by nature.

She was glad to find the Irish breakfast tea in the cupboard and sipped it slowly. It had been a staple in her home while growing up. Early on she found that a cup of Irish breakfast with a splash of milk and a dash of sugar could calm the most tumultuous inner storms. Erin needed this steaming cup of support this morning.

The bedroom door opened, and Erin's dad came out dressed in a pair of baggy jeans and a sweat-shirt. His white hair was combed back, and aside from looking a little winter pale, he looked like the bright blue-eyed father she had always known.

"Top of the morning, Glory."

Erin grinned. It was the standard greeting she had heard from him ever since she was a child. According to her dad, the greeting originated with his great-great-great-grandfather from a wee village near Dublin and was the duty of the O'Riley family to bestow on to the rest of the world. He always would wink after he made the declaration.

"Are you interested in having the best breakfast you've ever had in your life?"

"That's quite an offer," Erin said. She knew her father didn't cook. At all. So either Delores was a notable chef or her dad had a favorite place in town where he liked to go. In Irvine it had been a tiny place called Johnny's Donuts. The café's coffee was awful, but the donuts were amazing.

"I thought you and I could go on over to Jenny Bee's Fish House."

"A fish house, huh?"

"Best breakfast you've ever had. I guarantee it. Homemade bran muffins and perfect omelets. You ready?"

"Sure. Is Delores coming?"

"She doesn't eat breakfast."

"Oh. Okay. Let me get my jacket. I'll drive, okay?"

"I thought we'd walk. It's less than a mile."

"In this weather?"

Her dad put on a baseball cap and reached for his jacket waiting on a hook by the door. "What's the problem? You still opposed to exercise?"

Erin's greatest concern was for her dad and whether he should be hiking a mile in such blustery conditions. After being a physical education teacher for more than thirty-five years before taking to the classroom to teach U.S. history, her dad did push-ups, jumped rope, and jogged until he was sixty. If he hadn't had the scare with the blood clot traveling to his brain, a morning hike with him would have seemed normal.

She took the responsibility for his need to take it easy and said, "I don't want to walk. Let me drive us, okay?"

"Suit yourself."

By all outward appearances, he looked good. His sentences were clear and cohesive. Erin found it hard to believe that yesterday at this time he couldn't carry on a conversation over the phone. Erin wondered how she would know when she was supposed to leave. She had purchased a one-way ticket and would do the same for the return when it was time to leave. But what sort of indicators would make that clear? Hopefully, a call to his doctor would give Erin the information she needed.

Out of curiosity, Erin watched the odometer in the rental car as her dad directed her into the tiny town of Moss Cove. The distance to Jenny Bee's Fish House was two miles. Not "less than a mile," as her father had said. If they had walked, it would have been two miles into town and two miles back. Was her dad really planning to walk four miles in this fierce wind and chilling temperatures? Or was he trying to put on a show to convince her he still was his former self so she wouldn't have to worry?

On the drive into town, in spite of the misty white fog that covered them, Erin could see what she had missed driving in the dark. On the right side of the road rose an expansive forest of

71

soaring evergreens. Every so often a house appeared, tucked in here and there under the branches that dripped with moisture from the sea as well as from the sky. From several of the homes a vapor of smoke rose from the chimney.

On the left side of the road a variety of beach houses lined up near one another, each sporting a unique color and personality. Erin noticed a quaint oceanfront lodge called the Shamrock Lodgettes. Each of the lodgettes looked like a small log cabin, but the name did somehow add to their charm.

"I'm guessing this place reminds you of Ireland."

"It does indeed. We have plans to go to Ireland this summer. All depends on Delores, though, at this point."

Erin wasn't sure why the decision would depend on Delores. He certainly hadn't made choices that way while married to her mom. She wondered if his thinking was similar to his statement that they should walk to the café this morning. He would, of course, want to give the impression that he was strong and capable of anything. Was he hoping Delores would be the one to call off the trip due to this new turn of events? Erin thought she remembered hearing before that people who took blood-thinning medication or had a history of blood clots were advised not to take long plane flights or long car rides.

"Park over there," her dad said, pointing to the only open space in front of an undistinguished-looking storefront next to a Laundromat. A handmade sign out front announced that they had fresh halibut today and buckwheat pancakes. Erin hoped that didn't mean the two items came together.

Her dad entered the small shop first, and everyone greeted him—the waitress with two short pigtails and with a tattoo running up her bare right arm, the mustached cook behind the window, and the five morning diners. All of them knew him by name, and all of them seemed happy to see him. That didn't surprise Erin. Her father could be charming when he wanted to, and he always was the initiator when it came to collecting cronies.

Jack repeated his "Top of the morning, Glory" to one and all. Then, as if he were the traveling thespian here to announce the next community theater production, Erin's father scooped his cap from his snowy head and tipped it in Erin's direction. "So, what do all of you think of my one and only daughter? You can see where she gets her good looks, right?"

"Welcome to Moss Cove!" the waitress said. "You want some coffee?"

Caught off guard, Erin managed to say "Sure" before following her dad to a corner table. The other guests all took their time giving Erin a good looking over. A few nodded politely. One of them, a crusty, old, frowning sailor-type, just stared. This wasn't what she had expected when she rushed to Oregon to be with her father. She didn't know how a person was supposed to act the day after a stroke, but this wasn't what she had pictured.

The waitress, whom her dad introduced as Jo, placed two mismatched mugs of steaming coffee in front of them. "The usual, Jack?"

"Not today. I'm having my Sunday morning special. And bring the same for my girl."

As soon as Jo walked away, Erin asked, "What are we having?" The advertisement of halibut and buckwheat cakes lingered in her mind.

"A mushroom and Swiss cheese omelet with fresh crabmeat, red potatoes with basil, and honey wheat toast with homemade raspberry jam. Wait till you taste the jam. It's the best in Oregon, I'll tell you that. The raspberry harvest last year was a good one."

Erin decided to stop trying to figure out what was going on in this alternate universe where her father was very much at home. He apparently was okay. The meds were working. He wasn't in need of convalescence. Her trip was apparently for the purpose of seeing him and making some inroads with Delores. If that was the reason, then it had been a fairly expensive success, and she could book a flight home later today.

"So what do you think of the place?"

"This place?" Erin asked.

"No, our place. Hidden Cottage. What do you think?"

"It's nice."

Her dad's expression drooped, and Erin quickly bolstered her comment. "You and Delores have worked hard on the place. It's really nice."

"Not a place you would want to come to unless you had to, though, right?"

Erin wasn't sure what he meant by that comment. "Do you mean would I like to come up here for vacation?"

He gave a slight nod of affirmation. It seemed as if his feelings were hurt. That wasn't an expression she remembered seeing on him very often.

"It's pretty far away from Southern California."

"Of course it is. That's the point. Can't you see the boys down there, poking around in the tide pools? Mike can fish all he wants. You can sit on the deck and read a book all day long. At night we can have a cookout. Crab is the way to go around here. Couple of my pals have all the equipment. The boys can set the traps down at the pier and catch the crabs, then we'll boil 'em in the big pots. Not a bad way to spend a summer evening, don't you think?"

Her dad's idealized comments scrambled her brain. He had projected a scenario of an entire vacation based on the family gathering together at his Hidden Cottage. Had he forgotten how old the boys were? They weren't Tom Sawyer age, eager to go hunting in tide pools for their summer vacation. And Mike had never fished a day in his life, as far as she knew.

"The boys are pretty much on their own now when it comes to how they spend their vacations."

Her dad's countenance dipped again.

"But Mike probably would like to come up here sometime. Maybe he and I can come back this summer for a few days."

"Sure." He turned and glanced over his shoulder as the door opened and another local man entered. The turn-and-look-the-other-way gesture was familiar. Erin knew that was her father's way of indicating the end of that conversation. She knew her responses had disappointed him, but that wasn't a new experience. Erin never felt as if she had managed to garner his approval.

The man who entered came over to the table and introduced himself to Erin. He had a joke for her dad and a nod for the waitress before sitting down with a newspaper as his breakfast companion. Erin enjoyed seeing her dad like this, cheery and surrounded by "chums." It was especially good to see how enthusiastic he was again about eating. Ever since her mom died, he had been apathetic about many things, including food. And her father was definitely a foodie. That he had never turned his hand to cooking always mystified her. Her mom had been a pretty adept home chef and was always trying new things.

"Does Delores like to cook?" Erin asked.

"Not at all. She knows how to steam vegetables, and once she cooked a whole chicken. She's yet to make me a cup of coffee." Jack put his lips to the rim of his mug as if he had nothing further to say on the subject.

"I'm glad you have this place, then, Dad. You always did like having nice big meals with people you enjoy."

"Must come from all those years in the teachers' lounge."

Erin grinned. "I bet you're right. Do you miss that world?"

"Sometimes. I don't miss California, though."

Erin felt the same twinge of pain she had felt yesterday while talking with Sharlene. Knowing that she was a big part of the California he did not miss stung.

"Well, I miss you." She offered a smile that made her feel as if she were seven years old.

He conveniently lifted his coffee mug to his lips and murmured something she couldn't understand.

Erin took a sip of her Jenny Bee's coffee and coughed involuntarily, barely swallowing the coffee in her mouth in time.

"What's wrong?"

Once her throat had cleared she said in a low voice, "I'm afraid I've become a coffee snob. This is pretty strong."

"Can't handle the high-octane stuff, is that it?"

"I guess so. What about you? Are you supposed to be drinking coffee?"

"Yes, I am," he growled. Erin knew that was the end of that discussion.

In an effort to launch a less volatile topic, Erin said, "Jordan has a girlfriend. Did I tell you that?"

"How serious are they?"

"Pretty serious. He met her in Hawaii last month."

Erin's dad put down his coffee mug. "Did Jordan see Tony while he was there?"

"No. Jordan was on Oahu taking photos on the North Shore." Erin's only brother had been a difficult topic for many years. She hadn't seen him since their mom's funeral, and they had barely spoken to each other then. Years ago, Tony had dropped out of everything mainstream and moved to Maui. Erin knew Tony and her dad hadn't shared much of a relationship for more than twenty years. The strain had weighed on her mother and was a daily theme in her prayers.

"I have pictures of them." Erin reached for her phone and saw that she had missed a call from Mike. She flipped to her digital photo album and held up her phone so her dad could see the cute young couple standing by a palm tree at Sunset Beach. "Her name is Sierra."

Her father raised his eyebrows. "What kind of a name is that?" Without waiting for an answer, he studied the shot more closely. "She certainly has a lot of hair. Your grandmother used to have curly hair like that. Red, not blond like this girl, Sarah."

"Sierra," Erin corrected him. "Her name is Sierra, not Sarah." She was aware that several other diners were leaning over, unabashedly trying to catch a glimpse of the photo on Erin's phone.

"Have you met her yet?"

"No, not yet."

"She could have some Irish blood in her with hair like that."

The crusty old sailor who openly had stared at Erin when they entered rose, walked over, and leaned in to see the photo. Erin's dad held up the phone so he could get a better look. He made no comment. Just had a look and returned to his breakfast.

"When are they getting married?" Erin's dad asked.

"They just met last month." Erin took back her phone and placed it in her lap.

"By the time they decide to get serious, you might have that wedding business of yours up and going."

"Actually, I don't think I told you yet, but my

friend Sharlene and I launched our wedding planning business."

"Well, that's news. When did this happen?"

Erin let the true answer slip out. "Yesterday."

Her father made an expression that clearly reflected disapproval. "Yesterday. Then what are you doing here?"

"I wanted to come. I wanted to . . ." She almost said ". . . make sure you were okay" but with the audience that certainly was listening and the way her father had been acting as if nothing was wrong, she left her sentence unfinished.

"Well, you don't have to stay on my account. We appreciate your coming to see the place now that we have it all fixed up, but you don't need to turn this into a vacation. Not your first week on the job. If I were you, I'd be on the next flight home."

One of the women at the table just inches away turned to them. "You don't want to go home yet, Erin. This storm is on its way out. We're expecting full sun by tomorrow. Highs in the low sixties. It's going to be beautiful. You should stay and enjoy the weather."

Erin tried to make a lighthearted comment. "Highs in the sixties, you say. I suppose I shouldn't tell you that where I live as soon as it dips into the low seventies we wear wool sweaters and sip hot cocoa to warm up."

The woman didn't appear amused. However,

the leather-skinned sailor chuckled to himself.

The omelets were delivered just then, and she was happy to put an end to their group conversation. The toast arrived a moment later along with the acclaimed jam. All of it was delicious. Especially the jam. Erin's opinion of Jenny Bee's Fish House went up another notch with each bite.

They talked only a little as they ate. That seemed fine to her father, and it was fine with Erin. She spent her chewing time thinking through the phone calls she was going to make as soon as she could do so in private. She would send a text to Mike, letting him know she would call as soon as she could. She planned to give the doctor a call just to make sure, but at this point Erin saw no reason not to book a return flight for that evening or the next morning at the latest.

When she and her dad returned to the cottage, Erin dropped him off and left her engine running. "I need to drive back to town to buy something at the grocery store."

"What do you need? We might have it."

"It's a personal item." That excuse had worked for years with her dad. He never wanted to hear about any personal "feminine" item she needed at the store. In this case, her true personal item was personal time on the phone with her husband in the grocery store parking lot.

With a wave of his hand he dismissed her and

took the steps on the front deck with ease. She waited until he was inside the cottage before backing up the steep gravel driveway and driving the two miles to town.

Parking the car in front of the small Wayside Market, Erin called the doctor and left a message with the on-call nurse, then Mike and gave him a report of how things had been going.

"You might as well come home unless the doctor calls back and says otherwise. If your father is well enough to go out to breakfast and eat shrimp omelets with you, I'm guessing he's not in any immediate danger."

"I think you're right. It was a crabmeat omelet, actually. Not shrimp. By far the best omelet I've ever had."

"Really?"

"Yes. And the raspberry jam was homemade and delicious. I can see why my dad loves going there. On the outside it doesn't look like much. If you don't mind sharing your conversation with a handful of locals, it's a really great place to eat. When you and I come up here sometime, I'll take you there."

"Why don't you tell your dad that? Tell him you have to come home, but you and I plan to visit in a few months and to stay longer for a vacation."

A car pulled into the open parking spot next to Erin. She turned her face away from whoever it was that just pulled in. If it was one of the breakfast cronies from Jenny Bee's, she didn't want to get roped into rolling down her window to engage in a conversation.

"What about Delores?" Mike asked. "Does she like it there?"

"I'm not sure how to gauge what she likes. It seems whatever her favorites are, they're on a short list that she keeps to herself. I will tell you one thing, though. While I still don't have much of a liking for her, I can understand a little better what my dad sees in her and why he married her."

"And what exactly is that?"

"She's a workhorse. And good with her hands, just like my dad. She's also abrupt like him, too. With my mom it was definitely a case of opposites attracting each other. With Delores it's—"

There was a tap on the window. Erin jumped. She turned to see Delores's stern expression gazing in on her just as it had last night in the dark.

"Delores!"

Mike asked, "What about her? You were saying with their marriage it's—"

"She's right here. I'll call you back." Erin hung up her phone and turned the key in the ignition so she could roll down the passenger's window. She tried to adjust her expression to one of calm and innocence. Her mind was busy working to replay the last few minutes of her call to Mike so she could remember what she had said about Delores in case she had overheard through the closed-up car.

"Jack said you needed something at the store. I do, too." Delores stood her ground, apparently waiting for Erin to lock up the car and come inside with her.

Erin put her phone back in her purse, closed up the car, and locked it with the press of a button. "I guess I should have asked if you needed anything before I came back here." Erin realized she was apologizing once again to Delores.

Delores didn't pay any attention to Erin's apology. Instead, as the two of them entered the market, Delores said, "What did your father say at breakfast?"

"About what?"

"About his condition."

"He didn't talk about it."

Delores's brows caved. She walked over to the salad dressing aisle where no other shoppers were. "He's in denial. I've tried to tell him that he needs to change his diet, but he won't listen to me. I thought the best thing about your coming was that you would be able to convince him that he has to change."

Clearly Delores didn't need anything at the grocery store either. She just wanted her chance to corner Erin away from Jack's listening ears. What a crazy dynamic was at work in her dad's life.

"What did Jack eat for breakfast?"

Erin gave a rundown, even though she felt as if she were betraying her father by reporting on one of his loves—food—and speaking negatively about the fish market hangout that replaced the teachers' lounge of long ago.

Delores scowled. "He's eating himself into the grave. Eggs and cheese . . . I told him if he's bent on going to that wretched place he should order oatmeal or at least nonfat yogurt with blueberries. He should concentrate on his cholesterol and get more antioxidants."

Erin didn't know how to respond. Her dad had never been a tofu-and-granola sort of man. Was that how Delores ate? Was that why her dad said she didn't cook or make him coffee?

"You have to help me, Erin." Delores now looked more approachable than she ever had. She was only four years older than Erin, and yet this was the first time she seemed to be speaking to Erin as a friend.

In another uncharacteristic move, Delores reached over and clutched Erin's upper arm. With a look of desperation she said, "Please say you'll help me talk some sense into him. He has to stay strong and healthy. Erin, if anything happens to him . . ."

"I know, I know. I feel the same way." Erin placed her hand over Delores's, partly to comfort her and partly in hopes that she would ease up on her grip. Erin's heart was touched by Delores's words and expressions in a way she never expected. "I don't want anything to happen to my dad either."

Delores released her terror grip on Erin's arm. "You understand what I'm saying, don't you?"

Erin nodded. She felt as if she finally believed that this woman truly loved her dad. "Yes, I understand," Erin said softly.

With a relieved look, Delores pulled away her hand. "Good. I'm glad you understand. Because I mean it. If Jack becomes an invalid . . . I can't stay with him. Do you understand? I'll have to leave him."

6

May God be with you and bless you
May you see your children's children.
May you be poor in misfortunes
And rich in blessings.
May you know nothing but happiness
From this day forward.

Erin relayed the details of her trip to Sharlene the next day after returning to Southern California. She felt the same emotional ache pressing against her chest that she had experienced after Delores's announcement at the grocery store in front of all those salad dressing bottles. Delores had made it clear that she wasn't willing to remain committed to Erin's father "in sickness and in health." The revelation was a brutal one since Erin was almost ready to accept Delores and appreciate her for all the ways Erin's father had chosen to set his affections on her.

"What did you say when Delores said she would leave him?" Sharlene was standing in their office's corner with her arms folded, expressing the same sense of anger that Erin was fighting.

"I didn't say anything. To be honest, I was in shock. I thought she was going to say she loved him too much to bear the thought of anything happening to him. That's what I was thinking at that moment."

"Of course that's what you were thinking. That's what anyone who loves another person should be thinking at a time like that. I want to scratch out that woman's eyes. What did you say to your father? Did you at least leave him with some sort of hint that the woman he had married was self-serving?"

"No. I couldn't say anything. I really couldn't. The whole time was so awkward. I left their place at one o'clock and barely made it to my seven o'clock flight home. Mike said he doesn't think I should go up there again unless he's with me. He doesn't want them using me as the Ping-Pong ball in their odd match."

"This is pretty awful, if you ask me."

"I know. But it could be much worse. At least his health seems stable, according to my short conversation with the doctor." Erin rubbed the back of her neck. "I plan to call my dad each week, and then Mike and I will go up in May."

"Okay." Sharlene unfolded her arms and headed for the computer. "That's that, then. You're back, and we have work to do. Let me show you where we are with the agreements for the church venues on our list."

Erin and Sharlene dove back in with a shared enthusiasm for their venture. In many ways, it seemed as if Erin had never been gone. She thought about her dad more often as the weeks rolled by. She prayed for him more than she had before his stroke. And true to her plan, she called almost every week.

Their conversations were short and focused mostly on questions her dad asked about his grandsons. He appeared to be in good health. Several times he thanked her for "checking in." Occasionally Delores would be the one to answer the phone. She would give updates on how Jack had built new shelves in the garage or painted the front deck. Everything seemed to be back to normal.

Business picked up for Erin and Sharlene with a gust of energy toward the end of April, and by the time May arrived, they were experiencing almost more success than they could handle. They hadn't anticipated so many Christmas weddings. Erin's favorite triumph was the agreement they secured with Patio Galaxy for the rental of outdoor luxury furniture groupings.

Since Erin felt no urgency to make another visit in May to Oregon, she and Mike talked about taking a two-week vacation in the fall. They planned to fly to Portland, rent a car, and then, after visiting her dad and Delores, they would drive down the Oregon and California coasts.

August zoomed by, and they were a full week into September before Mike and Erin talked again about their plans for a leisurely fall vacation.

"To be honest," Mike said, "unless you see things differently, I would rather put the money into getting all the boys home for Thanksgiving. Especially since Jordan is bringing Sierra with him."

"Then let's do that," Erin said. She paused a moment and said, "I could invite my dad and Delores to come for Thanksgiving."

Mike wasn't quick to reply.

"Do you think that would be good or not?"

"I'm not opposed to your dad and Delores coming. It's just that this is the first time we'll all be together in a long time. With Jordan bringing Sierra, I want to make sure you feel like you have time to focus on them and not get hung up on any bickering between your dad and Delores. Why don't you think about it some more?"

The first week of November Erin brought up the topic again with Mike. She had been thinking about inviting her dad and Delores and she had also been thinking about inviting her brother, Tony, and his wife and daughters.

Mike's expression said it all. "Erin, honey, why would you do that to yourself?"

"I thought that maybe, just maybe, if my dad and Tony were together again, they might mend their torn relationship. It's what my mom hoped and prayed for every day."

"That's what you should do, too, Erin. Pray. Hope. Those are two things you can do every day. There's nothing wrong in wishing for the two of them to be reconnected, but do you really think you can facilitate that sort of restoration over Thanksgiving dinner?"

Erin didn't reply. They were sitting at the kitchen counter having their conversation, and she knew they had only five more minutes to discuss this before Mike had to leave and Sharlene would show up for their usual workday.

"Where are you going to put all these people, by the way?" Mike asked.

"We have air mattresses."

Mike gave her another look that expressed he thought she was nuts.

Erin stood and loaded the dishwasher, making more noise with the rattling of the dishes than was necessary. "Okay. Fine. For Jordan and Sierra's sake I won't invite Tony and his family. I'm sure it's a long shot that they could afford the airfare anyhow. I just wanted them to feel wanted and included and . . . I don't know . . . welcome in the family regardless of the past."

"Then why don't you invite your dad, Delores, Tony, and his family to all come for Christmas? The boys, too, of course. Jordan can bring Sierra. Joel and Grant can bring some friends home, too. Ask everyone to stay through New Year's."

Erin turned to look at her husband, stunned at his sudden gush of hospitality.

Mike put up both hands. "Kidding! I was only kidding, Erin! Don't even think of filling the house with a warring clan of the fighting Irish for Christmas."

She flicked her fingers at him, sprinkling him with water from her wet hands.

He seemed to enjoy the teasing that had been so much a part of their early years of marriage. "I have to go. Too bad. Staying and having a water fight with you would be so much more fun."

"I can arrange to schedule a match later tonight."

"Promise?"

She walked him to his car in the driveway and gave him a kiss by his car door. Mike gave her two kisses in return along with his usual pat on the backside. "Remember, water fight tonight. You promised."

Erin grinned. She had a wonderful husband, and she knew it.

Sharlene pulled up as Mike was driving away and Erin was smiling at him and blowing kisses.

"Aren't you the blushing lovebug this morning? Did I show up for work too soon? We can work out a signal system, you know. You can tie a ribbon on the front door if you want me to go away and come back later. I mean, The Happiest Day doesn't always have to be about our brides."

Erin laughed. "Today it does. We've had four more requests come in on the website since yesterday."

"I know. I saw them this morning. You know, I've been thinking . . ."

"Uh-oh, should I be worried?"

"No, you should be amazed and supportive of my fantastic idea. I'm thinking it will be especially favorable to you on mornings like this one."

"Does this have anything to do with your idea of moving our headquarters?" In the past four months, boxes of brochures and pamphlets had overflowed Erin's home office and spilled into the garage as well as half the floor space in the guest room of their three-bedroom home. Sharlene and Erin often had talked about renting a storage shed or looking into renting office space.

"Yes and no, it has something to do with the idea of sharing," Sharlene said. "Just hear me out."

The two friends entered the house as Sharlene unfolded her plan. By ten o'clock they had reached a mutual decision. They would run the business out of both Erin's and Sharlene's homes. The two of them would meet at Erin's home office every Monday and Thursday for planning and face-to-face updates, but the rest of the week they would divide the clients, as they had been doing, and would run everything from their separate locations. Sharlene already had cleared space in her garage for half the boxes.

"This will make us more efficient," Sharlene said as she pulled out her laptop and plugged it into the wall.

"That's true." Erin settled in the desk chair in front of her computer and remembered their first morning when they had toasted with their paper latte cups. "I know this is a good solution, but I'm still sad. The only other solution I see is for us to take on fewer clients. But things are going so great and running so smoothly, I would hate to put on the brakes now."

"Exactly."

The restructuring of their fledgling business took place right away. When more than half the boxes had been moved to Sharlene's house, Erin even managed to park her car in the garage.

By the time Thanksgiving arrived, Erin was grateful to have some of her house space back. She also was secretly relieved that she didn't have a lot of guests coming. Her goal was to make this the happiest, best, most memorable Thanksgiving ever for the five important people who would put their feet under her mother's dining room table.

The day before Thanksgiving Jordan and Sierra arrived just as it was getting dark. They came in through the garage and entered the kitchen. Erin had an apron on over her jeans and sweater and was pulling two pumpkin pies from the oven. She nearly dropped them when she saw Jordan walk in.

"You're here! I didn't think you would arrive until tomorrow." She quickly put the pies on the stove and wiped her hands on her apron before rushing to wrap her arms around her tall son and kiss him soundly on his scruffy cheek. "Oh, it's so good to see you, honey!"

The older Jordan got, the more he resembled Mike. His dark hair was longer than Erin had seen it in a long time. His jaw was firmly set, and his clear eyes hinted at deep inner happiness. He stretched his arm back and took Sierra's hand, drawing her forward. "Mom, this is Sierra."

Erin grinned wildly at the earthy young woman standing in her kitchen. Sierra's curly blond hair tumbled over her shoulders. Her no-makeup, no-nonsense expression was refreshing, and her soft blue green eyes were bright with honesty. "Welcome, Sierra. I want you to make yourself at home. Completely at home."

Erin considered giving Sierra a hug, but she hesitated, not knowing if Sierra was the type of girl who felt comfortable getting hugged on the first meeting.

Sierra quickly answered that question by stepping forward and being the one to give Erin a simple, sweet, spontaneous hug. "I'm so happy to finally meet you."

Erin loved her immediately.

As the evening continued, Erin's happiness grew. Mike came home with pizza for all of them. Jordan carried in the luggage, and Sierra offered to help in the kitchen. She chopped onions for Erin's famous stuffing recipe, washed dishes, and talked about the years she had spent working in Brazil. It was a dream come true for Erin to have another woman to work with side by side in the kitchen. She had waited a long time for the day when one of her boys would bring home a young woman who made his heart happy. Without a doubt, Sierra was that woman for Jordan.

Early on Thursday morning a persistent rain started about the same time that Erin put the obscenely huge bird into her new, bright red roaster and closed the oven door. By noon the rain had lifted, and when they sat down to an opulent meal at four o'clock, the late-afternoon autumn sun was coming through the freshly sprinkled front windows, casting tiny prisms of light on the rims of the crystal goblets.

The scene reminded her of the drive to the Hidden Cottage in February when the sun broke through the fog-shrouded woods and lit up the strings of glimmering ice droplets on the pine tree boughs. That trip seemed so long ago. It now felt like a vivid dream and not something that had really happened.

They joined hands around the table, and Mike

led their family in a prayer of gratefulness. Erin whispered another prayer silently, thanking God that her father's health was good and asking that he and her brother would somehow, someday, be peacefully reunited.

An echo of "amens" sounded around the table.

When Erin looked up, she saw that Jordan and Sierra, who had been holding hands during the prayer, hadn't let go after the "amen." Both Jordan and Sierra had their backs to the window, and when Erin looked at them, the sun had backlit their profiles, igniting the glow in their eyes.

That impression was extraordinary in and of itself. But the brief moment that pressed itself into her memory was the look on Jordan's face as he gazed at Sierra and the way that look was mirrored on Sierra's face. It wasn't a giddy glimpse born of infatuation or a heady gaze of passion ignited by human hormones. Jordan and Sierra gave each other the sort of look that remains the same at ninety-five when exchanged between two people who have set their sights on going the distance together as one. It was the look of lifetime love.

Erin choked up. Her son was in love right before her eyes.

Not wanting to give away any clues of what her maternal instinct was telling her, Erin uncovered the mashed potatoes in the china serving bowl that had been her mother's and passed the steaming spuds to Mike on her right. Ever since she was a child, at every family gathering, this beautiful bowl had served one purpose and one purpose only. This was where the garlic mashed potatoes with sour cream and chives were put and topped with a pat of butter before being covered and placed on the dining table to wait for the prayer of thanks.

Jordan held the bowl for Sierra. "Wait till you try my mom's mashed potatoes. These are the ones I said were worth the long drive. Seriously, Mom, this is what I came home for—your famous mashed potatoes."

Sierra looked across the table at Erin. "He really has been talking about your potatoes for two weeks now. If you don't mind sharing your recipes, I'd like to get this one along with your secret ingredient."

Erin swallowed a smile and answered with the same reply her mom always gave when anyone complimented her on this same recipe. "You add lots of love and an appalling amount of real butter."

Sierra's lips turned up in a compelling smile. That's when Erin knew she would be passing on more than just this recipe to Sierra. One day, this serving bowl would be hers as well. These mashed potatoes just wouldn't taste the same in any other bowl.

Erin had a deep longing to excuse herself from the table, go into the back room, and cry. She wanted to pick up the phone and say, "Mom, guess what? Jordan is in love. He's really in love. Her name is Sierra, and she's lovely and sweet, and you should be here to meet her."

Instead she drew in her stomach and let her shoulders roll forward. Then she held her chin up and smiled. She had found this was the best posture to take in moments like this when she missed her mother so much it felt as if a cannon-ball had blown a hole through the middle of her soul.

When Sierra slipped off to the guest room after dinner, Jordan took the opportunity to sidle up to his mom and put his arm around her. Jordan was the same height as Erin, so the two of them could look at each other eye to eye.

"Well?" It was the only word Jordan said.

Erin replied with a single word of blessing, "Yes."

7

May the road rise up to meet you.
May the wind be always at your back.
May the sun shine warm upon your face,
The rains fall soft upon your fields,
And until we meet again
May God hold you in the palm of his hand.

Jordan proposed to sweet Sierra on the beach in Santa Barbara in January. He went over all the details with Mike and Erin on the phone three days prior and said he had selected that particular day because it was exactly one year since he first had met her at Sunset Beach, Hawaii. At Jordan's insistence, Mike and Erin drove up to Santa Barbara to be there, waiting in the wings with a small gathering of friends and Sierra's parents to celebrate with the newly engaged couple.

The giddy clan cheered as the couple came walking back from the beach at sunset, bundled together in a blanket. Her ring was a simple, custom-designed etched band that Sierra convinced Jordan was all she wanted. She wasn't a diamond sort of girl. Her choice was to have a series of thin bands that she would add to her ring finger as the years went on, like the assortment of bangles she often wore on her arm. Unconventional, but as Erin had discovered, it was very much Sierra.

Jordan and Sierra were radiant and remained so during dinner. The group dined under a portico laced with twinkle lights and thick, gnarled grapevines at a beachfront restaurant. The owner was a friend of Sierra's dad.

Mike leaned over as Erin was midbite into the best calzone she had ever tasted. "This is good stuff," he said.

"Delicious." Erin dabbed the corners of her mouth with the red-and-white-checkered paper napkin.

"I'm not talking about the food. I mean life. Us. This. This is good stuff."

Erin leaned over and kissed her husband on the side of his neck. "Do you know that I love you more now than ever before?" Erin whispered.

Mike slipped his arm around her shoulder and drew her close. "I had a clue or two."

"Oh, really? What were your clues?"

Drawing back and looking closely at Erin's face he said, "It's your smile. I can always tell what you're thinking by the way you smile. And right now, you're smiling as if you love the whole world but especially me." He pressed his forehead against the side of her head and whispered in her ear, "And I love you more than ever, too."

Jordan and Sierra's wedding was set for August 7. Everyone assumed the two of them would zip through the planning because, after all, his mother did this for a living.

Within a week Erin knew that if she wanted to maintain a strong relationship with Jordan and Sierra, she would have to turn the planning connections on this one over to Sharlene. Erin had far too many opinions about what the couple should do, and like all young couples, the two of them had their own ideas.

"So I'll be the backup planner," Erin explained once she had Sharlene, Jordan, and Sierra on the phone the second week of January. "I need to be just the mother of the groom, if that makes sense. I'm here, and I'll do whatever you two ask, but from here on out, Sharlene will be the one to provide you with your personally designed portfolio and follow up with anything you need."

"Mom, you have no idea how much that helps us. Thank you. We were feeling uncomfortable with some of your suggestions, but we weren't sure how to tell you."

"I hope you don't feel as if we don't appreciate everything you put together for us." Sierra sounded concerned.

"Don't worry about any of that. I got a little over-eager and started to run ahead without taking the time to listen to what the two of you had in mind."

"Thank you for being so understanding," Sierra said. "I can already tell you're going to be a wonderful mother-in-law."

"Oh, I hope so, honey. I hope so."

Sharlene took over like the pro she was, and Jordan and Sierra were pleased with all the recommendations she pulled together for them. Since the wedding was going to be in Santa Barbara, Sharlene and Erin had to expand their connections beyond Orange County's borders. It turned out to be a helpful addition to their website and their business.

When the invitations went out, Erin followed up with a handwritten note to her brother, inviting him to stay with them after the wedding. She didn't hear from him until two weeks before the big day.

"I just can't pull it off, Erin. Sorry. I had hoped I might be able to come. It would be the first chance I've had to see you guys since I've gotten clean and sober." For the next twenty minutes he told her about the recovery program he had been in and how his life had been turned around.

Toward the end of their phone call, Erin told her brother, "I'm really glad to be able to talk with you like this, Tony."

"It's good to talk to you, too. Let's try to do this more often."

"I'd like that. I'm so glad the recovery program

has worked out for you. This is really, really good news."

"My wife and the girls think so, too. I was a mess for so long. The guy who heads our group has gone the distance with me, you know? It's what I needed. I wish I could come to Jordan's wedding. I really do. I think camping on the back-side of Maui is about as far as I'm going to make it anywhere during the month of August."

"I understand. Maybe Mike and I will have to come over there and see you guys."

"Now there's an idea. I'm ready to see you. I'm able to handle the real world, if you know what I mean. So come on over. I'm not sure you'll recognize me, though."

At their mother's funeral Tony's hair was long and hung in front of his face. He didn't make eye contact or have a conversation with anyone. Apparently he already had been using drugs for some time, but Erin, in her sisterly naiveté, told people he was in mourning and as shocked about the loss of their mother as she was. Had she known what was really going on, she would have responded differently to him.

"You haven't said anything about Dad," Tony said. "I'm assuming he's coming to the wedding with his wife."

Erin noted that Tony didn't seem to remember Delores's name. Either that or he chose not to speak it.

"Yes, they're coming. Dad said he wanted to drive so he would have his own car while they're here. He said they had big plans to go to Ireland earlier this spring, but they had some financial adjustments to make before they could go. I think they rescheduled their flight for the fall."

"What sort of financial adjustments?"

"I don't know. He's put a lot into the place where they live on the Oregon coast. All those remodeling expenses might have caught up with them. I didn't ask him. All I know is that he said they plan to take their time, drive down the coast, and stay here in Irvine after the wedding for at least a week."

Tony didn't reply.

"I really wish the two of you could be back in communication."

"I know. I'm almost there. Give me a little more space. I'm working on it."

Erin held on to the thought of "a little more space" as the final wedding details came together. Sierra and her mom were handling everything in Santa Barbara. All Mike and Erin had to work out were the details for the rehearsal dinner as well as transportation and accommodations.

Somehow those few arrangements kept hitting snags. Erin needed more space in her packed calendar.

The last week of July Sharlene showed up at Erin's with the newly altered mother-of-the-groom dress hanging in a zipped-up garment bag, compliments of the family dry-cleaning business.

"You are a lifesaver on so many levels, Sharlene. Thank you for having this done for me. I don't know what I'd do without you."

"Well, I can tell you what you're going to do *with* me once the wedding is over. You're going to sit down and go over these applications for assistants. I marked the ones that I think have the best potential. Our goal should be to have someone in place by the first of September, if not sooner."

Erin knew that Sharlene had been doing far more than her share over the past few weeks. Once the wedding was over, Erin would be able to go back to a regular workload and that assistant could work mostly with Sharlene. They both knew it was a nice problem to have, needing to hire someone.

As Erin spent the evening packing for the wedding weekend in Santa Barbara, she thought about all she had to be grateful for: Jordan's darling wife-to-be, the screaming success of The Happiest Day, and most recently, the great conversation she'd had with her brother.

She was almost ready to zip up the suitcase and go to bed when she decided she couldn't ignore the rumbling in her stomach any longer. It was hard to tell if the grumbles were over not eating enough in all her scrambling around that day or if she was feeling more nervous about this huge event in their son's life than she was letting herself believe.

Padding barefooted out to the kitchen, she told Mike, who was watching the eleven o'clock news, "I'm almost ready to go to bed. How about you?"

"I'll be there in a few minutes."

Erin opened the refrigerator door and stood for far too long, staring at the contents as if one of the uninteresting items would suddenly change into a Boston cream pie and start singing to her, "I am your midnight snack. Yum-yum! I'll calm those nerves and be nutritious for you, too!"

All she saw was a warehouse-sized glass jar of artichokes, a carton of orange juice, and four square plastic containers of leftovers.

"Did you eat the last of the broccoli salad?" she asked Mike.

He didn't answer. The sportscaster was giving the scores of the baseball teams that were World Series contenders.

Undeterred, Erin moved the containers around and peeled back the corners of the lids to determine if any of them held promise for a snack. As she reached her arm in for the large container at the back of the middle shelf, the huge jar of artichokes inched forward too far and toppled off the shelf.

Before she could catch it or move out of its path, the heavy glass jar came crashing down on the big toe of her left foot. She let out a scream as if she had been run through with a sword. Losing her balance in the wake of the sudden, over-whelming pain, Erin collapsed onto the floor and sobbed.

"What happened?" Mike towered over her, looking around for a clue.

The jar of artichokes had rolled, unscathed, across the floor and into the pantry, where it seemed to be hiding like a child who knew he was in trouble.

Mike's voice escalated. "What is it? What's wrong?"

Erin rocked back and forth, cradling her foot with both hands. "My toe," she managed to gasp.

Mike grabbed a kitchen towel, ran it under the cold water, and handed it to her to hold as a compress.

Catching her breath and feeling ridiculous for the dramatic burst of emotion, Erin tried to explain. "A jar fell . . . on my toe."

Mike leaned down to have a look. "Do you want an ice pack?"

"Yes."

He pulled out a frostbitten ice pack and handed it to her. "What else do you need?"

"Help me to get up." She couldn't believe the intensity of pain that was still shooting through her big toe. The metal rim of the jar must have hit right at the cuticle line. She had a sinking feeling that her whole foot was going to be in convalescence for the next few days. This was not good. The last thing Erin wanted to do was show up at the rehearsal dinner tomorrow wearing a sock with lots of padding around the big toe on her left foot. She could see herself hobbling around and watching people's expressions as she explained that a jar of artichokes fell on her toe.

Mike tried to help her to the bedroom but first she wanted him to see the culprit. As soon as he spotted the huge jar he winced. "Ouch! Oh, sweetheart, I can see how that would hurt."

She iced her toe and calmed down long enough to sleep, but it was a fitful night.

They rose early to get on the road, and the first thing Mike wanted to do was have a close look at her toe. It had turned a deep shade of purple and still was throbbing.

"You'll probably lose the nail." He said it as if he were familiar with these sorts of injuries. He had been the one their boys went to with their sports injuries and was handy with an ACE bandage. This time his recommendation was sandals so that her toe could breathe, whatever that meant.

Erin babied her foot to the car, kept it padded with a rolled-up towel, and iced it for the first hour of the drive. By the time they arrived at the hotel, it didn't hurt as bad.

Erin wasn't big on having her toenails painted.

When she got a pedicure, which was a rare treat that she didn't stop to take time for very often, she always had the manicurist buff her toenails instead of paint them. On the drive up, she had sent Mike into a drugstore for nail polish. He returned with three different colors, all in the range of dark plum. Before they went to the rehearsal dinner that night, Erin would make sure all her toenails were plum colored.

That morning she had thrown into her suitcase three different pairs of open-toed shoes since the pair she had bought for the wedding were closed-toed and tapered to a point. For good measure, she tossed in her walking shoes just in case she wanted to wear something protective around the hotel room.

It turned out she needed the walking shoes right away when Jordan asked Mike and Erin to help set up the outdoor venue where the wedding would be held the next day. This was their way of cutting back on expenses. Mike went to work helping Sierra's dad and two of her brothers set up tables and chairs. Dozens of strings of tiny white lights were already in place, strung from the trees that canopied the beautiful location. Sierra had collected dozens of Moroccan lanterns and hundreds of tea lights that were waiting until tomorrow to be put in place. It was easy to see that the wedding reception in this private park would be magical.

Erin pitched in, helping to wrap the plastic cutlery in a napkin and tie the bundles with colored yarn. She listened in on all the details of the plans Sierra and her mom had made with Sharlene's help for this picnic-style celebration.

She had heard a lot of the particulars along the way as Sierra would share some of her ideas and as Sharlene would update Erin. The experience gave Erin a new appreciation for what it was like to be on the other side of the business as the groom's mother.

Erin convinced Mike to take her back to the hotel while the others were finishing up so she could change out of her jeans and walking shoes into the outfit she had brought for the rehearsal dinner. She had a feeling the others weren't planning to change, but she wanted to. She was the hostess, and Mike was the host. She thought they should show up looking and smelling a little fresher than she was at the moment.

Plus, she wanted to paint her toenails and give them a chance to dry.

Forty-five minutes later, just as they were ready to leave their hotel for the rehearsal, Erin received a call from Dolores.

"We're not able to come."

Erin knew that others who were driving into Santa Barbara that afternoon had called to say the traffic was worse than usual.

"How far away are you? Are you at the hotel yet?"

"No, we're not at the hotel."

"Okay. Well, you have the information on the restaurant where we'll be for the rehearsal dinner, don't you?"

"We got the directions you sent," Delores snapped.

"Okay, good. Why don't you just come directly to the restaurant? The rest of us plan to arrive at around seven."

Delores hung up abruptly, but that wasn't anything new. Erin was in such a scramble over last-minute details and her role as the rehearsal dinner hostess that she didn't think to ask where they were or what the problem was. Erin simply expected her father to come strolling into the restaurant in time for dessert and to charm the socks off all of them.

But her father and Delores never showed up.

8

Here's to me, and here's to you,
And here's to love and laughter—
I'll be true as long as you,
And not one moment after.

When Delores didn't answer her cell phone after the rehearsal dinner, Mike said they were probably at the hotel sleeping after the long drive. When Erin and Mike met with Sierra's parents for breakfast in the hotel lobby the next morning, she sent Joel to check at the front desk to see if her dad and Delores had checked in.

Joel came back with a no-show report. Erin tried to call again, but still got no reply on Delores's cell.

"They have all the information," Mike said, trying to calm Erin as they dressed for the wedding. "You know your dad. He's done this sort of last-minute grand entrance before. They probably stayed at a less expensive hotel, and Delores forgot to recharge her phone."

While Erin knew all of Mike's suggestions were plausible, she still felt nervous.

"He's a big boy." Mike gave Erin a pat on the backside. "He can find his way here. You have another big boy who needs your undivided attention for the next few hours. Don't let your dad mess with you like this."

Erin took Mike's advice and headed for the ceremony all smiles like the rest of the wedding party. She watched for her dad and Delores while the guests were arriving and being seated. Then, as soon as Jordan held out his arm and walked her down the aisle to her chair on the right side, she tuned in to only Jordan and Sierra. Their beautiful, God-honoring ceremony was gorgeous.

When the photographer rounded up family members for photos after the ceremony, Erin sent Joel and Grant on one more search for her dad and Delores. They came back with only shrugs and cheese and crackers from the reception sampler platter. As soon as Erin could step away, she went to the bride's dressing room, took out her phone, and tried Delores one more time. Still no answer.

In a desperate attempt, Erin called their home number in Oregon. She was stunned when Delores answered the phone at the Hidden Cottage.

"Delores, what are you doing there? What's going on?"

In a matter-of-fact tone, Delores said, "We decided not to come."

Erin dropped onto a bench seat covered with clothes in the bride's room. "What did you say?"

"We decided not to come. We just couldn't do it." Delores's voice was as slate-cold as Erin had ever heard it.

"Let me talk to my dad."

"He's not able to come to the phone right now."

"Why not?"

"He's not here at the moment."

Erin's heart pounded in her ears. She pictured her father, uncaring and self-serving, sitting at the corner table at Jenny Bee's, chatting up the waitress and eating a blueberry muffin. How could he do this to her?

"I sent a card," Delores said with muscle in her tone. "Both your father and I wish your son and his wife the best. We hope this is a happy day for all of you."

"I don't even know what to say to that, Delores." Erin's jaw clenched. She was certain that Delores, the true decision maker now in their relationship, had convinced her father that she didn't want to come and be around all those people who didn't like her. "Why didn't you tell me sooner? I can't believe this. Why didn't you tell me you weren't coming when you called me last night?"

"Listen, Erin, you have to hear what I'm saying to you right now. Are you listening?"

"Of course I'm listening."

"This day is not about your father. It's about your son. It won't do you any good to spend the day mad at Jack. You'll be better off focusing all your emotions in a positive way on your son and his wife."

Erin was too much in shock to reply to Delores's firm comment. *How dare she say that to me! Why is she telling me how I'm supposed to feel?*

Delores was in control of this conversation, as she had been in control of so many things since she had married Erin's father. Erin knew she didn't have the emotional energy to stage a coup d'état over Delores's reigning position. Not now. Not here. Not over the phone.

Erin hung up without saying another word.

The anguish Erin felt brought on a headache such as she hadn't experienced since her pregnancy with Joel, when her blood pressure skyrocketed. Mike came looking for her.

"Is everything okay?"

She spewed her anger, and Mike listened patiently. He didn't say anything at first. Then he told her to stay right there while he went for some aspirin. He returned with a bottle of cold water and a tiny bottle of painkillers.

After she swallowed two of the pills, Mike said, "Let's go on from here. Shake off whatever you're feeling about Delores and your dad. This is Jordan and Sierra's day."

Part of her hated that his conclusion was the same as Delores's. Another part of her adored her husband for patiently and tenderly helping her to get back on track.

Erin felt herself calming down.

"How's your toe doing? Is that adding to your stress?"

"No, it's fine. It doesn't hurt."

Sharlene popped her head in the bride's room. "There you are. They sent me to find you two for the family pictures." With a closer look at Erin, she asked, "Are you guys okay? Please tell me those are happy tears."

"My dad didn't come."

"I noticed that."

"I don't know why he married her, Sharlene. Delores is the most controlling person ever. I'm trying to take Mike's advice and shake it off."

"Listen." Sharlene motioned for the two of them to scoot out the door. "You can complain all you want about her on Monday when we're back at work. But for now, you have a lot of wonderful people waiting to congratulate you. You also have a son and a new daughter who need you to be here, in the moment, mind, body, and soul. So pull yourself together."

Erin put on some lipstick and returned to the reception to smile in all the photos. Being immersed in a sea of celebration had a cleansing effect on her wounded spirit. By the time she had danced with each of her sons and felt Mike's supportive arm firmly wrapped around her waist, thoughts of her father's absence were put aside. The current of this river of the next generation's joy carried her through the night and brought her safely to shore in her husband's arms when they slid under the sheets late that night.

The next morning Erin peeled back all the gauzy layers that had covered her heart wound, and she could feel the anger seeping its poison into her spirit once again.

Crawling out of bed, Erin quietly lifted her cell phone from her purse. She closed the bathroom door and punched in the phone number to her father's Hidden Cottage.

"Delores, please put my dad on the phone."

"He's not able to speak to you, Erin."

"Please, Delores. Just put him on the phone."

"Erin, listen to me. I can give him the phone, but he will not be able to speak to you."

The tiny confines of the hotel bathroom closed in on her. "What are you saying, Delores?"

"Your father had another stroke."

The energy flowed out the bottom of Erin's feet. "When?"

"Two and a half weeks ago."

"What!"

"He didn't want you to know. You have to believe me when I say that he didn't want you to know."

"Delores!"

"I'll tell you everything, Erin, and you can be as furious as you want, but listen. Since you were here a year and a half ago your father has had four more TSIs, small strokes. Each time he's felt weak and sick for a few days, and then he would bounce back. The doctor said it's not uncommon. The blood thinner he's on is supposed to break up the blood clots that form in his legs. I have taken him to the doctor for testing every month for the past year."

Erin could barely breathe.

"This last one, though, was different. He got up one morning, said he felt dizzy, and went back to bed. I checked on him later, and he was off."

"What do you mean, 'off'?"

"His eyes weren't focusing. He couldn't communicate with me. I called an ambulance right away, and he spent three days in the hospital, a week and a half at a convalescent facility, and then . . ."

"Then what? Delores, is he okay?"

"No, he's not okay. This time the clot lodged in his brain stem. Erin, your father is paralyzed on his right side."

Erin lowered herself to the floor with a thud.

"He's unable to speak. He can barely swallow."

The bathroom door opened, and Mike entered. "Are you okay?"

Erin shook her head. "My dad . . ."

Mike took the phone from her, pushed the speaker button, and went into warrior-husband mode. "Jack, what did you just say to my wife?"

"It's not Jack. She's talking to me, Mike." Delores's voice came across the speaker with a lifeless, metallic ring to it. "I just told Erin that her father had a severe stroke. That's why we didn't come to the wedding. You both can be as angry as you want, but you have to realize he didn't want to ruin your day. He made it clear he didn't want you to know. I had to promise not to tell you until after the wedding."

Delores relayed the same facts to Mike, adding more details as to the severity of the stroke, the very slim possibility that the paralysis could be temporary or that Jack might regain his speech due to the part of the brain affected by the lack of blood during the stroke. She said she had kept a list of the events, the doctors, the meds, and all the insurance information.

"I have a copy of all of it for you."

Mike turned to Erin. She still felt as if she couldn't form an expression, let alone a decisive word.

"We'll pack up our bags and start the drive up there today, Delores." Mike raised his eyebrows and dipped his chin, looking at Erin for a sign of agreement to his decision.

She nodded.

"We'll call you along the way and let you know

when we think we might arrive. Are you at the hospital?"

"No. They sent him home yesterday."

They sent him home to die. Erin couldn't stand the thought of her father, indomitable Jack O'Riley, unable to move. Or to speak.

"We'll drive straight through," Erin said quietly. "We have to."

Mike had his hand on her shoulder as he asked Delores something Erin wouldn't have asked if the phone had still been in her hand.

"Delores, put the phone up to Jack's ear."

"I can do that, but as I told you, he's not able to speak."

"He can listen. He needs to hear his daughter's voice." Mike held the cell phone closer to Erin and nodded to her.

Her look at him must have been one of desperation because Mike leaned closer. Calmly and quietly he said, "Tell him you love him. This might be your last chance."

Erin swallowed and focused her attention on the phone as Mike held it up to her. She could hear Delores's voice in the distance say, "Jack, Erin wants to say something to you."

"Dad?"

Before Erin could say another word, she heard a great groan come through the phone followed by what sounded like choked sobs. She looked up at Mike. Was her father crying? Jack O'Riley never cried. Not even at her mother's funeral. He was the strong one who comforted everyone else.

"Dad? We're coming to see you. Mike and I are coming. We're driving up today." Erin spoke loudly over his groans, even though she felt as if her voice were barely squeezing out the words. "You take it easy, okay? We'll be there as soon as we can."

The sound that came over the phone as a response from her father barely sounded human.

"We're leaving Santa Barbara as soon as we can, Dad. Okay. I'm going to hang up now."

Mike nudged her onward with his expression.

"And, Dad? I love you." The tears overtook her before she could stop them.

Mike took the phone back. "I love you, too, Jack. You hang in there, okay? We'll be there as soon as we can."

Closing the phone, Mike knelt in front of Erin, and the two of them fell into each other's arms as Erin cried into the curve of her husband's neck.

Erin felt numb as she packed their clothes. They left the hotel as soon as they could with a hasty good-bye to friends and family who were still there. Erin could tell that Mike was at the same thin place she was emotionally. After the high of the wedding the day before, neither of them was prepared for the drop-off that came with this news.

As he'd promised, Mike made sure they

checked in with Delores every few hours. Her reports were always the same. "Jack is resting. No change."

With a stop outside of Redding for fuel and another in Medford, Mike made what he called an executive decision and told Erin they would drive only a few more hours to Eugene before finding a hotel.

"I can drive some more if it would help," Erin said. "It looks like it's going to be light for at least another few hours. Don't you think we should keep going?"

"I think we should eat something and get some sleep."

"But what if my dad . . ."

"He's stable for the time being. You and I won't be of any help to him if we push the rest of the way. Last time you drove there it took more than four hours from Portland, right? Trust me on this. We need to be ready for anything when we get there. Right now both of us are wrung out."

Erin knew Mike was right. After a good dinner of fresh salmon and asparagus at a small restaurant in Springfield, Oregon, they wearily made their way back to a tidy little hotel room where they pulled down the shades and immediately fell asleep.

The next morning, as Erin laced up her walking shoes, Mike asked, "How is your toe, by the way? You seem to be doing fine. Is it still hurting?"

"No. It hasn't bothered me. It's going to be okay. I thought it would be a lot worse than it is." She wished those words would be true of her father's condition as well, but she knew that was too big of a wish.

Driving through a quirky little espresso hut, Mike ordered a regular coffee along with Erin's usual nonfat, decaf latte.

"Really? Nonfat, decaf?" the young woman taking the order responded.

Erin was caught off guard by the remark. "What's wrong with that?" she spouted back.

The girl didn't hesitate to say cheerfully, "I'm just saying that, on a morning like this, if I were you, I'd order a 'why not.'"

"And what is a 'why not'?"

"Three shots of Italian espresso with Mayan dark chocolate powder, extra foamy half-and-half with whipped cream and cinnamon on top."

"Fine. I'll have one of those."

"Why not, right?" The girl looked pleased.

Mike looked surprised.

"Why not?" Erin repeated.

Once they were back on the freeway, Mike asked, "So, how is it?"

Erin licked the dash of cinnamon and whipped cream from her upper lip. "Quite possibly the best latte I've ever had. Or should I say, the best dessert. It's like a mocha cream pie only hot. Do you want to try it?"

"No thanks. This coffee is definitely the best I've had in a long time. They certainly know how to brew their beans here in the Northwest."

"At least that must be some comfort in their long, wet winters. Although you would never believe they endure all that rain by the looks of things since we entered Oregon. All the grass along the road is dried, and how hot was it when we drove through Medford? Didn't that sign at the bank across from the gas station say it was eighty-six?"

"It's August." Mike took another swig of his coffee. "It can't rain here all year long."

The fully caffeinated espresso not only got Erin's eyes all the way open, but it also worked at opening up her mouth to process with Mike the churning thoughts and feelings that had been bumping around in her head and heart the previous day.

"I don't know what I'm going to say to Delores when I see her."

"You might try starting with 'Thank you.'"

"Thank you for what? For not telling me about the strokes my father was having? There is no excuse for her keeping that significant information from me."

"Actually, there is an excuse."

Erin looked at her husband in disbelief. "Are you taking her side?"

"I'm saying she honored your father's request

to not let his condition affect Jordan's wedding. Erin, think what a different day it would have been for everyone if you had known why your dad and Delores weren't there."

She didn't want Mike to be right. She wanted to stay angry. If she couldn't keep her anger going against Delores in all this, where was she supposed to put it?

"It's a brutal mercy when things like this happen. But you and I both know if you dig past the brutal part, you'll find the mercy. That's what you need to think about now. Our son's wedding would have been a different day if we had known about your dad. He wanted you to be free to celebrate. That might well be the last gift he's able to give you. Just receive it, sweetheart."

Erin let her tears tumble over her warm cheeks. "You know, we've hardly talked about Jordan and Sierra's wedding. It was beautiful, wasn't it?"

"Yes, it was." Mike's calm voice filled the car, and the rest of the miles slipped by buoyed by memories of their son's "Happiest Day." Erin was beginning to understand what Mike had said earlier. It would have been a different day if Delores had given them the news earlier.

By the time they arrived on the outskirts of the coastal town of Moss Cove, Erin felt surprisingly calm. The area looked different from the way it had in the winter. Instead of closed-up buildings along the main street, the place had come alive with commerce. On the corner was an ice cream shop advertising saltwater taffy and displaying dozens of colorful pinwheels and streamers that twirled in the fresh breeze.

Mike slowed down to meet the twenty-mile-per-hour speed limit on the narrow two-lane road that wound through town.

"Charming place," he said.

"The sunshine helps. And all the flower baskets hanging from the lampposts. I assure you, this was a different town a year ago in February. When I was here, it felt like a dismal junkyard for amnesiac sailors."

Mike turned to Erin with a startled look. "How can you say that? This place is great. I can see why your dad wanted to move here. This is like something out of a movie. Look at the ocean. And these houses. This is a town that time forgot."

"It's rustic, I'll agree with you there."

"Those houses up there on the hills, now those look like the place to be, surrounded by the forest. This is good stuff."

"You really like it, don't you?"

"Think of all the open land we passed on our way here. We live in a cubicle in Irvine. A single honeycomb that's part of a huge, standardized hive. Look at that house right there. Now that's the work of some individualist. Did you see that huge piece of driftwood stuck in the ground to support all those birdhouses? Now that's the way to live."

Erin studied Mike's expression. "You're being sarcastic. Tell me you're being sarcastic."

"No." His unchanged face validated his answer.

"I can't believe it. I thought I knew everything there was to know about you. Never in a million years would I have guessed you would like a place like this. Next you're going to tell me you would like to live here."

"No, don't worry. That's not what I was thinking."

"Okay, so at least you haven't gone completely nuts on me. Oh, turn right here at the gravel drive just beyond that phone pole."

Mike put on the car's blinker. "I wouldn't want to live here because I wouldn't want to try to find work in a place like this, and I wouldn't want to commute anywhere. But I would like to come here for a vacation."

"Or retirement?" Erin asked as Mike headed down the gravel decline that led to Hidden Cottage.

"Maybe. I'll tell you one thing. I'd definitely take up fishing if I was here for vacation."

"Fishing? Do you like to fish?"

Instead of answering, Mike slowed the car to a crawl and peered out the front windshield trying to see past the dotted collection of smashed bugs. "Wow. Is this the place?"

"This is it."

Hidden Cottage shone like a sparkling gem in

the full sunlight. The front door, painted a warm persimmon red, looked welcoming and inviting against the sunflower yellow paint that covered the rest of the cottage under the dark pitched roof.

"It's a different color," Erin said. "I remember its being gray. Everything was gray the last time I was here. The sky, the sea, the house." She had to admit, the summer cottage they were now parked in front of looked charming and welcoming. It was a different place from the one she had visited a year and a half ago.

Erin also knew that the scene that would greet them inside would be vastly different from what she had experienced a year and a half ago.

"You ready?" Mike set the emergency brake and offered Erin a brave smile.

She nodded. But inwardly she knew she wasn't. What daughter is ever ready to see the hero of her life diminished in stature and confined to a state of partial mobility?

As she shuffled through the gravel to the makeshift wheelchair ramp that led up to the deck, Mike took her hand in his. He gave her hand two firm squeezes.

Biting the inside of her cheek, Erin returned three "love-you-too" squeezes to the man who now stood by her side, hand in hand, heart in heart. With Mike beside her, Erin felt ready to face whatever awaited them behind the persimmon red cottage door.

9

**May joy and peace surround you,
Contentment latch your door,
And happiness be with you now
And God bless you evermore.**

A surrealistic, alternate life began the moment Delores opened the door of Hidden Cottage and welcomed Erin and Mike inside.

Erin went directly to her father, as she had on her last visit when he was tucked under a blanket in his recliner. That time her father had barked at her about taking so long to get there and then gruffly received the kiss she planted on his cheek. Erin remembered how she had teased him and said, "I'm here now. . . . Isn't that good enough for you?"

His reply had been "Never good enough, you know that."

This time Erin could barely bring herself to plant a kiss on her father's cheek, which glistened with streaks of his own saliva. Nor could she find any words of cheer, charm, or comfort. The man propped up in the recliner seemed a poor imitation of her father.

He didn't bark at her. Instead he wept. He sobbed odd, guttural sounds as huge tears rolled down his pale face and dampened the washcloth that seemed to be an improvised bib under his chin.

Erin had no bravery in her. She cried quietly, all the while keeping unbroken eye contact with her father, her blue eyes mirroring the terror in his matching blue eyes.

She glanced at his right hand where it rested on his stomach, curled into a gnarled fist. His knuckles protruded in a crumpled tangle. He looked so thin. His beautiful white hair had been cut unevenly and was shorter than Erin had ever seen it. He appeared to her as a great lion, captured, wounded, and shorn.

"I'm so sorry," she finally whispered.

Those tiny words threw her father into an even deeper state of wailing, like a wounded animal. The sound went into her bones, and Erin knew she would never forget it.

Mike placed a firm hand on Erin's shoulder and pulled her back, breaking the eye-to-eye contact between daughter and father. With strength and boldness, Mike moved closer. He reached for a dry washcloth from a stack on the end table and began the work of an orderly, wiping away Jack's tears and drool. Mike leaned closer, spoke calmly, and told Jack they came as soon as they could.

"The wedding was wonderful," Mike said. "We'll show you all the pictures as soon as we get them. Jordan married a beautiful young woman. I think you'll like her very much. She feels like part of the family already."

To Erin's surprise, her father's demeanor seemed instantly to change with Mike's ministering touch. Her dad's left eyebrow went up, as if indicating interest to hear more. Mike moved the pillow under Jack's head without asking if he wanted it moved. But as soon as Mike adjusted it the taut muscle in Jack's neck relaxed, and it seemed as if it were easier now for him to look at them.

Mike made himself comfortable by sitting in the wheelchair parked beside the recliner. He went over some wedding details, describing the location, the bridal party, and the ceremony. Jack listened expressionless but his eyes showed he was clearly engaged. He was as calm as a contented cat.

Erin had been aware of Delores's presence behind her as she watched her husband say and do for her father what she wished she had been able to say and do. Turning to Delores, Erin asked, "May I use your bathroom?"

"Of course. You know where it is."

Excusing herself, Erin used the private moments in the bathroom as a chance to blow her nose, summon all her courage, and let the reality of the situation settle on her. She had a long list of questions forming and knew that she and Mike would have to make some difficult decisions before this day was over.

When she returned to the living room, her father was asleep. "Is he okay?" she whispered to Delores.

With a condescending look Delores said, "Obviously he's not."

"I mean, right now. Did he just fall asleep?"

"Yes. He does that. He sleeps most of the time." Getting right to business, Delores said, "I made reservations for you at the Shamrock Lodgettes down the road. You passed them on the way here. If you would rather stay here, one of you can sleep in the twin bed in the upstairs room and one of you can sleep down here on the sofa."

"Thanks." Erin turned to Mike, who was now standing beside her in the small kitchen. "What do you think we should do?"

"We'll stay at the Shamrock," Mike said. "We can check in now, settle in, and then come back here, if that's okay."

"Of course." It seemed to Erin that Delores looked as bad as her father did. Her hair was very short and looked as if she had received a bad haircut and then hadn't washed her hair for several days. She looked exhausted.

"How about if we bring dinner for you, Delores?"

"No. I have my own food here. I don't have food for the two of you, so you should eat before you come back."

Erin glanced at her father, sleeping in the recliner in the other room. "When he wakes up, tell him we'll be back." Seeing him the way he was right now made it difficult to estimate if his condition was going to be long term or if he was limited in the number of days, weeks, or months he had left.

Mike and Erin walked out to the car, holding hands. Fast-moving clouds from the east covered the sun, blocking the bit of summertime warmth that barely had visited this jagged coastline. Erin wrapped her light sweater around her and knew she would have to find some warmer clothes if she was going to survive here.

They drove in silence to the Shamrock Lodgettes and checked into the sparse wooden cabin with a round of information from Sylvia, the talkative motel manager. She was a large woman with a deep voice. Around her neck she wore an exotic long chain of beads. On the end of the chain was a large pair of reading glasses with rims that were equally colorful and exotic-looking. As she handed Erin the key to their lodgette, she said she had a tender spot in her heart for Jack and wanted to know if she could pay him a visit.

"I don't see why not," Erin said. "He brightened up when my husband told him about our son's wedding. I think it would do him good to have some company."

"Tell that to Delores, will you? That wife of his seems bent on keeping all of us away from him as if we're carrying the next untreatable disease. She even said to my face that it wouldn't do him any good to have visitors. She's a heartless you-know-what if you ask me. Never joins him at any of the community gatherings. But when it comes to your dad, I'll tell you what, he's the most popular man in town. Always the life of the party. Why, if he had moved up here when he was still a widower, I would have married him myself. Don't tell my husband that."

Mike and Erin politely excused themselves from the office and the friendly Sylvia. They agreed that Jack should have some visitors. He was a people person to the core. For Delores to lock him up in that small cottage and not allow the townsfolk to come see him was unkind. Erin was determined to change that.

Mike agreed with her but disagreed with how to go about making the change. Erin wanted to return to her father's place that evening with several of his cronies in tow. Mike felt strongly that they shouldn't catch Delores off guard by doing so.

"We need to talk with Delores about it," he said. "It's her home, too."

Erin preferred to forget that fact. All she cared about at the moment was doing all she could for her dad.

"He doesn't look good, does he?"

Mike wrapped his arms around her and drew her close. "No, he doesn't look good. I'm guessing he's been on a rapid downward path ever since you last saw him. He couldn't have gotten to where he is now in just two weeks. I think he's been keeping his condition from you for a long time."

"I should have come back up sooner. I should have checked in on him."

Mike hushed her. "You're here now. That's what matters. And we're here together. This is the new normal. We need to work from this point out."

Mike opened his arms, releasing Erin. She wasn't quite ready for him to remove his cocoon of comfort. She watched as he went to his luggage and pulled out his laptop. Turning it on and sitting at the small table in the corner of the room as if setting up his new office, he said, "Let's make a list. We need a plan."

Erin was familiar with the way her husband approached most everything in life with his "research and development" mind-set. He loved to look at things from every angle, brainstorm the possible directions they could go, and then come up with a step-by-step plan for implementing the strategies.

Before they returned to Hidden Cottage that evening, Erin and Mike had agreed that Jack needed to be moved back to Irvine, where he could receive prompt and highly qualified medical attention as his condition progressed, or more likely regressed. Mike said he would present their plan to Delores that evening and see what she had to say. Neither of them expected Delores to hesitate to move back to California.

When they returned to the cottage, Jack was still asleep.

"Mike, would you mind sitting with Jack?" Delores reached for her jacket on the peg by the back door. "I'd like to talk to Erin. Outside."

Mike looked at Erin. She gave a slight nod, letting him know she was okay with being left alone with Delores.

"Sure," Mike said.

Delores opened the door and led the way. Instead of sitting on the built-in bench that lined the deck's edge, she strode through the freshly cut grass on the top of the bluff. Then, winding through a path cut in the flourishing brush, she made her way to a flat area at the crest of the cliff. A cement bench waited there, facing the sea and the sunset.

Erin stopped to take in the immense view. "This is beautiful."

"The bench was Jack's idea." Delores took a seat with her hands in the pockets of her coat, her face to the wind. "That's why he paid a ridiculous amount of money to have the cement poured and make sure the bench wouldn't blow away in a winter gale. He used to spend a lot of time out here."

Erin sat beside Delores, folding her arms and pulling her sweater close. As far as she could see to the immediate right, immediate left, and directly ahead was nothing but the sea. It was like being on the front bow of a tall ship. "I can see why my dad likes it here."

"He hasn't been out here in at least eight months."

"Delores, why didn't you tell us how bad he was doing?"

"It's what he wanted. He was adamant about it. He didn't want anyone to know."

Erin felt a rise of unconventional compassion for Delores. "I can't imagine how hard all this has been on you."

"You're right. You can't imagine. He wasn't honest with me, you know."

Erin gave a small shiver and wished she could reach over and take Delores's hand, but she didn't feel that Delores was the sort of woman who wanted to be comforted.

"Jack told me a month ago he had been having small strokes for the past five years."

"Five years?"

Turning to Erin with a slight air of superiority, Delores added, "You didn't know that either, did you?"

"I knew he had headaches sometimes. But, no, I never heard they were related to strokes."

"Did he ever tell you he felt as if he had been hit in the head with a sledgehammer?"

"No. I remember he said he had a migraine a few years ago when Mike and I asked him to go to the movies with us. But I thought he wasn't interested in what we wanted to see."

"Do you remember his getting dizzy and then sleeping it off?"

"Maybe. A few times. I'm not sure."

Is Delores trying to get me to share the blame or responsibility for not detecting his condition sooner?

"Your father wasn't honest with me about his condition. He should have told me these things before he asked me to marry him. I was completely honest with him about my situation. He knew what he was getting into. He gave me no indication that he had been having any problems."

Erin wasn't sure what to do with Delores's impromptu confession.

"The man I married led me to believe he was strong and full of life. He promised to show me the world. Instead we got stuck here." She sighed, and her frustration was evident. "This wasn't our plan. You don't know what I've been going through. I'm sure you can't imagine how difficult it's been to care for him. I can't keep doing all that I've been doing for him. I just can't do it. I think anyone would agree I have gone above and beyond."

Erin took the opportunity to propose the solution she and Mike had come up with. "What do you think about coming back to Irvine? Mike and I have talked about it, and we think we can be of more help if you and Dad are nearby."

Delores stood up as if their conversation was suddenly over. "I thought that would be your solution."

"So you agree?" Erin stood, too. Her height helped her feel as if she still were able to respond to Delores as an adult and not as a child being shamed for something that wasn't her fault.

"I don't know how you're going to transport him all the way down there, but I'm sure you can figure that out. Now that he has the catheter and G-tube in his stomach for the direct feeding, the doctor said he doesn't need to be in a convalescent-care facility quite yet. All the information is in the file I've been compiling. It won't take long to pack up this place. I have everything organized."

"So you're in agreement this is the best thing to do?"

Delores turned to her. Her face was still expressionless. "Of course." She then turned her view back to the sea.

"Mike and I want you to know we are willing to do whatever we can to help. Mike is taking his vacation days this week so he'll be here until next Monday."

A strange, condescending look crossed Delores's face. Or perhaps it was a shadow of sorrow. It was so hard to tell what Delores was thinking. "You should know one more thing. The doctor said that sometimes physically fit men like your father can live quite a few more years after a brain stem stroke, especially if their heart is strong."

"Okay. Well, we'll have just to take each day as it comes."

The chill of the ocean spray rose from the cliffs below and brushed their faces with a fine misting of salty moisture.

"That's all any of us can do at this point." The chill in Delores's voice matched what Erin was feeling all around her.

Without any verbal signal, the two of them turned and walked back to the cottage without exchanging words of courage or comfort. Erin thought about the conversation they had shared over a year ago in the grocery store when Delores made it clear that she would leave Jack if he had serious health problems. Apparently she had changed her mind or at least accepted the part of her wedding vows that promised "in sickness and in health."

As they entered the warm house, Erin saw that her father was awake. She smiled at him. He stared with a glassy-eyed look as if he couldn't make out who the two women were. When she came to his side, his left eyebrow lifted, and he started to cry again. The gut-wrenching wails seemed to rise from his soul and overtook the small space.

Erin looked at Mike and gave him a nod, indicating that she had had the important discussion with Delores. Taking her father's hand, she said, "Dad, we've been talking about what would be the best thing to do, and we would like to take you back to California."

"No!" The word jumped from Jack's mouth so forcefully it seemed to surprise even him. He looked at Erin, blinking. She looked at Mike, not sure what to do or say next.

Delores, who had hung back in the kitchen, spoke up. "I didn't say he would go to California willingly."

Erin watched as her father raised his agile left arm. He pointed his finger down with three staccato movements. Clearly he was indicating this was the place he wanted to be. He wanted to stay put.

"Well, then," Mike said, keeping his focus on Jack. "We'll have to continue discussing this and see what works out best for everyone."

Jack let out a heavy sigh. He seemed to be trying very hard to concoct a sentence or even just another word. All that came from his sluggish lips was gibberish. The expression on his face changed to one of discouragement or despondency. It was impossible to distinguish the difference. He closed his eyes as if dismissing all of them and slipped back into a place of numbing sleep.

The first thing Mike did was convince Delores to hire a day nurse to care for Jack. Mike also rearranged all the furniture in the living room so that it was easier to get the wheelchair around. It was clear, though, that Jack wasn't able to lift himself into the wheelchair. Lifting and moving him was an arduous task, which is why they both smiled when Marge, a sturdy fortress of a woman, showed up from the nursing agency the next day. With Delores running out of steam, Marge was the sort of assistant they had hoped for.

On Wednesday morning Delores left, saying she needed to go into town. Erin thought she might be doing some shopping or taking a much-needed break now that she had reinforcements in place. When Delores returned six hours later, she looked red in the face and windblown, as if she had been driving around with all the windows of her car open.

"How are you doing?" Erin asked cautiously.

Delores was in the kitchen, opening a can of chicken and rice soup. "I've been better." She placed three saltine crackers on a plate and poured the soup into a mug.

"Is there anything I can do for you?"

Delores looked surprised at Erin's offer. "There's nothing to be done beyond what you're already doing." She sat in a chair next to Jack, eating the crackers first and then slowly drinking the soup. When she finished, she calmly thanked Erin and Mike for being there. Then she went to her room and closed the door.

Erin was beginning to understand the ways that different personalities deal with stress. Delores seemed to be coping by removing herself emotionally as well as physically from the hub of it all. Mike clicked into planning mode. He made calls, bought groceries, and fixed the broken garden hose on the side of the cottage. He was determined to have everything ready to move Jack and Delores to California as soon as possible, in spite of Jack's resistance to the idea.

Erin tried to take each hour as it came and not to let her emotions dictate anything she said or did. She felt steady if she continued to process things only moment by moment.

Late Thursday night she told Mike that she felt like a fish caught in a net. If she tried to flap around and break free of the situation, it made her only tired and discouraged. If she relaxed and went with the flow, she felt okay. But she still knew she was caught.

Mike finished brushing his teeth and stood in the bathroom in his new navy sweatpants and green fleece with a Paddy's Crab Shack logo. They had stopped at a souvenir shop on their way back to the Shamrock that night because Erin said she was tired of feeling so cold. They bought matching outfits, which was something they had never done before. Erin was already under the covers and wearing her fleece zip-up jacket and sweats. For the first time since they had arrived, she felt toasty warm.

"Speaking of fish, does your sweatshirt have a fishy smell?" Erin asked.

Mike sniffed his forearm. A string of dental floss hung from his mouth. "No. Does yours?"

"A little. Or maybe it's just me. I still smell the clam chowder we had for dinner."

"That was pretty good chowder. What did you think of it?"

Erin shrugged. "It was okay."

Mike kept his focus on his reflection in the small bathroom mirror as he meticulously wove the dental floss between his teeth. Erin couldn't remember the last time she had flossed. Yet Mike did every night. She leaned back and watched him, deciding this was one of the many tiny reasons she loved him so much. Mike took care of things. Even little things like his teeth. He was consistent and practical. And he loved her.

Erin suddenly realized how rare and wonderful it was to have someone so dependable and patient to walk with through life.

"Mike?"

He turned toward her.

"I love you."

A slow smile came to his closed lips. He tossed the dental floss into the trash can, turned out the bathroom light, and came to bed with her. "So, what got you interested? Is it the new sweatshirt?"

She leaned into him and cuddled up. "No. It's just you. You're wonderful. I love you."

Mike kissed the top of her head. "I love you, too."

They drew close, sharing a lingering kiss and then curling into each other's embrace. This was familiar. This was good. In the midst of everything else that was challenging and unsteady, settling into Mike's strong arms felt true.

"I wish I didn't have to go back home without you," Mike said.

"I know. Me too."

Erin knew that Mike had been working hard to make arrangements to set up a place for Jack and Delores in California. The details were as numerous as the obstacles, and Mike had to get back to work on Monday. Delores had quietly gone along with all their suggestions, and it was agreed that Erin would stay on another week while Mike prepared everything in Irvine.

She could float along in this big fish net for another week. She had to.

"I feel as if our roles in life are reversing," Erin said. "My dad is now the child, and I'm the adult telling him what he has to do. It's so awkward with Delores being detached the way she is. I think she has shut down even more than when we arrived."

Mike agreed. "She's not doing well, is she? This has been hard on her. It will be good for both of them to get back to Irvine."

Erin tried to imagine what her life was going to be like with her dad and Delores living nearby. Nothing would be the same again.

She pressed in closer to her warm husband. She kissed him once and then kissed him again. Life was going by too fast. Tonight she needed to feel alive—vibrant and youthful and very much alive. Mike had no problem making that happen.

10

These things I warmly wish for you:
Someone to love,
Some work to do,
A bit o' sun,
A bit o' cheer,
And a guardian angel
Always near.

On Friday morning, Erin's cell phone rang before she was awake. Mike was in the shower of their room at the Shamrock and for a moment she had forgotten where she was. She reached for her phone and saw that the call was from Sharlene.

"Sorry to call you so early," Sharlene said. "I have back-to-back appointments this morning, and I needed to hear from you on a couple of details that have to be decided today. Did you see my e-mail?"

"No, I didn't see it yet. I'm sorry, Sharlene. Are there some things we can figure out now over the phone?"

For the next few minutes Sharlene ran down a

list of office details that required their mutual agreement. They were able to settle the pressing details, and Erin apologized again for not checking in sooner. She had talked to Sharlene only once since the wedding a week ago.

"I really appreciate your carrying all this, Sharlene."

"Well, you've been carrying a lot yourself the past few weeks. We'll get on track Monday when you're back in the office."

Erin squeezed her eyes shut and wished she had let Sharlene know yesterday about the decision she and Mike had made for her to stay on another week. Telling her friend now made it seem as if she didn't take her responsibilities at The Happiest Day seriously.

"Listen, Sharlene. Mike and I had to make a tough decision yesterday. He's flying home this weekend, but I'm staying on another week. We don't have the details in place yet to get my dad and Delores set up in Irvine. Mike is working on it."

There was a pause before Sharlene said, "When you called earlier this week I thought you said that you had found a day-care nurse for your dad."

"We did."

"So why do you need to stay?"

Erin didn't have an immediate answer.

"I don't mean to sound callous," Sharlene said. "I know this is really difficult for all of you. I just didn't expect you to stay up there another week. We have a lot happening right now. I thought you were going to be back on Monday so I scheduled appointments for you."

Erin's still-groggy mind spun.

Sharlene stepped back into the conversation and said, "But listen, I understand the stress you guys are going through. I can work out the appointments for next week. It'll be okay. You just do what you need to do and come back as soon as you can. I hope I didn't add more stress to you by calling, especially so early."

"No, it's okay. I should have called you yesterday."

Erin and Sharlene talked for a few more minutes, and Erin got a better picture of how much her friend had been carrying of the business load over the past several weeks while Erin was wrapped up in Jordan's wedding and now her father's needs.

Sharlene emphasized again before she hung up that she was going to work things out for another week and Erin should stick with her plan to stay at Moss Cove.

Erin hung up and still felt awful for leaving Sharlene with the full burden of the business. She also knew she would feel awful if she left her dad and Delores right now before things were in place for the move to California. This net she was caught in had many layers to it.

All day long, Erin struggled with her decision to stay. Marge was doing a fine job taking care of Jack. Delores was gone for most of the day, doing who knows what. Mike spent hours on the phone while Erin went through all her e-mails and tried to catch up on the things she could do to help Sharlene with work. It turned into an exhausting day. Both Erin and Mike fell into bed as soon as they returned to the Shamrock and slept deeply.

On Saturday morning, Erin's phone rang at seven thirty. This time it was Jordan.

"Hey, Mom."

"Hi! How are you guys?" Erin pulled herself up in bed and tried to collect her thoughts.

"We're both doing great. Sierra's right here. I have the phone on speaker."

"Hi," Sierra chimed in.

"Is everything okay?" Erin wasn't sure she could handle one more crisis right now. Why else would they be calling?

"Yes. Everything is fine. We're doing great. But listen, we got Dad's message about Grandpa, and we decided we want to see you guys and Grandpa."

"But you're on your honeymoon."

Erin could hear both of them laughing.

"Yes, we noticed that," Jordan said. "Here's the thing. We're in Portland right now, and we were able to arrange a layover. We'll rent a car and come see you and then fly back to Santa Barbara tomorrow."

"Are you sure you want to do that?"

"Yes. So don't try to talk us out of it."

With a breath of resolve Erin said, "Okay. I'll tell your dad."

Deep inside, Erin was delighted they were coming. She saw this as a horrible way to end their honeymoon but an honorable way to begin their marriage as part of the extended family.

Once Mike and Erin were up and going, they bought some cinnamon rolls at the small bakery in town and let themselves into the cottage. Delores wasn't around, but Marge was there, using the suction machine to clear Jack's throat. Erin was used to the routine and went to her dad's side, slipping her hand into his. He was patiently enduring the assistance of the machine the way a dental patient opens up for a squirt of water and suction from the curved tube.

"You have some surprise visitors coming to see you today, Dad."

His left eyebrow rose. Two days earlier, Erin had arranged for Sylvia and three other pals of his to come see him, but Delores had intercepted them at the door and sent them away. Jack had been sleeping at the time and didn't know the guests were there. Erin didn't see how Delores could object to the guests this time. Jordan and Sierra were family.

"Jordan and Sierra are coming, Dad."

The announcement sent Jack into one of his tearful wails. Erin was becoming acquainted with what his different sounds meant. She found it easy to interpret this one: he hated being in such a distressing condition.

Erin leaned closer and patted his chest as he quieted. "You're still the same you, Dad. And that's who they're coming to see. All you have to do is give Sierra one of those half grins of yours and one of your charming winks, and you'll capture her heart for sure. She's an incredibly sweet young woman. She wants to meet you. And I want you to meet her."

Jack's chest gave a tremor the way it did when he was trying to rumble up some words and push them through his lopsided mouth. All that came out was "Whann?"

Erin took that to mean "When?" so she answered with "Sometime this afternoon, I should think. Marge will dandy you up nice and fresh to see them. Does that sound good to you?"

His lopsided grin went up on the left side followed by a wink. She grinned back. His limitations no longer frightened or repulsed her. He was still her father, locked up in the prison of his failing frame.

Erin went to the kitchen. "I'm going to make some coffee. You guys want some?"

"I wouldn't mind a cup," Marge said.

"Sure," Mike agreed.

"Yaaaah." Jack raised his good arm.

The three of them looked at one another as if they weren't sure it was okay to laugh. All of Jack's fluids and nutrition now came to him through tubes. Only the smallest tastes of liquid went into his mouth or down his throat since his gag reflex often made him choke. All three of them chose to ignore his request.

Erin set about brewing a fresh pot of ground Italian roast she had purchased at the grocery store a few days earlier. Ever since the "why not" espresso she had enjoyed from the drive-through in Springfield, she had craved dark Italian roast, fully caffeinated coffee. As the fragrant morning offering wafted through the close quarters, she opened the window above the sink a few inches to let in the morning air.

It was foggy outside. A thin, faint sort of hazy fog was clearing just as it had the past few mornings. Through the open window came the ocean's constant rumble. The tides had become a sort of metronome inside Erin's head, swinging evenly back and forth, marking off the moments, helping her keep in rhythm with the cacophony of life around her.

Erin turned and noticed her dad across the room. His nose was up, sniffing the air like a bear.

"You love the smell of this coffee, don't you?"

"Yaaaaa."

Her father closed his eyes and yawned. This, too, was a familiar rhythm of the past few days. He seemed to dip in and out of the reality going on around him. With a close of his eyes, he would turn back inside himself. To Erin it seemed like a coping mechanism incorporated in his system. Whenever he didn't have the strength to stay in the moment and process the emotions or thoughts, he would shut off.

Mike was working alongside Erin in the kitchen and had started making some instant oatmeal, as had become their simple morning routine the past few days. "Marge, do you know if Delores is up yet?"

"She left right after I arrived at about seven thirty."

"Did she say where she was going or how long she would be gone?" Mike was holding the box of instant oatmeal. The last two mornings he had made a small bowl of oatmeal for Delores, and she had eaten it. They were down to three packets left so Erin guessed Mike was trying to parcel out the supplies.

"She didn't say. She had a suitcase with her."

Mike and Erin exchanged puzzled glances. No one said anything for a few minutes. The coffeemaker sputtered. The teakettle whistled, and Mike poured the boiling water into the two bowls, stirring in the instant oatmeal. Both Mike and Erin stood as they held their bowls and spooned the oatmeal into their mouths, their eyes darting back and forth.

Before Mike finished his oatmeal, he placed the bowl on the counter and motioned for Erin to come with him. They slipped through the rearranged living room, and Mike politely tapped on the closed bedroom door even though they had been told Delores wasn't in there.

Mike turned the knob and opened the door to reveal the neatly made bed. Erin held her breath. She knew what Mike must have known when he motioned for her to follow him. The empty closet and the sealed envelope on the end of the bed confirmed the biting reality.

Delores was gone.

All week she had been busy packing boxes, organizing and sorting, separating out everything that was hers. On Friday Delores had loaded the car with six storage boxes that were sealed with packing tape. Mike and Erin had assumed she was going to take them to the Salvation Army drop-off as she had done with two other boxes earlier that week. Erin had noticed that one of the boxes was sealed and addressed as if it were prepared to be mailed. She didn't think about where Delores might be sending that box until this moment. Perhaps it had been mailed to Dolores's new residence.

Mike walked over to the bed, picked up the

envelope, and let out a few raw words under his breath. "She addressed it to your dad. She knew we would have to read it to him." He shook his head and added a few more ragged words to his evaluation of Delores's character.

"How could she do this? I thought she had resigned herself to my dad's situation." Erin lowered herself to the edge of the bed. "She spent all week acting as if she supported the idea of moving back to Irvine just so we would do everything we did to prepare him for the move."

"She had both of us fooled." Mike, her steady, problem-solving husband, grew red in the face.

The reality of the responsibility that had now landed in their laps hit her with full force. Intense anger replaced her initial sense of numbness, rushing over Erin like a wave. She wanted to read the letter to her father right now so they could see what Delores had to say for herself. Mike hesitated and then convinced her they should go for a walk, try to calm down, and come up with the best way to frame the information. Jack was the real victim in this. He was dependent on them now for everything.

The bracing salt air and their brisk walk down to the tide pools did much to clarify their thoughts. The anger toward Delores was still there but a shared empathy for Jack redirected their emotional energy, and soon they had talked through their plan.

Even with their logic lined up, it took several hours before both of them were in a stable enough place to stand in front of Jack and present him with the envelope. They waited until Marge had stepped out to run an errand. She hadn't asked Mike or Erin what had happened to Delores or why the two of them were so shaken. Certainly Marge figured out what was going on. To her professional credit and to Erin's deep appreciation, Marge kept to herself and focused on her required tasks. It would make sense that she didn't see the need to insert herself into this family crisis.

Jack was fully awake and seemed interactive when Mike sat beside him, looked Jack in the eye, and said, "We have something to tell you that, quite honestly, has really upset Erin and me."

Jack's left eyebrow went up. Mike showed him the envelope with Jack's name on the front. "Delores left this on the bed. Would you like me to read it to you?"

"Yaaaa." A breathy sob echoed from his deflated chest before Mike had even opened the envelope.

Clearing his throat, Mike read the short note aloud.

My dear Jack,
Since I've already told you all this in person, this note is more for Mike and Erin's benefit than for yours. I've put everything in order

and made sure Erin knows where all the papers are. No one regrets more than I that things turned out for us the way they did. I know you'll be well cared for, and that's important to me. You are a very dear person, Jack. I love you. You know that.

Delores

The forthrightness of the note caught Erin off guard, even though she knew she should be used to Delores's abrupt, self-first attitude by now. "She told you this, Dad? She told you she was leaving?"

Erin expected her father to wail. Instead he remained strangely still, blinking at them. He then drew in a deep breath and closed his eyes, shutting them out, folding up into his own reality. He seemed much more resigned to the situation than Erin expected.

But then, at this point, she didn't know what to expect. Her sense of balance was off-kilter. Erin had to go outside again and let the sharp air expand her lungs. She reached for her fleece jacket and exited quietly.

Making her way through the carved path in the brambles, she walked out to the bench and took her seat on the edge of the world. The wind was still, and the waves were calm, cresting with small curls of white foam. The tide eased in and rolled out without sending shooting sprays of salt water into the air.

"Why? Why would you let my dad have this stroke and then just let Delores walk away? I don't understand any of this."

Erin had asked God enough "why" questions after her mother's death to know that the continual asking resulted in an exercise in silence from the courts of heaven. She had come to understand that the asking was for her growth and her sanity and not necessarily for an answer. It was in the asking that Erin turned her heart toward listening. And in the listening came a humbling sense of awe at the all-encompassing majesty of Creator God.

As she stared out at the ocean, Erin remembered afresh some of the comforts that had come to her during stretches of quiet listening after her mother's death. What Erin heard in the silence was that there were, indeed, specific answers to each earthly pain. Every "why" had a "so that" response handwritten by God himself. She believed that.

She also believed that those answers were carefully recorded and stored somewhere in heaven, out of mortals' reach. It was only for her to believe that every time she sent a "why" into eternity that the answer was lovingly written beneath her question and tucked away, waiting for the day when the books were opened and she could read all that was recorded there.

A memory came to Erin as she sorted through

her thoughts there on the bluff. It was a memory of her grandmother, sitting silently in her bedroom the day her grandfather passed away. Erin was only eight, but she never forgot the way her grandmother had looked. She was listening. Waiting. Quieting her spirit. There was such a sense of calm and peace on her face that Erin knew her grandmother wasn't alone in that room. An invisible presence was there, sitting with her in silence, comforting her. Erin remembered quietly closing the door and wondering what it would be like to experience that otherworldly sort of calm.

Today was that day.

For nearly an hour Erin sat and listened. Only listened. She didn't dwell on any of her anger or confusion. She just observed. In the quietness she heard the staccato call of the seagulls as they stretched out their long white wings and soared above the water. She heard the steady ebb and flow of the tides. She heard the delicate rustling sound the wind made in the woods that lined the far side of the cliff.

Two small brown birds hopped closer to the bench as she sat motionless. Cocking their heads, they looked at Erin, looked at the ground, pecked for a seed here and there, and then flew off, their simple needs fulfilled.

I will give you the treasures of darkness.

Erin knew the line was part of a verse. She tried

to think of where she had heard it. Was it from one of the entries in her mom's diary? Or was it one of the many Old Testament verses her grandmother had worked hard to get Erin to memorize when she was young?

As a child Erin had resisted her grandmother's strict recitations of verses loaded with "thees" and "thous." Erin valued the experience now, knowing that some of those verses had gone into her head, and many of them had sifted down and found their way to her heart, where they remained. Her grandmother's efforts weren't wasted.

Over the years, whenever Erin remembered one of the verses, she had made it a practice to look it up and write it in her journal. First she would write the verse in her grandmother's King James Version. Then she would look it up in her Bible, a more modern translation. Tonight, when she returned to the Shamrock, she would make sure she looked up this verse and recorded it in her journal.

The hour of solace accomplished its work. Erin stood and realized she wasn't chilled. The sun had warmed her. God's abiding presence had calmed her. This was going to be a long journey with her dad. She knew she needed patience and peace—deep-down settled peace—to go the distance.

Strolling back through the cleared path in the

brambles, Erin stopped when she reached the grassy area in front of the house. Marge's car was parked to the side. That meant she was back from running her errand. Perhaps Mike had told her about the letter's contents.

From the top of the long gravel driveway Erin heard a car approaching. It was a silver compact, just like Delores's car.

Did she change her mind? Is she coming back?

Erin hurried toward the car as it came to a stop behind Mike's BMW. It wasn't Delores who crawled out from the driver's side. Jordan emerged from the rental car that was uncannily similar to Delores's.

Sierra popped out from the passenger's side and immediately came to Erin with her arms open and ready to offer a warm, empathetic hug. The two women held each other a moment as Sierra whispered in Erin's ear, "I'm so sorry this has happened to your dad."

Erin's love for Sierra grew deeper. Ever since Erin lost her mother no female relative responded to her with this kind of warmth. Sierra was now that woman, that relative. From the beginning Sierra had offered her friendship to Erin in daughterly ways, and Erin knew Sierra was a gift not only to her son but also to her.

Jordan now wrapped his arms around both the women and rested his forehead against the side of his mother's head. "How are you doin', Mom?"

"Better. Much better now that the two of you are here." She pulled back and drew in a breath. "Delores left Grandpa this morning. She did it in secret. Packed her bags and left."

Jordan and Sierra both pulled back and stared in disbelief.

"How did Grandpa take it?" Jordan asked.

Erin wasn't sure how to answer. "He didn't react much. When you see him you'll know why. I don't know what he thinks of her. I don't understand their relationship."

"Can we go in and see him?" Jordan asked.

"Sure. I don't know if he's awake. Dad's with him. And listen—don't let Grandpa's appearance startle you. From everything we can tell after being with him all week, he's still very much in tune with what's going on around him, at least most of the time. The stroke took his ability to communicate, but mentally it seems he's pretty much still all there."

"How awful," Sierra said.

"Can he talk at all?" Jordan asked.

"Not with full words. But you'll see. He communicates in other ways."

Clasping hands, Jordan and Sierra followed Erin to the persimmon red door.

"This cottage is darling," Sierra said. "It's like a fairy tale."

"My dad did a lot of the restoration, so be sure to tell him that you like it. He probably would like for me to show you the pictures. I'll try to remember to pull out the scrapbook." Erin felt bittersweet as she remembered how Delores had put the scrapbook together. When she and her dad showed it to Erin during her February visit, she had felt a sincere appreciation for Delores and the way she was doing things for her dad that her mother had never done. But all the kindness she had felt toward Delores was gone.

11

Grant me a sense of humor, Lord,
The saving grace to see a joke,
To win some happiness from life
And pass it on to other folk.

Erin opened the front door a few inches and found that her dad was in the midst of routine hygiene procedures.

"Jordan and Sierra are here," she told Mike quietly. "I think we'll make a quick run to the grocery store while you finish up."

"Good idea. Give us another twenty minutes."

As they drove past the Shamrock Lodgettes, Sierra said, "Are those 'lodgettes' only for 'leprechaun-ettes'?"

Jordan grinned at her joke, and Erin said, "Believe it or not, that's where we're staying. We reserved you guys a room for tonight, too."

"Then I guess we'll see if any 'leprechaun-ettes' are staying there," Sierra said. "The hotel where we stayed last week on Maui had a notice about the *menehune* being at work doing repair on the pool. We found out that the *menehune* are more or less the Hawaiian equivalent of leprechauns."

"How was Hawaii? I'm sorry, I haven't even asked," Erin said.

"It was perfect." Sierra turned around in the front seat and gave Jordan a big smile.

"Mostly perfect," Jordan added from his spot in the backseat. "There was one major problem."

"What was it? The pool being repaired?" Erin glanced at him in the rearview mirror.

"No. The pool was only closed for an hour one of the nights. The problem was that we didn't want to leave. We're determined to save all our pennies so that next time we go, whenever that might be, we'll be able to stay longer."

Erin parked the car, feeling grateful to have Jordan and Sierra with her. The three of them entered the small grocery store. They were greeted loudly by Sylvia, who was wheeling her cart to the checkout. "A few of us have decided to stop by tonight to see Jack. Do you think that will be a problem now that the dragon lady has left town?"

"How did you know that Delores left?" Erin noticed that four other people in the immediate area had stopped what they were doing and were looking to Sylvia for the latest info.

"Clint at the post office said she shipped a lot of boxes the other day to some place in Mexico. He asked if she wanted insurance and she said yes, the maximum amount. Then Clint told her that he heard she and Jack were moving to California. And she told him he shouldn't assume things about people."

The clerk at the cash register clucked her tongue. Erin felt a twinge of regret that Sierra and Jordan were hearing these embarrassing specifics about Delores. Yet in a way it relieved her from trying to explain to them what she herself didn't understand.

"So," Sylvia said, "what do you say to a little gathering tonight? Would around six thirty be okay with you?"

Sylvia's reading glasses were balanced on the end of her nose. The gems embedded in the brightly colored frames caught the light from the overhead lighting, and with each birdlike movement of her head, Sylvia sent tiny sparkles of refracted light onto their faces.

Erin tried to view the visit in terms of what her dad would want. "You know, I think my dad would enjoy some company. Six thirty would be fine."

"Great. We'll make it a cookout."

"A cookout?" Erin hadn't expected that.

"Sure." Sylvia gave a sweeping gesture to the others in the grocery store. "You're all welcome to come. I'll take care of everything. Paddy can bring a fresh haul of crabs. Jack has the steamers in his garage. We'll come over early and set it all up. All you need to do is get Jack in his wheelchair, put a hat on him, and park him on the deck. Trust me, it'll be the happiest day he's had in a long time."

"Happiest day," Erin repeated under her breath. What a different meaning those words were taking on since she and Sharlene had selected them for their wedding consulting business. As alternate a universe as all this felt, Erin somehow knew Sylvia was right. Being with friends on Jack's deck, even though he would have to be in a wheelchair, would be her father's happiest day in a long time.

They bought a few groceries and some chips and soft drinks for the cookout. The dour-looking woman at the checkout softened her expression as Erin paid for the groceries.

"Your father always made my day when he came in here," the clerk said. "He would say, 'Top of the morning, Glory,' even if it was the middle of the day. I'm really sorry to hear about his stroke. If you don't mind I'd like to come to the cookout, too."

"Yes. Please come." Erin didn't know the woman's name, but she had seen her every time she'd gone to the grocery store.

"I'll bring a salad."

"Okay. Thanks." Erin tried to catch a glimpse of the woman's name tag, but it was hidden underneath a sweater.

"We'll see you later, then."

"Everyone is so friendly," Sierra said as they drove back to the house. "This is a darling place."

"I can see why Grandpa likes it here," Jordan said.

Erin still wouldn't give Moss Cove the high marks everyone else in her family did.

When they arrived at the house, Erin found that Mike had slipped away to the dormer bedroom for a nap. Jack was awake and sitting in the recliner. A sturdy half grin and airy sound of happiness came from his mouth when he saw Jordan. He held out his left hand. Jordan grasped his grandfather by the wrist, and the two men locked into a wrist-to-wrist hold as Jordan introduced his bride.

Jack turned his head to take in a full view of Sierra, who was hanging back shyly. His eyebrow went up. His grin lifted higher. He looked at Jordan and out of his mouth came, "Buuufoo."

Jordan broke into a broad smile at his grandpa. "You got that right. I married the most *beautiful* woman in the world."

Then Jack cried. Jordan teared up, and so did Sierra. Jack managed to keep the wailing sounds curtailed between his closed lips, but as he did, a string of spittle trickled down the side of his jaw.

Erin stepped in with a washcloth and dabbed his mouth. She had already done so much crying during moments like this that she somehow remained dry-eyed as she cared for him. She proudly watched her son treat his grandfather with respect.

Sierra stepped closer and slipped her left hand into Jack's left hand, giving it a squeeze. Jack lifted her hand to his dried lips and placed an awkward kiss on the back of it, as if she were a princess and he was a loyal subject. Sierra smiled at him warmly.

Erin was amazed. Her father had never been like this with her, all tender and gushy. Nor had she seen him this way with her mother or any other woman. She remembered him, as a physical education teacher, always in coaching mode. The limitations on his ability to express himself and the way the stroke had affected the emotional centers in his brain revealed a big teddy bear in the man she had known only as disapproving and never satisfied.

Jack drew Sierra's hand back and blinked as he held it up so he could take a good look at the wedding band on her finger. Jordan held out his hand to show the wedding band on his finger. "See? We're official. Husband and wife."

Jack winked at Sierra and let go of her hand so he could give Jordan a hearty thumbs-up signal. Jordan beamed as if he had proven at long last to his grandfather that he was a man of worth, even though he never had become the athlete Jack pushed him to be. The two men were communicating in front of Erin in a way that had never happened before. She couldn't help but think how rich and affirming this moment of blessing was for Jordan and Sierra. Erin knew that if her father had come to the wedding in the same state he had been in emotionally and physically all his life, Jordan wouldn't have received any of this.

This small treasure was hidden away in the vast darkness of her father's condition. She only wished Mike had been there to see it revealed.

Before Erin had a chance to tell her father about the party that was coming to him that evening, Sylvia arrived. Marge opened the door for her, and she walked right up to Jack and looked him over. He gave her an equal inspection with his one good eye.

"Well, I'll give you this, Jack O'Riley." Her voice was much louder than it needed to be. "You're a whole lot better off than you might think you are."

Sylvia didn't qualify if her statement applied to his physical condition or to the loss of Delores. It didn't matter. She had had her say.

"We're going to use your crab pots and steamer from the garage. You have any problems with that?"

Jack moved his head a bit and made a flipping motion with his left hand as if giving her permission to have at it.

"As soon as your nurse there puts you in the wheelchair, we'll push you out on the deck. The sea air will put a shine back in those baby blues of yours." Sylvia gave Marge a nod as if she was now in command. "He likes his navy blue stocking cap, don't you, Jack? Make sure he has it on when you bring him out. Although it's a gorgeous afternoon, and you might not need a hat at all."

Erin and Mike had been so occupied with caring for her father's basic needs that they hadn't even attempted to take him outside for fresh air. By the look on his face, he was eager for the opportunity.

Marge went to work with all his medical needs while Erin, Jordan, and Sierra followed Sylvia out into the tidied garage. With the four of them working together, it didn't take long to set up what Erin thought looked like the starting pieces of a distillery. Sylvia gave directions to Jordan, and he put the huge crab pots and steamer in place over a big portable propane stove.

Sierra made herself at home and set about decorating the patio with three strings of white Christmas lights she found in the garage. Two of Jack's cronies arrived in a truck that they parked on the grass and unloaded a beat-up old ice chest that took both of them to carry.

Mike came outside a few minutes later and stood back, taking in the free-for-all. "What's going on?"

Erin sidled up to him and slipped her arm around his middle. "It looks like the circus has come to town, doesn't it? Sylvia has arranged for a cookout." Leaning closer, Erin whispered, "Between you and me, I think she's celebrating Delores's departure."

A scowl rested on Mike's face. "You sure your father is up for this?"

"Yes, I am. I think he is."

"I guess it couldn't hurt him to have a change of pace. He seems stable enough. It's actually a good way to have a going-away party for him without calling it that."

"I think you're right."

"I'll help Marge to wheel him out." Mike went inside while Erin found a broom and swept off the deck.

Ten minutes later, the man of honor was wheeled out the door and onto the deck wearing sweatpants, a clean knit golf shirt under a fleece jacket, and his navy blue stocking cap. Erin realized at once that the green fleece jacket Marge had grabbed for her dad was Erin's Paddy's Crab Shack fleece.

The stunning part was that he was so slim now he could fit into her jacket. Never did Erin expect to see such a thing.

Paddy of Paddy's Crab Shack gave a cheer when he saw Jack on the deck. He had arrived earlier with an ice chest full of live Pacific crabs.

She had a feeling he would like that her dad was proudly "wearing the green" for his pal.

Marge had shaved Jack, tucked his ragged hair under the cap, and effectively hidden all the tubes from view. He was smiling his new crooked smile, and he looked happy. All the worry lines from his forehead were gone.

Eight guests arrived by the time Jack was out on the deck. All of them greeted him with dignity and lots of camaraderie. Sylvia was right, Erin thought. This was good. This was going to be her father's happiest day.

The large boiling pots for the crabs had been set up near the garage and carried a fishy scent. She was amazed at how everyone stepped in and went to work as if they hosted this sort of gathering every Saturday night. A folding table appeared from the back of someone's car, and it soon was filled up with paper plates, a big bowl of coleslaw, a plate of baby carrots with hummus for dipping, vinegar and sea salt potato chips, and triangular wedges of watermelon neatly arranged on a serving platter made from an old stop sign that had been pounded up around the edges.

The people's spontaneity and the event itself put a steady smile on Erin's face for the first time that week. She soon noticed she wasn't the only one who couldn't stop smiling. Her dad was wearing himself out with delight. About a half hour into the gala, she noticed that he closed his eyes and dipped his chin. Erin went to his side and could tell that he was just checking out for a short break the way he did physically and emotionally.

She took it upon herself to release the brake on the wheelchair and attempt to push him back into the house. The movement roused him, and he made a horrible guttural sound in protest. "I was going to take you back inside, Dad. Just for a little bit."

"No!" Like a toddler he pointed his finger decisively at the ground the same way he had earlier that week when they told him about the plans to return to Irvine and he had made it clear he wanted to stay in Moss Cove. Now he wanted to stay on the deck in the middle of the party.

Erin acquiesced. It was his party, after all. She leaned over, looked him in the eye, and sang, "It's my party, and I'll sleep if I want to, sleep if I want to . . ."

Her dad laughed.

It was a wonderful sound. She hadn't heard him laugh in a long, long time. The laughter that rolled out in response to her silly song was the guffaw of a carefree soul. It was the sort of laugh that rolled from his barrel chest when she was in elementary school and he used to take her to the pool at the community college. He would send Erin and her brother up to the top of the high dive and then coach them from the water and watch them jump. Whenever either of them managed to accomplish the dive or jump the way he had instructed, Jack O'Riley would laugh instead of praise them.

Some of Erin's happiest childhood memories were of coming up from a carefully executed dive with water still dripping from her nose and eyelashes, and in her ringing ears she could hear her father laughing his happy laugh. That sound meant she had done something right.

It had been a long time since Erin had heard that laugh from her father. And here he was, sitting on the deck he had built with his own hands, confined to a wheelchair, unable to speak a full sentence, and yet he was laughing.

Erin spontaneously planted a kiss on her father's forehead, and he tucked his chin, returning to his turtle state of survival.

"Are you ready to dig in?" Jordan approached Erin with two plastic trays in his hand. On each tray rested a whole crab, steaming and ready to be cracked open with the implements included on the tray.

"Wow, is this for me?"

"Yes, all yours. This other one is for Sierra. Where did she go?"

They looked around and saw that she was coming their way from the car with something in her hand. Jordan called out to her, and she held up a pouch.

"Oh, I love that woman," he said.

Erin beamed.

"She's bringing her iPod and some portable speakers I bought for her. A little music will definitely get this party started." Jordan motioned with his head for Sierra to come over to where he was standing on the deck. "Here, you take this, and I'll take care of that."

Erin and Sierra sat beside each other on the built-in bench that ran along the edge of the deck. They simultaneously turned to face the ocean, preparing to watch the sunset as they figured out how to attack the well-boiled crustaceans in front of them.

"I've never eaten a whole crab before," Sierra said. "How do you start?"

"I'm a novice, too. I think we use this to crack open the shell and then use this slender fork to pull out the good stuff." Erin pushed up her sleeves. Sierra did the same. The challenge began. Both of them found it impossible not to get completely hands-on and pull off the legs one by one, cracking the shell, consuming the tender white meat.

"This is incredible," Sierra said after her second bite. "Is yours as good as mine?"

"Better," Erin said playfully. "Look at that sunset."

Mike came over and joined them. They watched reverently as the huge orange ball slipped behind a bank of clouds far out at sea. The lavender-shaded clouds seemed to bob along the surface of the deep like a lumpy mountain range belonging to some other planet. Erin had no difficulty believing she was, indeed, on another planet. Nothing was familiar; yet everything around her rang true. She was eating an entire crab for the first time in her life, sitting close enough to her husband to feel the warmth of his body. Next to her was the sort of daughter-in-law she had hoped all three of her sons would find. And only a few moments ago, her father had laughed.

The last drop of sun disappeared behind those otherworldly mountains, and as it did, another verse of Scripture from long ago skittered into Erin's thoughts from across the sea: *In quietness and confidence shall be thy strength.*

Quietness. Confidence. Strength. Those were the qualities she dearly needed in her life right now. She believed the Lord was at work doing more than she could see on the surface.

Just then the music started. Through the tiny speakers that Jordan had set on the outside kitchen window sill came a gently rolling instrumental intro followed by a mellow rendition of "What a Wonderful World."

Everyone looked around to see where the tune was coming from. Some of the crusty guys standing out on the lawn by the back of Paddy's pickup truck lifted their bottles of beer to Jordan.

He grinned at his new bride. She grinned back. Without a word, Sierra put her tray to the side and wiped her hands on a dish towel she had brought out earlier to clean off the benches.

With quick, dainty steps, Sierra went to her husband. The two of them met in the middle of the open deck, taking a waltz position as if they had been dancing together their whole lives. As everyone looked on, Jordan and Sierra treated them to a charming, loving dance as they stared into each other's eyes.

Then Erin remembered. This had been the music for the first dance at their reception a week ago. She hadn't been able to sit back and enjoy the moment then. This repeat performance was so much better.

The tangerine shades that illuminated the evening sky cast a warm glow over their small celebration on the bluff. The song's words encircled the young couple. Jack, who was only a few feet away, lifted his head, stuck out his chin, and made sounds like a baby.

Erin realized he wasn't crying. He was singing. Her father loved this song.

Erin leaned her head on Mike's shoulder. This happiness was so unexpected. It came from such a place of wreckage. Yet in the midst of all the loss, these elemental graces of life remained, and their beauty ushered in an unfaltering peace.

Mike kissed Erin on the lips. She curled in closer to him.

"Are you cold?" he whispered.

"No."

"Are you okay?"

"Yes."

Mike wrapped his arms around her and held her tight as the song ended. Twined together they watched as their married son gave his blushing bride a backward dip, held her until the final note ended, pulled her back to himself, and kissed her good.

Erin turned to see Mike's expression. The glimmer in his eyes told her he was feeling it, too. This night was a gift to all of them.

The next song was one Erin didn't recognize. It was a twangy country tune with a fast string of lyrics. One of the men by the crab boiler pots joined in, singing nice and loud. The enchanting "wonderful world" moment flitted away.

Mike stood and wheeled Jack closer so he could be in on their conversations if he wanted to. He had to be strapped up in the wheelchair due to the paralysis, and it seemed he was having difficulty breathing. Mike tried to adjust his position, but Jack pushed him away. Marge did a quick check of the tubes and his mouth. He pushed her away, too.

"Dad, what is it?" Erin asked.

He patted his chest.

"Is it your heart? Your lungs?"

He touched his hand to his nose. Others were listening in now, trying to discern why he was drawing in such deep breaths. He didn't seem to be in any pain or panic, judging by his facial expression.

"It's the sea air," Erin said. "You're just breathing it in, aren't you?"

The half smile rose. He drew in a long, deep breath through his nose, his chin held high.

"You just want to fill your lungs with this salty air, don't you?"

He drew in another deep draft like a prisoner who hadn't seen the outside world for weeks. In truth, that was the case. His face took on a more robust hue. Two of the men whom Erin recognized from the Jenny Bee's breakfast a year and a half ago came over and talked with Jack. She watched as he made good use of his eyebrow, his pointed finger, and the washcloth Marge had left in his lap. He was able to wipe his own mouth now, bending his left arm straight up and patting it dry.

Erin went back to her meal, enjoying the time-consuming, messy venture more than she had expected to. Extracting the fleshy good stuff from the crusty ole crab seemed a not-so-coincidental parallel to what was happening with her dad right now.

Only one thing weighed heavily on Erin. How could they take him away from this? Who besides Erin and Mike would visit him in Irvine? All his old friends had moved out of the area. Everything there reminded him of Faith and the forty-five years they had lived in that community and watched it grow from bean fields and strawberry patches to a crowded city jammed with traffic. He would be confined to a room. It would be like caging the lion once again.

Not ideal, but it had to be done.

Erin looked around at the salt-of-the-earth folks gathered in the grassy area and on the deck. Two more had walked down the gravel driveway and were at the folding table scooping up hummus with potato chips and greeting others who were offering them something cold to drink. Tomorrow she and Mike would be down to only two more days to finalize transportation arrangements and move her father to Irvine. Did these folks know this was Jack's going-away party? Was it, in an odd sort of way, her father's wake? A wake that he got to attend?

In the same way that Jordan and Sierra's wedding celebration had been just perfect for them, the impromptu cookout on Hidden Cottage's deck during the beautiful August evening turned out to be just perfect for her father.

Erin glanced toward the sea that had now closed its shades and turned out the light for the night. All the vibrant glow of life, love, and laughter was gathered around them now, under the twinkle lights strung by Sierra as well as in the sparkling glimmers from the heavens.

12

May brooks and trees and singing hills
Join in the chorus too
And every gentle wind that blows
Send happiness to you.

As the evening festivities wound down, Erin and Mike talked through the arrangements for the night. Someone needed to stay with Jack now that Delores was gone. Marge had assured them she would be back at seven thirty in the morning, but in his condition, someone needed to be near him at all times.

They decided Mike would stay at Hidden Cottage that night. He said he wanted Erin to get a good night's sleep, and he didn't think that would happen if she stayed at the cottage. Her dad's throat needed to be suctioned every few hours, and the machine's noise was impossible to sleep through.

Erin returned to the Shamrock along with Jordan and Sierra. Sylvia already had arranged for the still honeymooning couple to stay in the "deluxe" unit two lodgettes down from where Erin was staying. From the outside Erin couldn't see why their unit was "deluxe," but they were quick to cozy in for the night, and she didn't ask to take a tour of their cabin.

Sleeping only in snatches, Erin wished she had just stayed at the cottage with Mike and her dad. Being alone was dreadful. In a very small way, she understood her father's choice to marry Delores after being alone.

Erin fretted about how things were going to work out once they transported Jack back to Irvine. The last conversation she and Mike had on the topic landed them on the same page. Since no openings currently were available in any of the convalescent facilities near their home, the only answer was for Jack to live with them.

The darkness that surrounded Erin in the empty motel room provided a blank screen for her fast-moving thoughts throughout the night. Before her, images played out as she tried to think through where they would install the wheelchair ramps at their house and how they would clear the guest room to make space for her father and his equipment. They would need to find a proper hospital bed; the recliner he was using now wasn't the answer.

Erin felt her chest constrict as she thought about all the ways her life was about to change now that she and Mike had become her father's caregivers by default. She knew better than to give way to her rising anger, but she disregarded the nudge to pull back. Instead she followed the trail of a few precisely placed thoughts that led her right to the smoldering campfire of her resentment. With only the slightest breath, she rekindled the angry flames.

How dare Delores leave! How unbelievably cruel. Not only did Delores abandon my dad, she also abandoned Mike and me.

Erin's anger grew until it filled the room, and she wanted to scream. Any lingering sweetness from the "wonderful world" moments at the cookout was gone. All sense of peace from her "be still and know" exercise that afternoon while gazing on the ocean also was gone. She was alone. Alone in a place where all she could see were images of how restricted her life was about to become.

The sourness stayed with her into the new day and hung on her the same way the coastal fog hung over the cottage. She didn't bother Jordan and Sierra in their cabin when she woke up but rather dressed and drove over to the cottage at 7:20, feeling groggy and grumpy. When she entered, the cottage's closeness and the strong smells coming from the living room caught her off guard. Mike opened one eye and lifted his hand in a halfhearted wave to her from his reclined position on the couch but didn't say anything. He looked exhausted.

Trying to be as quiet as she could, Erin opened the kitchen window to let in some air. She was relieved to see Marge's car heading down the gravel drive. Erin went outside to greet her, blinking back her tears.

"Is everything okay?" Marge asked.

"I just needed some air. And I wanted to say thank you."

"For what?"

"For taking care of my father."

"It's my job."

"I know. But it's a job that not everyone could do, and you do it so well. I just wanted you to know I appreciate you."

"Thank you for saying that. I like your dad. He's not like most patients I've had over the years. He has a strong spirit."

"He does."

"It's going to take a lot out of him when you move him from here. You know that, don't you?"

Erin nodded.

"I thought the party last night was good for him."

"It was."

"Did you see how engaged your dad was with everyone? Not the whole time, of course, but clearly he was having a great time."

"Yes, he was."

"Is anyone with your dad right now?"

"Yes. Mike is on the couch. I've only been here for a few minutes."

"I better go in there and get to work."

"Thanks, Marge. Again, I really appreciate you."

Marge went inside to go about her duties. Erin realized she had never come right out and told Marge that Delores wasn't coming back. Perhaps Mike had said something. It didn't really matter because, aside from everyone in town knowing everyone else's business, Marge was, as she said, doing her job. She was professional enough not to ask about personal family matters.

For a moment Erin considered going back to the Shamrock and trying to catch a few more hours of sleep. Instead she decided to stretch her legs. Her restlessness led her across the grassy area in the fog and through the woods. She came out of the gathering of trees and found she was standing on the top of a stack of black volcanic rocks. Below the rocks the waves were receding, revealing tide pools and a pebble-filled cove under the over-hanging cleft of rock. In the same way that the cottage was hidden from the road, this cove was hidden from the cottage and the main road.

Erin's first thought was of how her three boys would have reveled in this sort of a secret pirates' cove when they were younger. The rocks formed a jagged path down to the tide pools, and Erin decided to attempt it. She slipped once but caught herself. It wasn't a difficult descent. But the rocks were slick.

When her feet were planted in the pebbled cove, she looked up at the tree-lined cliff. The fog clung to the trees, hiding their evergreen tops from view. Here, in the sheltered cove, the air was damp from sea mist. The shallow waves crept among the tide pools, fingering the anemones and causing them to respond with faint shivers.

Erin lingered in this place of sea sounds and scents, bending close to examine a colony of tiny mussels clinging to the unmovable rock. Unusual, mosslike growths covered one of the boulders with a deep green softness. Her shoes were wet. Her nose dripped. Her fleece jacket had kept out only so much moisture, and now she was legitimately cold.

Even so, she liked it there.

She lingered a little longer. This was a place where a different sort of life unfolded in time with the tides' ebb and flow. Tiny creatures called this place their home. All the basic elements of air, water, and light found their way to this unobtrusive place and carried out their own steady life cycle.

Many analogies to what was happening in her father's inner life could be drawn from this shaded cove. But Erin didn't want to dwell on any spiritual lessons or nuggets of hope the way she had yesterday when she sat on the bench. This morning she wanted to hold on to her anger.

That anger gave her strength as she scaled back

up the slick rocks and returned to the cottage with soggy tennis shoes. Mike was in the kitchen. He greeted her with concern.

"I didn't know where you went."

"There's a small cove through the woods. I went down to have a look. I can see where the 'moss' comes into the name of this place." She pulled off her wet shoes and placed them on a rack in the bathroom.

Mike followed Erin with a cup of coffee he had made and motioned for her to follow him upstairs where they could speak in private.

With his voice lowered, Mike said, "I don't see how I can leave you here and go home tomorrow. We still have too much to figure out before we can move your dad down to Irvine."

For the next twenty minutes Erin and Mike discussed the possibilities of what could be done and reviewed all the inroads they had made earlier that week in settling the specifics. In spite of all of Mike's attempts at lists, he had failed to come up with a workable plan. Not that Erin placed any blame on him. Both of them had become caught up in her dad's daily care and the sleep deprivation that came with it. Mike's frustration and exhaustion now were coming through in his voice.

"Did you sleep at all last night?" Erin asked.

"Not much. That's another reason I don't want to drive all the way back home by myself."

"Why don't you fly home? Jordan and Sierra are going to leave today. You could ride with them to the airport and catch a flight home this evening."

"Are you sure you want all of us to leave you here?"

"I'd rather all of you stay, of course. But that's not practical. You need to get back to work and so do Sierra and Jordan. I don't like that I need to stay here by myself, but at the moment, that's the only option I can see."

They talked a little more about how to ready their guest room for Erin's dad and set up a schedule with a day nurse in Irvine. Mike agreed with Erin that he would be able to work out an arrangement more quickly once he returned home. At the moment he was leaning toward finding a room in an extended-care facility, even though they had been told none was available. Mike wanted to try some face-to-face visits instead of just phone calls before he gave up on that option. As soon as he had everything in place, he would fly back up, they would have some sort of workable transportation figured out, and they would take it from there.

Until then, all Erin could do was wait.

After Mike left with Jordan and Sierra, Erin moved her things from the Shamrock and settled into the dormer room. She liked being at the cottage better than being at the Shamrock. Not just because she had immediate access to her father but also because of the view of the pine trees out the window. Just beyond the trees to the right, she could catch a glimpse of the ocean. That small slice of the vast horizon and sparkling sea gave her spirit a place to go, a place to focus and to think.

Sharlene called while Erin was in the midst of settling in and asked if she had time to go over a few things.

"Sure. I was planning to call you later, but I can take a break now." She sat on the edge of the upstairs bed and turned toward the window so she could watch the ocean as they talked.

"I think we need to go ahead and hire an assistant right away. I know we were going to talk about it when you returned, but the way things are shaping up, we need to make a decision now."

"I agree."

"I sent some résumés to you a few hours ago. Did you have a chance to look at them yet?"

"No. I haven't looked at them."

Sharlene paused as if waiting for a better answer.

"I can try to work on that next. Or, you know what, Sharlene? I trust you. Why don't you make the decision? You're the one who will be working with her right away. I hate to slow you down any further."

"If you're sure you're okay with that, then I do

have one person who rose to the top. Her name is Ashley. If you have a chance to look at the files, you'll see her résumé."

"By all means, go ahead and hire her."

Sharlene let out a sigh. "It's not been ideal for either of us."

"No, it hasn't."

"So, you think you'll be back in a week?"

"Yes. Maybe sooner if Mike can work out the details."

"Well, I feel for you guys. I really do. But I have to tell you, Erin, if you could still do a few things while you're there, like respond to e-mails, it would help me a lot."

"I understand."

"I mean, it's been almost a month since you've been able to give the business your full attention. First the wedding and then your dad. I'm spending most of my time dashing around trying to plug up holes, and I'm falling unprofessionally behind on everything."

"Hopefully this new assistant will help out."

"Yes, but you and I both know it's going to take several weeks of training before she has a good feel for what we do and how we want her to present The Happiest Day to our clients. That's why I was hoping we could wait until you returned before we hired someone."

Erin could hear the tension rising in Sharlene's voice. She had to admit that she didn't have an accurate concept of the amount of pressure her vacancy had placed on Sharlene.

"What can I do to help?" Erin asked. "Aside from coming back to Irvine today. What can I do besides e-mails while I'm here?"

Sharlene paused before answering in a calmer voice. "Let's just start with the e-mails. That would help a lot."

"Okay, I can do that."

"I'm not trying to complain; I hope you understand that. I know you're in a crisis situation. I just don't want our business to fail because of it."

Erin thought Sharlene's assessment of their business was exaggerated. That is, until she hung up and dove into all the e-mails waiting for her. She discovered they had several unhappy brides who had received incorrect information about services listed on The Happiest Day website that were no longer available. Erin worked for several hours writing e-mails, making phone calls, and coordinating with their web designer to put the long-overdue updates in place.

Two bad reviews of The Happiest Day had been posted to a website that evaluated local businesses in Irvine. It took Erin three days and dozens of phone calls and e-mails to set things right and to convince the reviewers to pull their negative words off the site.

As the week wore on, Erin fell into a routine

with the e-mails and Marge as well. Each night Erin made herself comfortable on the couch and slept in snatches, ready to quickly attend to her father whenever he had difficulty swallowing. She had become adept at using the suction machine, to clear his throat and mouth, and being back to a light sleep all within ten minutes.

During the day she tried to catch a nap upstairs before Marge went home. On Thursday afternoon, in the middle of her nap, Sharlene called with the news that she had acquired a partnership with Nannette's Creations, an exclusive bridal shop in Newport Beach that Erin had been pursuing for more than a year. Nannette was older, well established, exclusive, and had responded with cool indifference each time Erin had contacted her. She had made it clear by her aloofness that she didn't need to be associated with the likes of Erin and such a fledgling venture as The Happiest Day.

"How in the world did you get Nannette to agree?"

"You would be so proud of me. I went in yesterday with a gorgeous bouquet from Julianne's Floral. It's right there down the block from Nannette's."

"Yes, I know."

"I waited in the car until I saw Nannette through the front window. I went in and placed the bouquet on the reception desk and told her the flowers were a gift from me. She asked why, and

I said, 'Because you designed a wedding dress for one of our clients at The Happiest Day, and for that particular bride, how she felt about herself in that dress was ninety percent of the reason her wedding was the happiest day of her life.' "

"And what did Nannette say?"

"She was flattered. That's when I knew I had my opening with her. So I thanked her again, handed her my card, and started out the door."

"I don't understand. Why didn't you give her a brochure and tell her about how our service works?"

"Because you've done that already, right?"

"Yes. Twice."

"So she didn't need the sales pitch."

"Are you saying you left, and she called you and agreed to become one of our partner merchants?"

"No. I haven't finished telling you yet. I started out the door. And she asked if I had been in before. I told her I hadn't, but that you had, and we were business partners. I described you and she said she knew who you were."

"She remembers me?"

"Oh, yes. Definitely. She said you are one of only a few women of a certain age who are able to still wear jeans and look fashionable."

Erin frowned and switched her cell phone to the other ear. She wasn't sure she liked being the "woman of a certain age" in this story.

"So why did Nannette decide to sign with us now?"

"I told her about your father and that you were caring for him in Oregon and how the timing was horrible because your son just got married and you had to leave immediately after the wedding to be with your father."

"We didn't leave immediately after the wedding. I didn't even know about the stroke until the next morning."

"Well, the point is, the story is what sealed the deal. Turns out Nannette's mother had a stroke when Nannette was a teenager, and she said she knows exactly what you're going through. I told her I was trying to keep our business going despite your absence, and do you know what she did?" Sharlene didn't wait for Erin to respond.

"Nannette pulled one of the white rosebuds out of the bouquet I had just given her, handed it to me, and said with that gorgeous French accent of hers, 'You may fax me the agreement this afternoon. Strong women should help each other succeed, should we not?'"

"That was it?"

"Yup. Don't you love it? You are now a 'strong woman' in her eyes, and our list of partner merchants just went up to five-star status."

"Wow, Sharlene, this is good news."

"I hoped it would brighten your day."

Erin's phone beeped, and she quickly had to tell Sharlene that her battery had run out.

"No problem. Talk to you tomorrow."

When Erin went downstairs to find the charger and plug in her phone, Sylvia was in the living room sitting on the sofa, knitting. She looked up at Erin over the top rim of her glasses and gave her a small smile. Erin's dad was sleeping. Marge was reading a book, her usual downtime occupation.

Sylvia was early today. Her normal time to see Jack was later in the afternoon. She had been coming every day since the cookout. Arriving promptly at three thirty, she gave him the update on all the local gossip and was gone by 4:10. Jack perked up whenever Sylvia came. He didn't cry, smile, or wink at her, but he watched her as if she were the evening news anchor and it was his place to take it all in without a response. Erin didn't know why Sylvia was here now, except to be a comforting presence.

Paddy and two of his pals checked in on Jack later that evening. He seemed alert and interested in their company when they arrived. By the time they left he had become agitated and then despondent. Erin could only imagine the crashing emotions that he must feel. He was unable to speak while his cronies cracked jokes.

The progression of his friends' attempt to communicate was fascinating. They started off the visit by looking him in the eye and speaking more loudly than necessary. When each of them decided where to sit, they turned facing each other, as if Jack weren't in the room. By the end of their visit, her father seemed to have become little more than a faithful ole hound, worthy of a pat on the head or scratch behind the ears. He didn't have the ability to do anything other than sit with them and perhaps give an occasional howl.

What Erin witnessed that evening upset her. She was determined to find ways for her father to reengage and communicate at the level she believed he still could.

On Friday the morning fog that had lingered most of the week lifted before noon. Erin and Marge maneuvered Jack into the wheelchair and navigated the narrow pathway out the front door. As soon as they bumped the wheels over the threshold, Jack lifted his chin to the ocean breeze. They adjusted him so that the sun bathed his immovable right side.

A deep humming sound started in his throat and grew to a gurgle as it passed through his slanted lips. Erin smiled. She placed her hand on her father's shoulder and massaged his brick-tight muscles. "I love it when you sing, Daddy."

She couldn't remember the last time she had called her father "Daddy." But she could remember the last time she had heard him sing.

Not the way he had chortled along at the cookout. She remembered when he really sang, heart and soul. It was in the shower. Always in the shower. His rich tenor voice echoed through the house whenever he showered.

Once, when she was in the seventh grade, Erin had two friends come to their home for a sleepover. The next morning her father showered long before the girls were ready to wake up. The three sleepyheads were treated to a full rendition of "When Irish Eyes Are Smiling," followed by a number of Wayne Newton classics, and finally one of his favorite Sons of the Pioneers' songs about a tumbleweed.

For the rest of the school year, Erin suffered embarrassment as her friends took delight in doing imitations of her father's far-reaching voice.

Erin's mom had tried many times to convince Jack to join the church choir. He preferred his role as an usher, a job he volunteered for when he was forty-one and faithfully continued performing until he was sixty-two. He was the official greeter at their church and outlasted all the other ushers as well as three pastors. Jack O'Riley, with his snowy white hair, merry blue eyes, and strong right-hand grip was the first impression many received of the church. His wit and charm ensured that every visitor received a friendly reception.

One of the pastors often said during the worship service, "I trust all of you worshipping with us received the right hand of fellowship when you entered this morning." Everyone knew he was referring to being greeted by Jack and experiencing one of his memorable handshakes. Now here he was, unable to lift that once strong "right hand of fellowship" and unable to greet his friends with wit and warmth.

Yet he could sing. Or at least to him it must have sounded like a song.

As Erin rubbed his neck and shoulders, she felt the sun's soothing warmth on her right side as well. She drank in the ocean's seasoned air, tasting the tingle of salt on her lips and feeling the cool trail of tears on her face.

This wasn't easy.

And it wasn't over.

13

Where the wind has a sound like a sweet song
And anyone can hum it,
And the heather grows upon the hills
And shamrocks not far from it.

On Saturday afternoon, two weeks after the wedding and one week after the cookout, Erin left her father in Marge's capable hands and simply said she was going out for a few hours. She took her phone and walked to the bench on the bluff's edge. The sun was doing a nice job of making the smoothly rolling waves look freshly scrubbed with a "top of the morning, Glory" shine.

Erin zipped up her daily-worn green fleece jacket and sat for a few moments breathing in the clean air, trying to clear her thoughts. She missed Mike. Pressing Home on her phone, she waited for him to pick up. His groggy voice answered on the fourth ring.

"Do you want me to call you later?"

"No, I'm awake. I was just thinking about you. How's everything going this morning?" She pictured him in their bed with the phone to his ear and his eyes closed.

"The same. I'm sitting on the bench. Thinking of you, too."

They shared a pause over the phone the way best friends do when they're content just being with each other.

"Mike, it feels like we're not getting anywhere. With our exit strategy, I mean. I feel like I've been here for months."

"We're getting there. It's just slow. I talked to a contractor last night. He's coming Monday to give me an estimate on the wheelchair ramp. And did I tell you I checked on ordering a hospital bed? The company will deliver it as soon as we're ready. I also filed with the agency that provides in-home nursing. All they need is a start date and the reply from your dad's insurance company. We have to be patient. This is a detailed process."

Erin was already dreading the call she knew she would have to make to Sharlene after this update. The great news about Nannette's partnership had been the only bright spot in the business. Sharlene had made it clear that she was falling further behind as she was training Ashley. In their last phone call Erin had confidently said, "I'll be able to jump in when I get home next week." She knew now that her statement had been overly optimistic.

Erin and Mike talked for another ten minutes

before she hung up and wrapped her arms around her middle, drawing them close for warmth. She fixed her gaze on the massive view of the endless blue-gray world before her. At the edge of the horizon, where the curve of the summer sky met the steady stretch of water, all the world blurred into one color and one shape. She couldn't tell where the ocean stopped and the sky began. That's how her life felt at the moment. She was stuck in that place of blurred lines and constant gray. It was a place where time disappeared, out there, somewhere beyond the deep blue sea.

She recalled the "Be still and know that I am God" thoughts that had covered her spirit well over a week ago. This morning the exhortation seemed to be "Let go, and know that I am God." Hanging on by her fingernails was no longer working. If this was to be her life rhythm for a while, then she needed to go with it. She knew that. But she didn't like it.

Erin thought of her father. He was the one who coached the rest of them onward in the rough times. Images came to her of the motivational posters he had put up in his office while he was still teaching. Under the pictures of athletes pressing their toned bodies to go beyond normal human limits were phrases such as "Keep going in the face of opposition" and "Fight through the challenges until you can see the finish line."

This was her marathon, but she wasn't prepared.

Returning to the cottage, Erin checked on her father. He was sleeping. She gave his hand two squeezes and then told Marge she was going shopping.

This shopping trip wasn't to the grocery store. This time she drove an hour and ten minutes to the nearest superstore, where she loaded her cart with the survival items she needed to keep her going on this marathon. She started with some warmer clothes. Erin decided while sitting on the bench that she was tired of feeling chilled all the time in the damp, cool climate. She purchased a pair of sweatpants, two long-sleeved T-shirts, a sweater, a hooded jacket, socks, and shoes with thick rubber soles.

Moving on to the food section, she loaded up on basics and then added several boxes of snack food. She felt especially happy when she found her usual shampoo, which the store in Moss Cove didn't carry. She added some books to her cart, a CD of praise and relaxation music, and a dozen fresh washcloths.

Then she returned to the media section and searched until she found a gem. It was a two-CD pack with twenty-four songs performed by three Irish tenors, and the opening tune was "When Irish Eyes Are Smiling." She knew her dad would love it.

Erin paused in front of the televisions. Her father's cottage didn't have a TV. Delores had taken the small one that had been on the dresser in the master bedroom. Her dad didn't seem to miss it because he always had been opposed to television. During Erin's childhood her mother insisted they buy one when Erin was in fifth grade. Her father called it "the family idol" and never placed a TV so that it sat center stage in the living room of any home he lived in. He treated it more like a radio that provided news updates and not as a stage that provided entertainment.

Even as an adult, Erin took awhile to convince herself she could purchase a television if she wanted to. Today she decided she could put the TV someplace in her father's cottage where it wouldn't irritate him but would provide Marge and her with some welcome company, especially on the foggy gray days when there was no view to look at out the front windows.

She selected a small television with a built-in DVD player and managed to load the box into her cart without assistance. As she wheeled her way to the checkout counter, Erin stopped at a bargain DVD display and purchased four old movies she thought her dad might like.

Still feeling unsettled about buying the television, Erin decided it was because that's the sort of thing you do when you're moving into a new place and want to add your own touches of comfort to make it feel like home. She didn't want to do that. This wasn't permanent. She needed to get back to her own home, not make this into a home away from home.

Then she decided that once they were able to move her father to California, she would put the TV in her kitchen. Sharlene had a TV on her kitchen counter and said she often watched the news while making dinner. Erin told herself she would pop in cooking DVDs and make good use of the TV.

On the drive back to the cottage, Erin called Sharlene twice. When Sharlene didn't answer, Erin left a short message each time and chose not to deliver the news about her extended stay in a phone message. All she could hope was that Ashley was catching on quickly and would be able to fill in the gaps for another week or so.

When Erin drove down the gravel stretch back to the cottage, she noticed a truck parked to the side of the garage. An older man wearing a baseball cap was cutting the grass. He waved to Erin, and she smiled and waved back. The neighborly kindness of the folks in this community kept surprising her.

The man continued with his lawn work as Erin unloaded the car. Marge came out and helped her. The two of them carried the television inside and set it up next to the couch.

"I was about ready to buy one myself," Marge said.

"I bought some music, too, and some books." Erin held up the new CDs, DVDs, and the books in front of her father as if it were show-and-tell time.

He made no indication that he was interested in any of it. His eyes were open but it seemed as if nothing was getting through to him. Erin held off putting in the CD of the Irish tenors. Instead she turned on the TV without any sort of rebuttal from her dad. Since she hadn't called the cable company yet, she put in one of the DVDs she had bought of an old movie with Robert Redford. Jack stared at the TV for most of the movie but seemed more lethargic than usual. By the end of the day he had developed a rattling cough.

Erin rested little over the next few days since Marge had Sunday off. Her father needed constant care. The suction machine ran at least once every half hour.

When Marge arrived on Monday morning and took one listen to Jack's lungs, she was convinced his cough sounded like pneumonia and they needed to take him to see the doctor.

Getting him in the wheelchair and then in the car was hard work. Erin felt horrible that she hadn't calculated what was happening with her dad's cough.

The doctor who saw them treated Jack with dignity, and that meant a lot to Erin. He seemed thorough and knowledgeable enough to give Erin confidence in his diagnosis.

"It's not pneumonia," the doctor explained. "I'm

not saying it couldn't develop into pneumonia, but at this stage it's one of the many complications that come with a stroke of the magnitude your father experienced."

Erin and Marge both heard that Jack needed more consistent attention with the suction machine and that he needed to move around more. The doctor recommended that Erin rent a proper hospital bed so Jack's position could be raised and lowered. He also needed a pull-up device to hang above the bed so he could reach for it with his good arm and exercise.

As Marge and Erin worked together to maneuver Jack back into the car, he put in more effort to assist them than he had on the way there.

"Well, that's more like it," Marge said. "I had a feeling you were holding out on me. You have plenty of strength, Jack. We're going to get you started on these exercises. No more moping around for you."

Once they got him home and comfortable, Erin went upstairs and listened to one of several messages Sharlene had left for her that morning while they were with the doctor.

"I have some great news. I was able to arrange for three of our brides to attend an exclusive spring show at Mia's Bridal Boutique on Saturday. I reserved a place for you as well. It's going to be fantastic. Call me when you can, and let me know if you're back in the office."

Erin regretted that she hadn't managed to connect with Sharlene over the weekend to tell her that once again her time at Moss Cove was being extended. This was really getting difficult on both ends. She stretched out on the bed, exhausted, and tried to remember what it was like the other times she and Sharlene had taken brides to an exclusive bridal shop, nibbling dainty treats and watching models sashay around the room in the newest designs for spring weddings. That world seemed as if it were from another life, not the one she was stuck in now.

She listened to Sharlene's next message, which had been left on her phone an hour earlier. "Hey, I haven't heard back from you. It was my understanding that you were arriving home today with your dad. Is that right? My brain is on overload. I thought it was today, but I just went past your house, and no one was there. Call me if you need anything. Let's meet as soon as you're able. Hopefully, that'll be tomorrow. Just call me and we'll figure it out."

Sitting up and drawing in a breath for strength, Erin dialed Sharlene's number.

"Erin, how are you? How is everything going? Are you home now?"

Erin swallowed. "No, I'm not. I'm still in Moss Cove, Sharlene."

The other end of the phone was silent.

Erin tried to explain about the transporting and

moving details Mike was working on and the long weekend she had spent giving her dad twenty-four-hour care. The topper was the trip to see the doctor that morning. Her stomach was in knots as she said, "I honestly don't know what's going to happen. I have a feeling I'm going to be here for a while." She almost said "for a long time," but Erin didn't want to say it aloud.

Sharlene kindly asked how Erin's dad was doing now, and Erin updated her on his stable condition and the hospital bed that would be delivered for him that week.

After another pause Sharlene said, "How about if we set a time to talk tomorrow morning? Would eight o'clock be too early for you?"

"No. That would be fine."

"I'll call you at eight."

Erin hung up and sat on the edge of the bed, looking out the window at the sunlight on the pine trees' boughs. Her knotted gut told her she was about to lose her business and her closest friend.

All night, as Erin cared for her father through his bouts of deep coughing, she wondered how she had become so enmeshed there. She didn't have to be her father's caregiver. She could arrange for him to be moved to a nursing facility at any time and she could go home—back to her life, business, and husband. When her mother asked her and Mike to look after Jack, she certainly didn't mean this sort of full-time care.

This is crazy. He hardly even knows I'm here. What am I trying to prove?

By eight o'clock the next morning Erin was emotionally and physically exhausted. She waited for Sharlene's call, and finally, at ten minutes after eight, she dialed Sharlene's number. It rolled to voice mail, and Erin left a short message just as the delivery truck pulled up with the new hospital bed.

The delivery crew set it up in the living room facing the large front windows. The men also delivered a shower chair the doctor had recommended so that Jack could be wheeled to the bathroom and lifted into the chair to take a real shower. Marge wanted to get him in the shower right away. The steam would help to clear his lungs.

Erin returned upstairs to try Sharlene again and heard the bumping-around sounds as Marge coaxed Jack to "hold on to this" and "move your strong leg over the other way." Apparently the process was a success and didn't require Erin's assistance because rising up to the dormer was the strange guttural sound of her father's voice drawn out in long notes. He was singing in the shower.

For one moment Erin closed her eyes and let this single sweetness count as a small victory. Another "treasures in the darkness" sort of moment.

She stretched out on the bed with her face in the corner where the sun was coming through the window. In the luxury of that narrow strip of warmth, she let her weary body float off to sleep, knowing that Sharlene's phone call would awaken her. However, it was a call from Mike that roused her less than half an hour into her slumber.

Erin kept her voice low as she said, "I need to come home. I hate to do this, but we need to put him in a care facility up here somewhere until we can get everything in place to move him down to Irvine. I need to go back to work. I need some sleep. I need to be there, not here."

"You're sure that's what you want to do?"

"Yes. I'm worn out. I can't stay here, Mike. Can you help me to find a place for him here?"

"He already has pre-registration papers in place for a facility in Florence. All the forms are in the file there. Delores set it up."

Erin bristled at the thought that Delores assumed Erin would bail on her father the same way she had. Yet for a moment Erin understood how someone like Delores could make a decision to pick up and leave. Staying was really hard.

"Okay. Well, I'll pull out the papers and start working on that. Do you think this is the right thing to do?"

"I don't know. I thought I'd have everything ready here by now."

A long pause stretched between them. Finally Mike said, "Let's both pray about it and then talk again in a few hours."

"Okay."

Erin went downstairs feeling the knot in her stomach clenching tighter. She found her dad all cleaned up, freshly shaven, and sitting up in the new hospital bed with his left arm clutching the lift-up bar. She couldn't imagine he had heard any of her conversation since she had kept her voice so low. But she had a hard time looking him in the eye and felt like a traitor.

"We should have ordered this equipment right away," Marge said when Erin joined her in the kitchen. "He's like a new man. Look at him."

A hint of the old Jack O'Riley showed on his face as he methodically pulled on the bar. After a lifetime of regular calisthenics, Jack seemed happy to be back to his familiar routine. He looked more comfortable. The brand-new white sheets on the bed gave the room a freshness that was much needed. Marge had all the windows open. Sunshine poured in through the window in the kitchen, and the little cottage seemed to breathe once again.

It was a beautiful new day.

Erin unwrapped one of the instrumental praise music CDs from her big shopping trip on Saturday. She dusted off the old stereo in the corner and put in the CD. It took her a few attempts at pressing buttons and turning dials before sound came out of what her sons would call "vintage speakers."

For the first time since Sierra and Jordan had plugged in their iPod at the cookout, music enlivened the surroundings. And, oh, what a difference it made.

"Do you like that, Dad?" Erin turned the music low the way she knew he preferred and looked to him for a response even though it had been days since he had responded to her about anything.

A half smile curved up the left side of his face.

"How about the bed? Are you liking that, too?"

"Yaaaa."

Erin went to his side. He had stopped the self-directed exercises and was resting his wrist on the bar. "I heard you singing in the shower."

His grin stayed firmly in place.

"You're looking pretty handsome this morning. Marge did a good job on that shave." Erin smoothed the backs of her fingers across his warm cheek. She wasn't usually this compassionate as she cared for him and hoped he wouldn't suspect that she was about to leave him, too.

Her dad opened his mouth further, the way he did when it was time for suctioning.

"Do you need me to use the machine?"

"Naaaah."

"He's showing you his teeth," Marge said. "I

finally got him to let me do a proper brushing with the electric toothbrush."

"Oh, let me see. Look at those pearly whites. Very nice."

Jack lowered his arm and pointed his finger at her.

"What? Do you think I need to brush my teeth?"

"Naaaah." He pointed at her mouth again.

"Something about my teeth?"

"Yaaaa."

She smiled broadly for him, just as she had many times during her junior high years when he wanted to examine the progress of her orthodontia. Erin had had such crooked teeth that she had required three years of braces complete with headgear and retainers until she was in college. The results had been well worth it. She had a beautiful smile, and her father delighted in reminding her of that over the years.

"Are you checking to make sure my teeth are still straight after all those years of braces?"

He grinned. "Yaaaa."

"Your huge investment is still holding its value." Erin gave him an extrawide smile.

Then she remembered something her mother had confided in her years ago. The reason her dad teased her about her smile being his biggest investment in her future was because his insurance plan didn't cover orthodontics. To pay for the expense, her father had worked a second job three nights a week selling tools in the basement of a Sears department store in downtown Santa Ana.

When Erin was a teenager, her father having an extra job meant nothing to her. The ongoing orthodontics meant only pain, embarrassment, and aggravation. But when she was old enough to understand and appreciate the gift, her mother told her about the long and steady sacrifice her father had made so that Erin wouldn't have to go through life with a mouth full of jagged teeth.

Erin didn't think she had ever thanked her father for his silent act of giving.

Leaning closer and smiling, she said, "Thank you, Daddy, for all the years you worked the extra job at Sears."

He looked surprised.

"Mom told me. I'm sorry I never said thank you until now. I think I would be a different person if I hadn't had my teeth fixed. Thank you for investing in me and giving me my smile."

His eyes teared up. He reached for her face and cupped his warm hand under her chin. He struggled with much effort to form a blessing in a single word. "Buuufooo."

The word went deep. As a daughter she had waited her whole life to hear him say it. With all his gruffness, he never had. Until today. Her father pronounced her "beautiful."

Blinking quickly so her tears wouldn't overtake

the moment, Erin smiled at her daddy, eye to eye, heart to heart.

And then she knew.

She couldn't leave. It was her turn. This was her Sears department store basement. In the same way her father had given sacrificially all those years ago to improve her quality of life, now her turn had come to give selflessly to her father. She couldn't send him to the nursing facility in Florence. Not when she had it in her power to stay on a little longer and give back to him in this way while he was nearing the end of his days. She would not leave him the way Delores had.

14

May the lilt of Irish laughter
Lighten every load.
May the mist of Irish magic
Shorten every road.
May you taste the sweetest pleasures
That fortune e'er bestowed.
And may all your friends remember
All the favors you are owed.

As soon as Erin decided she was going to stay on with her father at Hidden Cottage, the knot in her stomach loosened. She kept thinking that if she were in the same situation as her father, she would want someone who loved her to care for her as long as possible.

Erin slipped outside after her dad fell into a restful sleep while listening to the soft music. She took her phone and called Mike to tell him of her change of heart.

"Are you sure you want to do this?"

"Yes. I want to give it a try. What do you think, Mike? Are you okay with my staying a little longer?"

"How much longer? A few weeks? A few months? What are you thinking?"

"I don't know. Probably a few weeks. Maybe a month. There's no way of knowing. He could have another stroke tomorrow, and that could be it."

"Yes, or he could live another ten years like this. He's a strong man."

"He doesn't want to go to Irvine or to a nursing facility. He wants to stay here. I can make that happen. At least for a little longer."

Erin didn't want to argue with Mike. She also didn't want to toss in a report about her gut feelings on this. Mike didn't always respond to her intuitive indicators, especially if he knew she was tired or emotional. At the moment she was both, but she still knew that staying with her father was the right thing for her to do.

"I don't know, Erin," Mike said after a heavy breath. "An hour ago you said you needed to come home. Now you're saying you need to stay there. I don't know what to think anymore."

Erin knew that if she could see Mike right now he would give her the same look he gave her when she said she wanted to invite her dad, Delores, and Tony and his family for Thanksgiving. It was the "why would you want to do this to yourself?" look.

Neither Mike nor Erin said anything for a moment.

Finally Mike said, "You need to be prepared to put him in the full-time care facility as soon as there's any indication at all that he needs more medical attention than you can give him."

"Okay. I agree."

"And we have to come up with some sort of limits. Either I need to go up there for a weekend soon, or you need to come down here and hire Marge to stay through the weekend."

"Okay."

"I have to get back to work. Let's talk about this more tonight."

"Thanks for understanding, Mike."

"I do understand. I know how it was when I lost my brother. Once they're gone you can't go back and make decisions like this. But I'm concerned about you. This is a lot to take on."

"I'm okay," Erin said. "Better now, actually, than before I called you."

"I love you."

"I know. And I love you, too."

Erin hung up and decided to call Sharlene again. This wasn't going to be an easy call; she didn't want to put it off. They would have to come up with a way for Erin to carry more of the business responsibilities during the next few weeks. She wasn't sure she could handle much more, but she knew Sharlene had to be close to hitting overload.

Sharlene picked up the call on the first ring and

in her usual breathless voice said, "Erin, I have to call you back. Sorry. I'm just about to leave an appointment, and I'll call you in about ten minutes."

Erin went inside and made a cup of Irish breakfast tea. She added a splash of milk and a dash of sugar. With the first sip, she thought of her mother. And when she did, she remembered her mother's words about how there were no shortcuts in relationships and how to experience the fullness of love, she must go the distance.

Only the strongest and bravest stay on the path. And you, my darling girl, have been given everything you need to be among the strongest and bravest.

Erin sipped her tea seated in a straight-backed wooden chair in the kitchen nook by the window. She hoped her mother's blessing was still true in her life. She didn't know how any of this was going to work out. All she knew was that the knots in her stomach had untangled the moment she decided to stay.

Sharlene's call came through, and Erin went outside to talk in private. She sat on the front deck with her back to the wind and said, "Busy day?"

"Yes. It's been full. How are you?"

"I'm okay. I have some . . ."

"Good. I was . . . Oh, sorry. Go ahead," Sharlene said.

"No, that's okay. You go first. Tell me your update."

"Okay. Well, I met with our CPA today."

Erin drew back. She thought they had been doing just fine financially. She didn't expect this sort of update. "What did Jan say?"

"I asked her to help me . . . to help us . . . to come up with an estimated buyout figure." Sharlene paused.

"Buyout figure?"

"I wanted to be prepared in the event that you would consider selling me your half of the company."

The air around Erin felt still, as if she had slipped into the eye of a hurricane, and from this position of stunned silence she could see everything in her life caught up in a massive swirl. The vortex moment sucked all the air from her lungs and all the words from her lips.

"Jan was able to come up with what I think is a reasonable price. I'll e-mail it to you, and we can talk some more. I don't know if this is what you want to do, but it's something we need to talk about."

Erin still had no words.

"I know you're in a really tough spot right now, and I thought it might help to relieve some of the pressure if you didn't have the business to worry about. Because as soon as you finally do get your dad down here, if he's living with you as you said, your days will be pretty well dictated by his needs. I thought the money might help you and Mike with the additional expenses you'll have."

If this plan was coming from anyone other than Sharlene, Erin would be certain that she was being undercut in some sort of slick deal. But this was Sharlene. Her trusted friend. Certainly she was sincere when she said she was trying to help relieve the stress for Erin. But this was Erin's business, her dream, as much as it was Sharlene's. She didn't want to sell her half of the business.

"Sharlene, I just need a little more time here with my dad. We haven't been able to work out the details to get him down to Irvine, and I don't want to put him in a nursing facility here. I need to stay on with him at Hidden Cottage."

"How long?"

"I don't know. As long as I need to." Erin felt a pounding headache coming on. Her words weren't forming the way she wanted.

"Erin, I don't know what to say. Here I thought I might be offending you by offering to buy your half of the business. But it sounds like you've already decided to leave."

"No, I don't want to leave," Erin said quickly. "And I definitely don't want to sell my half of the business. But for now, I need to stay here. I was hoping you and I could work out some sort of agreement to cover the time I'm away."

"What did Mike say about all this?"

"He's not thrilled. But he understands because he remembers what he went through when he lost his brother."

Sharlene cleared her throat. "Erin, I'm all for you doing what you need to do. I support you and your loyalty, and if I were in your dad's position, I guarantee you that you are the person I would want to be there every day, caring for me. But here's the problem. For a month now I've been working seventy-hour weeks. I've been doing the work of two people and training an assistant. I simply can't continue to do this indefinitely."

"How is Ashley working out?"

"She's fine." Sharlene sounded irritated that Erin had asked about Ashley, as if she were trying to change the conversation's direction. "She's doing a good job. But I posted the position as part-time, and that's all she can give me right now. She's barely able to come twenty hours a week. It's not enough. I don't want to lose what you and I worked so hard to build. And I have to tell you, it feels like we could lose it all."

"I feel awful that I've put you in this position, Sharlene."

"You didn't do it on purpose."

"I know, but I still feel terrible. This isn't what I ever wanted to happen to us or to The Happiest Day."

"I know. But we need to make some decisions.

I'll send you the e-mail with the offer for the buyout. At least consider it. Talk to Mike about it."

Erin knew she didn't want to consider it and she didn't want to present it as an option to Mike. Not right now. "I'll read the e-mail." It was all she could honestly agree to at the moment.

"Let's talk again tomorrow," Sharlene said. "My schedule is full all morning. Try me in the afternoon, or I'll try you tomorrow night, okay?"

"Sure."

Erin hung up feeling more alone than she had in a long time. The worst part was that in her intensely groggy state she couldn't think clearly at all. She wandered upstairs and took a restless nap before Mike called and she went outside again to have another difficult conversation in private. Mike's conclusion was the same as Sharlene's. He suggested they both think things through for another day and pray about them before making a final decision.

The next day Erin felt no different about her decision to stay. She felt only more tired. She prayed, talked to Mike, talked to Sharlene, prayed some more, and still knew this was where she belonged. Mike said he supported her decision and would come up in a week or so and stay with her a few days. Sharlene's response wasn't as comforting.

"I'm sorry to be the negative one here,"

Sharlene said, "but I just don't see this as a good decision. And as I said before, even if you are able to move your dad into your home in Irvine, you won't be able to keep up with work the way things have been going."

"We don't know that. I'm still working on e-mails here, and you can send more my way. I can do more than I have been doing."

Sharlene disagreed. She asked Erin once again to seriously consider the buyout offer.

"I don't understand why you're pressuring me to let you buy my half of the business. This is my dream, too, Sharlene. I'm not ready to give it up."

"But, Erin, in a way, you already have."

Sharlene's words dealt a stunning blow that left Erin's head pounding as her eyes welled with tears. "Sharlene, give me more to do, okay?" Erin tried not to let the emotion show in her voice. "Keep sending me e-mails, and let's see if I can paddle a little faster on my side of the canoe."

Erin heard Sharlene release a long, steady breath on her end of the phone. "Okay. We'll try that until the end of next week. Then we'll have to reach a mutual decision about what to do. Be prepared because I'm sending you a mountain of work."

"That's fine. That's good. I want to do my share."

The tears were still in her eyes and the tension still tightened her throat after she hung up. Erin knew she had to do something to help improve her sleep.

She changed the structure of her day the next morning when Marge arrived right on time. Erin didn't crawl upstairs to try to go back to sleep as she had on previous days. She felt rested because she finally had given in to freshening up the master bedroom downstairs and had slept in that bed, which was far more comfortable than the couch or the upstairs twin bed. Erin had arranged the master bedroom to her liking and moved her dad's clothes to the far end of the closet. Then, for the first time since she had been there, she took her clothes out of the suitcase and hung them up.

During the night Erin kept the bedroom door open so she could hear her father if he was in any distress. Now that Jack had a proper bed, he was sleeping far better than he had in the recliner.

It all took Erin back to when each of her sons was born. She remembered how when they finally slept through the night, she was able to do the same. That Friday morning, she had the same sense of rejuvenation.

Over the bed was a framed souvenir from one of her dad's trips to Ireland. It was in the shape of a shield and labeled "From the Shield of Saint Patrick." Erin had developed the habit of reading it each time she entered the room, but now decided she would read it each morning.

Christ be with me
Christ before me
Christ behind me
Christ in me
Christ beneath me
Christ above me
Christ on my right
Christ on my left
Christ where I lie
Christ where I sit
Christ where I arise
Christ in the heart of every man
who thinks of me
Christ in the mouth of every man
who speaks of me
Christ in every eye that sees me
Christ in every ear that hears me
Salvation is of the Lord.

After a refreshing morning shower and the simple happiness of using her favorite shampoo again, Erin worked on e-mails for an hour and then went for a walk in the glen across the road. She picked a bouquet of wildflowers and put them in a vase so her dad could see them. He gave a nod and a half smile.

While Marge got Jack in the shower, Erin changed his bedsheets and put on the music. She opened all the shades and two of the windows. Now that much of the furniture in the living room had been moved around to make space for the reclining bed, Erin kept the rearranging going.

"Dad, do you mind if I keep moving things around here?"

Fresh from the shower, Jack gave a wave of his hand, and Erin went at it, moving unneeded furniture and other items from the living room out to the garage with Marge's help. They dusted and vacuumed and then together adjusted the bed's position so that Jack had the best of everything. He could press a button and the back of the bed would lift him so that he had a perfect view out the front windows. The foot of his bed was now over the main heating vent in the living room so when it was cold enough for the heat to come on, his feet would be first to feel the warmth.

Erin then moved the stereo unit so that if her dad wanted to, he could use his left hand to start or stop the system. The carousel held fifty CDs. Only nine of those fifty slots were occupied. The one in the first slot was the Irish tenors. As soon as Jack found that he could push the button and the three tenors joined him and sang "O Danny Boy," his morning was the most tolerable he seemed to have had since becoming confined.

"This is good for him," Marge said as she and Erin stood in the garage after hauling out the recliner. "It's a generous thing for you to stay and make these arrangements."

Erin leaned against one of the stacks of boxes Delores had organized before her departure. She knew her dad couldn't hear them in the garage so she asked, "What's your assessment of his situation, Marge? You've been with patients like my dad before, right?"

"Yes."

"Delores said he could live another five or more years."

"Not with the condition of his kidneys. You know how I check for blood each time I change the bag?"

"Yes."

"This morning I saw blood for the first time."

"Are his kidneys beginning to fail?"

"Yes. It looks like that's what's happening. I will tell you this: if I had to make an estimate, I would say he might be with us another four months. Maybe less."

Erin stared at the garage wall and let that new piece of information sink in.

"Didn't you realize the shortness of time he had left when you decided to stay?"

Erin shook her head. "The doctor said he was strong. I thought Delores told me that the first doctor who examined him said he could live another five years or so even with the paralysis and the G-tube."

Marge shook her head. "No, that's not accurate. Delores knew. She knew he had months, not years. She read the charts. She knew about his kidneys."

Erin felt her teeth clench. Her slow-burning anger toward Delores returned. It took a big dose of self-control not to spill out her frustrations.

"Your father deserved someone better," Marge said with diplomacy.

"I know. And he did have someone better, much better. He had my mother. She was perfect for him." Erin and Marge lingered in the garage as Erin talked about her mother. It felt good. Therapeutic. She was better off focusing on the positive than retelling the negative.

Marge left to check on Jack. Erin remained in the cool, damp garage with the stack of unopened boxes.

Erin felt as if an invisible hourglass had been turned over. Four months. Could she stay here for four months? Mike would understand, especially once she gave him this new information. But would Sharlene?

"First things first," Erin told herself. The task at hand was going through those boxes. She could call Mike and Sharlene later. In the same way that she had organized for garage sales over the years, Erin sorted, stacked, and reorganized the remaining pieces of her parents' life.

She came to a box marked FAITH and recognized the handwriting as her own. She had packed this box for her dad after her mom died. It had all the things in it that Erin didn't think she should claim for herself. Now she felt differently as she lifted the lid and revisited treasures that she assumed her father never had looked at since his wife's passing.

Deciding the garage was no place for such a rendezvous with memories, she dusted off the box and carried it into the living room. Placing it on the floor beside the couch, she went to the kitchen to make some lunch.

When she returned to the couch, now bathed in afternoon sunlight, her dad was awake. He pointed at the box and raised an eyebrow.

"It's a box of Mom's things. I thought I'd do a little deep-sea diving for long-buried treasure. Do you mind if I do it here?"

His expression made it clear that she was welcome.

The small treasures were wrapped in tissue. Erin remembered the day she had carefully placed many of the trinkets into this box. The first one she now unwrapped was a figurine of a woman holding up her hand. Balanced on her finger was a tiny bluebird.

"Aawwgh."

"Do you remember this, Dad?"

"Yaaaah." He pointed at Erin.

"No, it wasn't mine. It was Mom's."

He pointed at her with firm determination. She didn't know what that meant. Turning the figurine over, she looked at the bottom and noticed the letters EMO and the numbers 5/22. That was her birthday.

"Erin Melody O'Riley. EMO. Is this mine?"

"No."

"Mom's?"

"Yaaaa."

"Did she get this when I was born?"

His eyes lit up.

"Mom got this little statue when I was born. I didn't know that."

Jack vigorously patted his chest.

"I know. That makes me happy, too."

"No." He pointed at the figurine and then pointed to his face.

Erin took a wild guess. "Did you give this to Mom when I was born?"

He started to cry and made one of his happy wails.

"Oh, Dad, that's so sweet." She looked at the statue again. Fifty-two years ago her father had seen this little treasure of a woman with a bluebird on her finger, and he had thought of her mother. And of her. His baby bluebird.

Erin wrapped the statue in tissue and placed it on the side of the couch that would be her "keep" pile.

"Nooo."

"Do you want me to leave this out?"

"Yaaaa."

Erin placed the figurine next to the vase of wildflowers. Creating a grouping was so like something her mother would do. She was good at displaying art around the house. Erin remembered how the kitchen table always had a centerpiece of some sort. If no flowers or bowls of fruit were available to brighten the table, a candle with a shell beside it or a china cup and saucer with her mom's favorite teapot next to it took center stage.

That was the extent of her mom's artistic expression. She wasn't good at decorating or scrapbooking the way Delores was. Erin's mom didn't see the whole picture or the entire timeline. Her life was a scattering of small moments, bits of meaningful conversations, and bright dashes of beauty where least expected. She held life like a bouquet.

Going through the box of favorite things was a reminder of her mother's cheery, spritely spirit. Erin had been in the midst of mourning the loss of her mother when she had packed away those trinkets. Holding them now turned into a sweet celebration of her mother's life. And it was just between her and her father. If Delores were still there, things would have been quite different.

Erin knew that if the circumstances were different, she wouldn't be there having that moment with her father. This was for her. It was an important and filling moment. She was so glad she was there.

Four more months.

15

May you enjoy the four greatest blessings:
Honest work to occupy you,
A hearty appetite to sustain you,
A good woman to love you,
And a wink from God above.

Erin became sidetracked from her project of going through the boxes from the garage. She left the box marked FAITH in the living room by the couch and put her full attention to e-mails and laundry and a list Sharlene sent her of phone calls that needed to be made.

The next morning, as soon as Marge arrived, Erin bundled up and walked up to the bench on the cliff. She called Sharlene, and as the wind whipped her hair, she calmly told her friend, "I know for certain that I need to be here. It doesn't look like my dad has much longer. Marge thinks it could be four months or less."

Sharlene offered a quiet "Oh, my."

"I wanted you to know that because it might

help you to see that I think we can keep pressing on for a few more months."

It took Sharlene a moment to respond. "I don't know, Erin. I received a call from a bride yesterday, and she said you were talking to her on the phone and in the background she could hear someone gagging and moaning."

Erin knew which call that had been. She had tried to make the call in the kitchen but was cut short when her dad woke and started to choke.

"I know. I need to find a better place to go when I make the calls. My phone gets the best reception from the kitchen or on the deck, but it's not always convenient to sit outside and my dad's hospital bed is too close to the kitchen."

"Where are you right now? Because I'm only catching every three or four words before it seems to cut out."

"I'm outside. It's windy." She tried to shelter the mouthpiece with her hand to cut out the wind.

"You know, as hard as this is for both of us, I have to be direct about this, Erin. If your dad lives another four months, that's still six months that you will have been on this sort of part-time schedule and part-time leave of absence. Six months is a long time."

"I know."

"And what if he improves, and he lives another two years? Are you going to stay that whole time? Would you expect to be able to keep the business

237

partnership the way it is that whole time? I need a full-time partner in this. Since you can't fulfill that position, why not cut me free so that I can find a new partner and keep the business going? I feel like you're drowning right now, and I'm trying to save you, but in the process you're pulling me and the business down with you."

The reality of the situation hit Erin more intensely than it had in their previous conversations. This wasn't fair to Sharlene. Simply acknowledging that it was difficult and apologizing didn't make it better.

"I have to go," Sharlene said. "How about if we talk on Friday? That's what we agreed to last week. We need to come to a conclusion on this. I'll call you Friday evening, okay?"

"Sure. I'll talk to you then."

Erin returned to the house and spent the next two days trying to catch up with the e-mails and make all her phone calls without interruption. She ended up using the musty, drafty garage since she got good reception and could talk privately.

By Friday afternoon, Erin knew what she wanted to say to Sharlene. She had talked to Mike about it and was ready for Sharlene's call that evening. Until then, it seemed like a good idea to finish the project of going through the box of her mother's mementos that she had left by the couch. Her father awoke when she sat on the couch and watched as she unwrapped the faded tissue paper and revealed the hidden items.

One small treasure that particularly caught his attention was a heart-shaped frame. Inside was a photo of Erin's parents when they were in their early twenties. She knew the photo was taken at Huntington Beach when they were dating. Her dad had a basketball under one arm and the other arm around Faith, who was wearing a scarf around her neck that fluttered in the ocean breeze. She had on a full skirt cinched at the waist and a white blouse with the short sleeves rolled up. Her naturally blond hair was pulled up in a bouncy ponytail, and behind them was the vast Pacific Ocean. In the black-and-white photo, the crest of the waves looked like a jiggly silver line. Her dad was so strong. So sure of himself. So invincible.

Erin held out the framed photo. Her dad took it with his good hand, blinked, and stared for a long time without making a sound. Then he coughed, choking on his own saliva. Erin reached for the suction tube and ran through the usual routine. When she finished and turned off the noisy machine, he sighed.

"Do you want me to leave this one out, Dad?"

He didn't reply. He just held the frame and stared. Then, pressing it to his chest, he closed his eyes and went away. Erin watched his face and had a pretty fair idea of where he went. It was to that place where there is no time. The place where the gray of the sky meets the gray of the ocean.

That squiggly silver line somewhere beyond the deep blue sea.

Staying with the task in front of her, Erin dredged up and sorted the treasures. She pulled out another framed photo and carried it into the kitchen where she put it aside. When Sylvia stopped by right on time for her daily afternoon gossip fest, she saw the framed photo and helped herself to a long look.

Erin quietly answered the question she knew Sylvia was about to ask. "That's my brother."

"Good-looking young man."

"That was in high school." Erin looked at it again with Sylvia. The uncanny thing was how similar this photo was to the one of her dad and mom at the beach. This one was taken in the driveway of their childhood home. Her brother, Tony, was wearing a basketball jersey with number 17 on it. Their father stood next to him with his arm around him the same way he had had his arm around Faith, and under Jack's other arm was a basketball. The expectation was written all over Jack's face. His son was as tall as he was and was smiling at the photographer with the handsome charm of the O'Riley men through the ages.

What Erin didn't know until her recent conversation with Tony and what she guessed her parents never knew was that Tony experimented with drugs when he was in high school. He could have been on something the day the photo was taken.

"Jack, why didn't you ever tell me you had such a handsome son?"

Jack's eyes opened wide. Sylvia carried the picture over to him, and Erin didn't stop her. She was curious to see his response when he looked at his son now that his emotions were in such a state of immediacy.

Sylvia held up the picture. Jack stared at it. He didn't reach for it as he had the picture of him with Faith. At first he just stared. Then the sobs came. These were different sobs from those Erin had heard from him before. It sounded as if the pain in his heart was leaking out.

Apparently Sylvia could tell the difference as well because she quickly backed up and handed off the picture to Erin. "That wasn't a good idea, was it?"

"It's okay," Erin said softly. "Talk to him. Change the subject. Tell him what's been happening at the Jenny Bee, and he'll perk up."

As Erin predicted, her father was easily redirected. Sylvia took it upon herself to be more entertaining than usual, and for that Erin was grateful. While Sylvia was with her dad, she went outside to make a phone call. She had considered making this call several weeks ago but didn't want to sound the alarm until the right time.

With Marge's comments about the state of her dad's kidneys in mind, Erin left her brother a message. It was time for him to come. He had asked for "a little more space" before reconnecting with their father. They were running out of life space, and Erin didn't think either of the men needed any more. What they needed was to get face-to-face.

She wished she and Sharlene could have been face-to-face when they had their conversation that evening. Erin was in the garage, wearing her well-used Paddy's Crab Shack fleece jacket and holding a cup of Irish breakfast tea. The tea was as much for support and cheer as it was to keep her hands warm. The coastal chill slid under the closed garage door and sent shivers up her legs.

Erin started the conversation by saying, "I want you to know I've given this a lot of prayer and thought, and I really don't want to sell my half of the business—"

Sharlene cut in. "I thought you might say that. So I went ahead, and I met with an attorney today, just so we could both know what our options are."

"Wait." Erin put her cup of tea down on the garage floor. As soon as Sharlene said "attorney," Erin's hand shook, and she didn't want to spill hot tea down the front of her. "Are you saying you're going to bring an attorney in on this?"

"Only if we need help with clarifying the terms on the contract we signed with each other."

Erin couldn't believe Sharlene was saying this.

Was she going to force Erin out of her share in the company?

"Before you say anything else, Sharlene, let me tell you the rest of what I started to say. I do not *want* to sell, but I recognize how unfair this is to you. I know that I need to stay here for as long as I need to stay here, and so I've decided to sell you my half of the company."

Erin didn't expect the tears that puddled in her throat and choked her as she spoke those last words.

Sharlene seemed as surprised at Erin's statement as Erin had been when Sharlene said she had met with an attorney.

"So . . ." Sharlene didn't seem to know where to go next.

"So I agree to the terms in the e-mail you sent earlier. You can have the papers prepared, and I'll sign them." Erin was trying hard to keep her voice steady. "Again, this isn't what I want, but it's what's fair to you, and that's what's most important to me at this point."

The last few minutes of their conversation were awkward and felt like trying to offer a hug to a person who doesn't like to be touched. This was a far cry from their easygoing friendship all the way through their business partnership.

After Erin hung up, she picked up her cup of tea and sipped the cooled comfort in three big gulps. It was done. Over. For now, this was her focus.

This place. This time. This opportunity to be there for her dad. Mike understood and agreed. In the grand scheme of life this was what mattered.

Erin called her brother again and left another carefully worded message on his voice mail. He returned her call the next day when she was picking up some audiobooks in a bookstore located in the next town up the coast from Moss Cove.

"I'm sorry I didn't call you sooner," Tony said. "I was camping, and the phone service isn't reliable where I was."

"Were you able to listen to my messages?"

"Yeah, how is he?"

Erin found a corner of the bookstore where she felt she could talk more freely and proceeded to give Tony her evaluation. She concluded by saying, "So I think you should come. You shouldn't wait too long."

She could hear her brother's long, low huff of air into the phone. "Okay." He seemed resolved. "I'll figure it out. You're right. I need to come."

"Let me know your plans once you make them."

"I will. And, Erin? Do me a favor and don't tell him I'm coming. At least not yet. If you're saying his emotional reactions are immediate and spontaneous, I don't want him thinking for a long time about my coming. Does that make sense?"

"Yes. I'll wait until you tell me what to say and when to say it."

"You're turning out to be a lot like Mom. Did you know that?"

Erin felt her heart swell. "Thanks for saying that, Tony."

"It's true. She was always the peacemaker. Now you are."

Erin wasn't sure she should be called a peacemaker. Her brother didn't know the secret thoughts she harbored toward Delores.

On her way back to the cottage, Erin pulled off at a turnout for a state beach that had caught her attention each time she had driven that way. The afternoon was sunny and windy. She didn't think it would be a problem if she stayed out a little longer.

The parking area had only a few open spots. Erin found one, got out, and followed the trail through a glen of tall, thin-trunked trees. The trail brought her to a wide beach. The sand was a light gray shade, which didn't surprise her. The surprise was in the astounding rock formations that rose from the sea near the shore. They were stunning in their rugged simplicity. In the same way that an expert gardener would take delight in shaping animals from large bushes, it appeared as if God had taken delight in shaping forms out of rock and leaving them for the wind and waves to reshape.

As far as spending an afternoon on the beach, the visitors there were doing the same sorts of things vacationers everywhere at a beach would do. Families were eating picnic lunches, couples in beach chairs were reading and napping, children were building sand castles.

The difference between this beach and the ones she had frequented at home was that so few people were here. More important, most of them were wearing sweatshirts. The wind was at work along this pristine stretch of coastline. Three people were flying huge kites.

Erin walked down toward the firm sand along the shoreline. She slipped off her shoes and let the stunning cold of the sand and water invigorate her feet. With her eyes focused on one of the huge rock formations to the south, she walked, feeling the salty air fill her lungs.

For a long stretch of the beach she walked and walked. She thought about her brother's comment regarding her being a peacemaker. Erin knew that deep inside she had built up a case against Delores, and toward that woman she felt absolutely no peace.

Worse than that, she had let her feelings of hurt and betrayal grow ever since her phone conversation with Sharlene. It wouldn't have been so painful, she decided, if Sharlene hadn't called in a lawyer. Erin was prepared to peacefully hand over the business; yet Sharlene was making preparations to move in and legally take the business.

What hurt the most was that Erin knew she had lost her closest friend. Their friendship couldn't go on with this separation that now stood between them.

With her frustration rising to the surface, Erin did something she hadn't done in a long time. She jogged. Just a short distance was all she had planned to run. But then her lungs seemed to fall into a steady pace with her feet, and she kept going, feeling the stretch in her long legs and welcoming the endorphins that the exercise released into her system.

Erin thought about how her father used to jog all the time. She had joined him off and on for a few years when she was in high school. She would rise at 6:00 A.M. with her dad and jog around the neighborhood. Erin didn't like running, but she craved her father's attention.

Knowing her limits, Erin stopped jogging and caught her breath as she continued walking in the sand, holding her shoes and filling her lungs with the brisk air. She reached down and picked up a small shell in the sand. It was a mussel, opened yet still hinged together so that it took on the shape of an ebony butterfly.

She trotted back to the parking lot, feeling the bottoms of her feet being massaged by the sand. It occurred to her that many women she knew would give anything to step out of their routines and come away to the wild Oregon coast where they could walk along the beach like this and take the time to reflect on their lives. When she put this extended sabbatical into that context, it seemed like an unwanted gift in the midst of a dark time.

Erin returned to the car with sand still clinging to her toes and thought of a verse she had read that morning.

"I will give you the treasures of darkness, riches in secret places, so that you may know that I am the LORD, the God of Israel, who calls you by name."

Erin got in the warm car and stared out the windshield at the vast blue sky streaked by thin, pale clouds. She tried to imagine what it would be like to hear God call her by name. It made her wonder what happens when a soul steps into that invisible realm the moment after death. What did her mother see? Did she hear God call her by name?

Starting the car and pulling back out onto the main highway, Erin realized that her normal life didn't contain space for her to contemplate those sorts of things. Everything had slowed down for her and had been sifted to the essentials. She liked having this sort of room in her thoughts.

Every evening after Marge went off duty, Erin had been reading aloud to her dad. She was reading through the Psalms, which he liked. That evening was especially chilly so, before she started to read, she put two logs in the stove and made herself some cocoa.

Her dad sniffed the air, doing his Smokey the Bear routine, as she settled onto the couch. "You can smell my cocoa, can't you?"

"Yaaaa."

She tilted her head and gave a feeble apology. "I hope it's not torturing you for me to drink this."

He looked at her and sighed.

"Does this bother you? To see people eat in front of you? I'm sorry. I didn't think of that."

He had become pretty expressive with his big blue eyes. The way he looked at her with the crinkled lines extending from his left eye, Erin knew she wasn't bothering him.

"You're glad I'm here, aren't you?"

"Yaaaa."

"I'm glad I'm here, too. I've been going so hard and so fast for the last few years I haven't had time to just think, you know?"

His eyebrow lifted, expressing his interest.

"I mean, I can't tell you the last time I read an entire book. And in only a few nights we have read through almost the entire book of Psalms. When was the last time either of us did that?" She reached over and gave her dad's foot a playful wrangle.

"Your foot is cold."

Erin popped up and went to the bedroom

dresser. She opened the top drawer and saw a file folder tucked under the neatly rolled-up socks. Taking the socks and the mysterious file with her back to the living room she asked, "Do you mind if I open this?"

He looked at it as if not able to place what it was.

"It was in the bottom of your sock drawer. Are these some important papers? Something personal, maybe? I won't open it if you don't want me to."

He motioned for her to go ahead. Erin put the socks on his feet and placed the file on her dad's lap so they could open it together. She turned back the top flap and saw a few notes in her dad's handwriting.

"So you don't know what these are?"

"Naaaaa."

Erin pulled out an old, faded Valentine's Day card. On the inside in her dad's handwriting was a little jingle she had forgotten all about. As soon as she saw it she remembered the way her dad used to recite the poem to her mother.

"Do you remember this, Dad?" Erin read it to him.

> Her smile is as wide as the ocean,
> She lives in the cottage by the sea,
> She's the wife of Jack O'Riley,
> So give her a kiss for me.

He responded with a short sigh.

"That never made sense to me, Dad. Who did you expect to kiss your wife?"

He pointed to the ceiling.

"The sky? No? The sunshine? The rain? The rain is supposed to kiss her?"

"Naaa." He pointed again.

"Heaven? God?"

He nudged her guessing forward with his eyebrow raised. She knew she was on the right trail.

"Oh! Angels. Is that it? Is it angels?"

He winked his left eye.

Erin remembered the mention of angels in other Irish blessings. After all these years, the jingle finally made sense. "You're saying that the angels should give her a kiss for you simply because she's your wife."

The look of delight on his face was grand. The two of them never had communicated this well when he had a voice and a full vocabulary at his bidding.

Erin laughed. "So all along you were asking the angels to give Mom a kiss. I never got that. I do remember when you used to quote this to her. She laughed every time. You would put on that brash Irish accent of yours and come across as Mr. Smooth, that's what you were."

He tried to laugh but started to cough instead.

Once she got him cleared out and settled down

again, he had a great look of contentment as she went through the file and read the rest of the letters to him. The tender part of it all was that either Erin's mom or her dad had saved the letters all those years. The odd part was that Delores must have seen these papers. How did she feel about all this? Had Delores decided to leave Jack alone with his memories of Faith here in his cottage by the sea?

Looking at her dad she said, "People are complicated, aren't they? Life is pretty unpredictable, don't you think?"

He raised his eyebrow in agreement and gave a somber nod.

The rest of the week continued at the same pace. Marge arrived at seven thirty each morning; Erin found time for a walk into town or along the beach in between laundry, phone calls to insurance companies, and going through boxes in the garage. Sylvia now stopped by every other afternoon at three thirty, and Erin read to her dad each evening. For the time being, this was her life, and she was okay with that. All feelings about Sharlene and the loss of The Happiest Day were set aside. She hadn't received the official documents yet from Sharlene for her to sign over her part of the business. Sharlene had stopped forwarding business e-mails to Erin, and Erin had no brides-to-be to call.

She felt as if she had faded into that same blue-gray space between the sky and the sea where she had imagined her father went when he tried to remember the past. The past was a blur. The future uncertain. For now, this was all there was, and it wasn't terrible. In fact, it was strangely serene.

16

Deep peace of the running waves to you.
Deep peace of the flowing air to you.
Deep peace of the smiling stars to you.
Deep peace of the quiet earth to you.
Deep peace of the watching shepherds to you.
Deep peace of the Son of Peace to you.

The next day Erin drove to the nearby state park. She decided that morning that she needed to go for a walk and use the time to think, pray, and listen.

The listening part of her life seemed to be the biggest surprise since arriving in Moss Cove. It was quieter there than at home without the city noises like cars and leaf blowers. Yet in the cove the sounds of nature—of the bigger world—were with her whenever she went outside. Sounds of the wind in the trees, the seagulls, and the constant ocean with its changing moods made their presence known.

Erin now could recognize the waves' varying sounds. She knew, just by listening to the intensity of the waves' roar through the open kitchen window, when they were crashing against the rocks and sending a spindrift into the air. She also knew when the sea was at rest, simply breathing in and out, sending the waves rolling to the shore and then curling them back.

Today the sea was feisty. With a curled-up fist, it hurled the whitecapped waves onto the shore. The salty avengers tumbled far up on the sand before receding in haste and preparing for their next pitch.

Erin kept a fast pace as she walked beside the agitated ocean. This place of walking, listening, thinking, and praying felt familiar. Walking beside the sea on a day like this was like sitting beside her father on one of his agitated nights. The ferocious breathing in followed by the rumbling exhale that rattled the deep didn't frighten her. She had been listening to those sounds long enough to know they signaled life grappling to do what it was created to do—breathe.

Erin returned to the car with sand in her hair. A gust of ocean breath had picked up the tiny grains and tossed them at her as she trounced along the shore. She closed the car door against the wind and inhaled the warmth the sun had created for her without the wind's opposition.

Pulling the rearview mirror toward her, Erin was surprised to see the robust color in her cheeks and how the color made her eyes look bluer. It had been weeks since she had worn makeup. Her hair was dearly in need of attention. Her natural auburn roots weren't too far off from the color her stylist used on her hair, but Erin could tell where her natural color ended and the assisted shade began. She could also see the gray much more clearly. It appeared that her hair had not only been speckled with sand during her walk but also sprinkled with flecks of silver.

She decided she looked more natural and earthy than she had in a long time. At home she kept her regular hair appointments and never left the house without makeup. She would never, not even around the house, be caught wearing a fleece jacket advertising Paddy's Crab Shack. Yet here she was, wearing the green jacket once again. She was zipped up to her chin in her coastal "career" apparel.

She noticed how short her nails were. A month ago she'd had them done perfectly for Jordan's wedding. A week ago she had purchased a bottle of polish remover at the Wayside Market along with a pair of clippers and a file and had gone to work trying to salvage the jagged mess they had become.

She tried to picture what Sharlene was wearing today. Probably a skirt, another one of her business decisions made earlier in the year. She had found a designer who made straight skirts with darling matching jackets that featured classy details on the collar and cuffs. The line was designed especially for petite women. When Sharlene tried on the first suit, she declared that all her business calls would be made in that outfit because it "rocks my tush."

Erin could envision Sharlene's nails. They would be shaped perfectly, polished with her new signature shade of pink, and on the little finger of her right hand she would have a gem design of some sort. Usually she went with a flower, but for Jordan's wedding she had gone with a heart and commented that the heart was a good subliminal message for brides to see when she made a presentation to them.

Erin looked down at her crumpled sweatpants, green fleece, and chewed-up fingernails. She was about as far away as she could get from looking like a CEO of The Happiest Day.

This all happened so fast. I lost everything, didn't I? Should I try to start a new company when I do go back home eventually?

The thought depressed her. She turned the key in the ignition and backed out of the parking lot.

One hour at a time. Don't wear yourself out. It's a marathon.

When Erin returned to the Hidden Cottage, Marge had her dad out on the deck in his wheelchair all bundled up against the wind. Erin sat quietly beside him looking out at the ocean. The wind still was creating mischief with the waves. The white spray from the water dashed against the rocks to the far right and rose high enough up the cliff that the fountain shot a fan of silver droplets for them to see.

"Oooo."

Erin smiled at her dad. "It's like having your own private fireworks show in the middle of the day, isn't it?"

"Yaaaaa."

Marge had gone back inside, leaving Erin to watch her dad. He seemed alert as he breathed in the salt air. Erin took a risk and asked him a pointed question. "Dad, why did you marry Delores?"

His eyebrow went up and stayed up.

"I know. It's none of my business. I just don't understand."

Jack calmly placed his hand on his chest and patted it.

"Did you love her?"

He didn't reply right away. Then a slow "Yaaaa" came from his lips along with a string of drool. Erin used the washcloth in his lap to dry his mouth. He still was looking at her intently, his deep blue eyes seemingly eager to communicate with her.

With his chin pressed forward, he expressed himself to her with a string of unintelligible sounds. Vowel groupings came tumbling from his crooked lips. His eyebrow rose and fell. Instead of getting frustrated as he did whenever he was trying to communicate but the words wouldn't form, this time he kept going.

The meter and the rhythm of the continuing stream of sounds made it clear what he was doing. Erin realized that her father was telling her a story—his story—distilled in his wounded heart and pressed through his lips in the only way it could come out. Just sounds and facial expressions from half of his face.

She fixed her gaze on him and listened as if she were six and never had heard such a wonderful story in her life. His eyes told her he was telling a love story. The story of his second love, Delores. Nothing about their marriage was conventional, but he had found contentment with her for those few short years.

Then, with a lowering of his eyebrow, he raised his finger and pointed at her the same way he did when she was young and was receiving a scolding. The guttural sounds were from no written language. But the expression made the message clear.

Erin reached for her father's wagging finger and enclosed his hand with hers. "I understand, Daddy. I do. And you're right. It's not my place to judge. Not you or Delores or the choice either of you made to be together and to move here."

His surprised expression made it clear that she had indeed "heard" him as clearly as if he had used English to communicate his message. He drew the back of her hand to his lips and kissed it twice before the heaving motions that started in his chest reached his throat.

Then Jack O'Riley let loose with a wailing moan that was beyond any cry he had yet expressed. He cried big, drippy, splashing tears, all the while holding fast to Erin's hand.

The feisty ocean was in his soul.

He had just confessed to his daughter the treasure buried in that deep darkness. She had pulled the gems to the surface and admired them in his presence. Then she had honored her father by declaring that she perceived the value of his hidden treasure. He had been heard and understood.

It was her gift to him.

When the tumult ceased and all the tears were mopped up, Jack dipped his chin and lowered himself into a deep sleep. His chest rose and fell as precious oxygen rolled in and out of the caverns of his steady lungs.

Snugly tucking the blanket around him, Erin drew in a deep breath and gave way to a tremor in her spirit. Being here for a moment like this was the reason she had willingly surrendered her half of the business to Sharlene. And she didn't regret it.

The rest of the day Erin felt weak, as if all her emotional muscles had been overused and needed to rest. She was up at midnight with an upset stomach.

When she got up to use the bathroom, she checked on her dad and found he was awake, too. He was running a fever. The liquid medication through his G-tube and the cold compresses she administered didn't bring down the fever. She sat beside him for more than an hour, softly singing all the old hymns she could remember. His breathing slowed. He wrapped his fingers around her hand and seemed soothed by the singing.

The night inched along. Erin started a fire to take the chill off the room and kept the cold compresses on his forehead. She checked his temperature every half hour and prayed. Just before dawn, when his fever spiked and the thermometer registered 102.4, Erin turned up the light beside his bed. He didn't flinch as he usually did when the light was turned on.

"Dad, how are you doing? Can you give me a little groan or squeeze my hand? Let me know that you can hear me."

He was unresponsive.

Erin called an ambulance.

The effort to maneuver her father onto the stretcher, out the narrow door, and into the ambulance was complex but not nearly as difficult as it had been previously when Erin and Marge had loaded him into the wheelchair and then into the car to drive him to the doctor's office.

Marge arrived just as they were pushing Jack into the ambulance. He still hadn't opened his eyes or tried to communicate.

"I'll call you from the hospital, Marge. I'm going to follow the ambulance in my car. If I end up bringing him home today, I'll let you know."

"I'd be glad to come with you. I might be able to answer some questions for the doctor."

Erin appreciated Marge's kind support and told her so. "You have no idea how glad I am that you were the assistant assigned to us. You are a wonderful woman."

Marge took all of it in stride—the compliment, the ride to the hospital, and Jack's condition.

Erin was much more rattled and soon understood why Delores had been so reluctant to take her father to the hospital when he first experienced his strokes. The waiting in the small curtained area was torture. Every aspect of the experience felt impersonal and small-town inadequate. But the good part was that the attending nurse immediately put Jack on an IV with a high dose of fever-reducing medication as well as the fluids he needed.

By noon they had seen the doctor, answered questions, and were waiting for the results of some blood work. At one o'clock Jack opened his eyes and looked around, surprised to see the surroundings.

"Hey, Dad. How are you feeling?" Erin slipped

her hand into his left hand and gave it a squeeze. His hand felt cool. That was a good sign, she thought. "You had a rough night. We brought you in because I couldn't get your fever down."

His lips were chapped, and his chest seemed to rise and fall more rapidly than usual, as if he were panting.

"You okay?"

"Auaaehh."

"Does it hurt anywhere?" Marge asked, coming closer to the side of his bed.

"Eeauuaa."

"Are you uncomfortable?" Erin asked. "Is that it? You're in pain?"

"Auuueeeu."

These sounds were different from any Erin had heard him make in the past. At least when he could say "Yaaaa" or "Naaaah," Erin could go through a list of questions. Mike called it the diagnostic check. Now she couldn't distinguish what he was saying.

"Where does it hurt?" Marge asked again.

He pointed at the opening between the curtains. Erin guessed he was confused. "We're at the hospital. A doctor came and had a look at you. They're checking the results of the tests they ran on you. We can't leave yet."

"Aaaaaaugg." He seemed exhausted, as if pushing the sounds out was as hard as running a race.

"Just rest, Dad. You don't have to try to say anything."

He looked up at her and seemed to try hard to focus. His right eyelid drooped more than it had in the past. The heavy lid now covered half his pupil.

Marge did an overall survey to make sure nothing was poking him. She couldn't find any indicators of what might be causing external pain. "The doctor will be back soon," she assured him in her efficient manner. "You just rest now."

The afternoon at the hospital dragged on. More tests were ordered, and Jack was rolled out for a scan. He returned with the sheet covering his middle but not his legs. His paralyzed right leg was curved in and his right foot followed inward, turning in and tightening up in a limping position. Both his legs looked uncharacteristically pale. All of her dad's years of going to work in Southern California in shorts and a polo shirt with a whistle around his neck were far in the past. His continually tanned legs and teaseworthy white sock line were gone. The legs that now replaced them were unrecognizable to Erin.

Marge readjusted the sheet to cover his legs as Erin checked his left foot. He felt cold to her touch. Erin pulled the thin blanket up from the end of the bed and tucked it in around him. He gave no indication that he was aware of her touch. His eyes remained closed.

Erin commented in a low voice to Marge that it never felt this depressing when they were at home with him. There he had light, music, and a manageable routine. Not to mention the view and the heating vent that blew warm air at the foot of his bed. The hospital was straight-backed chairs, beeping machines, and air-conditioned chill.

Erin checked her watch. "It's almost three o'clock."

"Don't worry about leaving on my account." Marge had pulled a paperback novel from her purse and looked at home in the corner chair. "I'm fine with staying here as long as I need to. You might want to call Sylvia in case she was planning to make her usual visit this afternoon."

"Good idea."

Erin slipped out to the emergency waiting area to make her call. She ended up having to go outside because she couldn't stand being in a room full of so many hurting people. It was as if her empathy antenna had sprouted since caring for her father. She could look at people and read more in their expressions than she had ever even tried to decipher in the past.

Stepping outside, she pulled out her cell phone, which had been turned off because use of cells wasn't allowed in the hospital rooms. She saw that she had missed a call from her brother.

"Hey, Erin. Listen, I'm working on trying to schedule a flight to see Dad like you said I should, but it's not coming together for me. To be honest, I'm not sure I'm ready for this. How is he doing? I mean, if he's stable at the moment, maybe I should wait and come when it's more urgent, you know?"

Erin called him back, and when she reached his voice mail she said, "Hi, Tony. I just listened to your message, and I think you should come as soon as you can. I had to bring Dad to the hospital this morning. He has a fever that wouldn't break during the night. That usually means there's an infection. They're still taking some tests. He's not the same strong, forceful man you remember him as being. As a matter of fact, he's lost a lot of weight. I don't know how long he has left, but I do think you should treat this as if these are the end of his days. Call me back and let me know what you decide. Love you."

Erin then found the Shamrock's number and phoned Sylvia to reach her before she headed to the Hidden Cottage for her afternoon visit. When Sylvia answered, Erin gave her an update, realizing that Sylvia was the unofficial town crier and that by six o'clock most of Moss Cove would know about Jack's confinement in the hospital.

The doctor was in the room with her dad when Erin returned. He was talking with Marge and showing her some details on Jack's chart. When Erin entered, the doctor looked up and said, "Are you the daughter?"

"Yes, I am."

"I was telling your mother that—"

"She's not my mother. Marge is his day nurse."

"My apologies." The doctor looked at Marge, clearly embarrassed.

"If you would like me to leave the room I'd be glad to." Marge rose from the chair, but Erin motioned for her to remain.

The doctor continued with the test results.

Marge nodded as the doctor relayed the test numbers. She seemed clear on all his medical terms while Erin got lost immediately. The main piece of information she gleaned from his report was that Jack's kidneys were failing.

"The average male his age and in his condition can function for an extended time on as little as one-fourth of one kidney. It's hard to say how well he'll do with the limited use he has at this point. He seems to have a lot of inflammation in his lungs, which would indicate he's fighting a common viral infection as well. I wish I had better news than this." The doctor closed the chart and leaned back. To Erin it seemed his next words would be "It's only a matter of time now."

Instead he said, "We can step up the fluids. I've prescribed a painkiller. It's fine for you to administer it any time you have reason to believe he's experiencing discomfort. The area around the G-tube looks very good." The doctor turned to Marge. "It's evident that he's receiving excellent care. I didn't see signs of any bedsores, which is also very good. Our objective at this point is to make him as comfortable as possible."

"So we should take him home?" Erin asked.

"I'd like to keep him overnight for observation to see if the inflammation in the lungs calms down. If it appears he might be headed for pneumonia, I can start medication. With the many other medications he's on now, I'd rather wait to see if he needs the other drugs."

"Okay." Erin leaned up against the edge of the bed and gave her dad's feeling leg a squeeze. He didn't respond.

"Can you think of anything I didn't cover? Any questions?" the doctor asked.

Erin had been watching her dad off and on during the discussion. She had a suspicion he wasn't asleep even though his eyes were closed. When the doctor was explaining the kidney failure his eyelids seemed to wiggle. When the doctor repeated the decision to keep him overnight at the hospital, Jack's mouth seemed to twitch, and his eyebrows dipped. But when she squeezed his leg, he didn't engage with her.

Erin couldn't imagine how it must feel to have people standing around discussing your condition and making decisions for you when you aren't able to protest or enter into the conversation.

Motioning to the doctor that she wanted to step away from the bed, Erin walked toward the waiting room, and the physician followed. Once she was certain she was too far away for her father to hear, she asked, "Is there anything else we can do for him?"

"Not that I noted. As I said, he looks like he's getting excellent care. Just keep him comfortable."

Erin's next question was painful and difficult to form in a way that didn't make her feel like an impatient or uncaring daughter. "Is there any way to know . . . I mean, how much longer . . ." She couldn't finish her question.

"You want to know how much more time he has. Is that it?"

"Yes."

"We don't have a way of knowing exactly, of course. But I'd say, based on his overall condition, he has a few weeks. Maybe a month. Again, we can't estimate with precise accuracy in cases like this. Patients surprise us in both directions. Does that help?"

Erin nodded. A lump had formed in her throat. If she answered aloud she was afraid the lump would burst.

"I'd recommend that you go on home and get as much sleep as you can. He'll receive good care here. You're going to need your strength for what's ahead of you."

Marge and Erin stayed another hour while Jack slept, seemingly unaffected by their presence.

"We should go," Erin said at last, resigning

herself to not being able to do anything more. They drove back to the cottage, and Erin said, "I'll call you from the hospital in the morning to let you know when I'll be bringing him home."

"You'll need help transferring him," Marge said.

"I'm sure I can make arrangements at the hospital. If you could be here when we return, you and I can get him inside. Besides, Mike will be here tomorrow afternoon. If my dad stays at the hospital most of the day, Mike might be here by the time he comes home."

Marge offered Erin a tender smile and comforting pat on the arm. "Get some sleep."

"I will," Erin promised.

She unlocked the persimmon red door and stepped inside Hidden Cottage. An eerie stillness surrounded her.

17

May the blessing of light be on you—
Light without and light within.
May the blessed sunlight shine on you
And warm your heart
Till it glows like a great peat fire.

Entering the vacant cottage had a powerful effect on Erin. She stood in the silent living room, gazing at the empty hospital bed and then turning her attention to the vivid tangerine sunset out the front window. The same sort of inexplicable peace that had come and gone in her thoughts over the past month returned and soothed her.

She walked out to the bench and sat with her face to the wind, absorbing every last drop of the orange sunset. Listening to the waves, she breathed in and out and did nothing more than appreciate God and his faithful hand of balance and mercy on all of his creation. Erin felt weak and small. Yet in that confinement she knew a deeper peace than she ever had known. And with that peace came strength.

I wonder if it's been the same for my dad. He's been drawing from that inner peace. I know he has. His body used to be his strength. He was a mule. He could do anything. Now he's been enclosed in such a vulnerable weakness. Yet in all my life I've never seen him this strong about what truly matters.

Erin took her time walking back to the cottage. She picked a handful of Queen Anne's lace and examined an interesting-looking cricket that was unafraid of Erin's slow approach while it remained perched on a bramble bush.

Inside the cottage, she opened windows to let in the twilight breeze and the nature songs of the night. She freshened up the living room, changed the sheets on her dad's bed, washed a stack of dishes, and had a piece of locally made blueberry pie for dinner.

Then, closing up all the windows, she readied for bed, anticipating the luxury of sleeping through the night without interruption. "Doctor's orders," she reminded herself as she slid under the covers. "He'll be fine without me tonight."

Erin pulled out her cell phone, ready to have a long talk with Mike. He answered her call on the first ring and told her he was packing and couldn't wait to see her. Erin gave him the update on her dad. They decided that Mike would call when his plane landed. If he needed to go directly to the hospital, he would meet her there.

Sinking under the covers, Erin fell into the deepest sleep she had had in over a month. She woke almost eleven hours later, blinking and quickly remembering where she was. It felt as if her life had turned another page. Or maybe it was about to turn another page. Something felt different to her. It wasn't just that she was alone in the cottage. Something in the unseen universe seemed to have shifted during the night.

Her wake-up shower was quick, and her selection of what to wear was simple, as was her entire wardrobe. She drove to the hospital under lumpy coastal clouds. She thought about Mike and couldn't wait to see him. They rarely had been apart for very long during all their years of marriage. She had a wonderful and understanding husband. She intended to tell him so as soon as he arrived.

Erin expected to find her father as she had left him, comfortably nodded off in the hospital bed with an intersection of tubes, cords, and machines monitoring his vitals. What she found shocked her.

Her dad was curled up in a semifetal position, quietly whimpering. The sheet and blanket had fallen by the side, his backside was exposed, and he was shivering under the chilly air-conditioning vent.

"Daddy!" She rushed to his side, speaking strong and confident words. "It's okay. I'm here. You're all right. Let's get you straightened up and under the blankets."

She pushed the nurse call button furiously and then pushed it again three more times for good measure. Pulling his arm forward as she had seen Marge do during their physical therapy sessions, Erin continued to speak firm, decisive directions, telling him how he was to use his arm to hold on to her and work hard to turn himself. "Come on, you can give me more than that. You can do this. One more twist. Come on, focus here. Use your muscles. Press harder. What are you holding back for? Show me what you've got."

Jack's cramped and feeble frame rolled over. Erin adjusted his paralyzed leg. She positioned his lifeless right hand in its usual curled position on his stomach.

"One more twist here, Dad. Let's level your shoulders. Come on, don't turn into a cream puff on me. Work it."

He laughed.

At least she thought it was a laugh. It was an odd sound, but it wasn't a wail. His swollen face showed a glimmer of relief.

"You liked that cream puff comment, didn't you?"

He made another light, breathy sound.

"Well, what goes around comes around, Coach O'Riley. This is payback for all those years you called me a cream puff, not to mention every student you ever yelled at during your illustrious career on the field. It's your turn to buck up, mister. You have to work every single muscle left in your body, and you have to do it now!"

With that, he strained forward with all the muscles in his neck popping out, and Erin was able to maneuver his shoulders the rest of the way. "One more time, hotshot."

He gave a weak effort, but it was enough for Erin to prop up the pillows behind him the way he needed them to provide the most support for his head. Marge had taught her well. She knew what he needed.

A nurse appeared and pressed the button by his bed, turning off the signal. She didn't look at all pleased.

Erin tried to remain controlled for her dad's benefit. She didn't want to cause a scene even though inwardly she wanted to pitch a fit. "My father has been neglected for some time, and I'd like to know when the last check was made on him."

"I'll have to pull his chart." The nurse looked him over and lifted his wrist to take his pulse. "His rate seems elevated."

Erin realized that the nurse hadn't seen what she saw when she arrived. All the nurse saw was her father rightly positioned and tucked into the bed as if nothing were amiss.

"He was curled up in a fetal position when I arrived," Erin stated firmly. "How could he have been so neglected that he ended up curled on his side and crying when I arrived? He had no blankets over him and was shivering."

The nurse glanced at Erin with a look of compassion. "I'm sorry to hear that. I'll check his temperature. He appears to be perspiring."

"That's because he just had a workout. I turned him. He helped, but I turned him."

The nurse appeared to assume Erin was exaggerating.

"I'd like to see the doctor as soon as possible. I'd like to make arrangements to take my father home."

"A hundred and two." The nurse seemed to be speaking to herself after taking her dad's temperature.

Erin paused. That was a pretty high temperature. Still, he wasn't receiving the kind of attention he would at home. "When may I see the doctor?"

"I'll check on that for you." She didn't look at Erin. Her focus was on Jack. "Are you comfortable, Mr. O'Riley?"

"Haaa."

It was hard to tell if his response was a "Yeah" or a "Ha!"—as in "What a joke," or if it was just his releasing a deep breath. His eyes stayed open after the nurse left. He looked at Erin with the expression of a frightened child.

"I'm sorry, Dad. I should have stayed with you last night. I'll get you home where we can take care of you. Mike is coming. He'll be here for a few days. We'll get you comfortable again. You'll see."

Jack lifted his left arm. His hand was shaking, but he managed to give her a wobbly thumbs-up sign.

Erin smiled. "You did good, by the way, with turning in the bed. You're a strong man."

He pointed a bent finger at her and managed a slight nod.

"I know. I make a good coach, don't I?"

"Haaa."

"Well, I learned from the best. What can I say?"

Her dad coughed a deep-chested, rattling cough. Erin quickly moved to do everything she knew to do and used the suction machine next to his bed to clear the mucus. She had to wonder if anyone had done this for him in the middle of the night. Was that why he had gotten so curled up and twisted? Had he coughed himself into that position somehow?

The next four days were long and arduous. The doctor put Jack on oxygen and continued to treat the viral infection that seemed to be elevating his temperature. He was having difficulty breathing so the doctor recommended he stay another night to watch for pneumonia.

Mike's visit was at just the right time. He came directly to the hospital from the airport, and for the next few days, he and Erin formed a tag team keeping vigil beside Jack's hospital bed.

It took three days for Jack to rally. The doctor released him to go home, saying that his symptoms were under control, and he had managed to dodge the pneumonia bullet. Erin called Marge, who agreed to be at the house waiting when Erin and Mike brought Jack home. Marge hooked up a portable oxygen unit Jack needed now due to the weakened state of his lungs. The three of them fell back into the familiar routine with the addition of more medications, occasional adjustments to the oxygen, and a more elaborate charting of his temperature readings. The chart beside Jack's bed looked like the chart hanging on the wall at Jenny Bee's Fish House that listed the rise and fall of the coastal tides as well as the moon's stages.

With Marge back on duty, Erin and Mike slipped out for a late breakfast his last morning there. They found a corner table at Jenny Bee's and attempted their first semiprivate conversation since Mike had arrived. Even though only two other locals were in the café at the time, Erin kept her voice low, and Mike followed suit. That is, until he had his first taste of the homemade raspberry jam. He turned around and gave a thumbs-up sign to Jo.

She grabbed the coffeepot and trotted over to refill his cup.

"Great jam," Mike said. "Really nice."

"One of our specialties here. You two want anything else?"

"No thanks," Erin said. She watched as Mike sipped his industrial-strength coffee from a thick white mug and thought about when she had been there with her dad a year and a half ago. What a different man he was then. He was so eager for her to approve of his Hidden Cottage and all she had said was, "It's nice." She had different feelings toward the place now, mixed feelings. In many ways it had become her home away from home. She never expected that.

Erin realized that one of her dad's wishes for the Hidden Cottage had come true the night they had the crab cookout and danced on the deck under the twinkle lights. Jack's family and friends had gathered at Hidden Cottage and enjoyed one another and the place's slow-paced beauty. No wonder his disappointment showed on her first visit when she brushed it off as a place her boys were too old to enjoy or too far away for her and Mike to visit.

Erin reached across the table and slid her hand under Mike's so that his warm, strong hand covered hers. Just that sense of touch, of immediacy, comforted her.

"You are wonderful, you know. I don't think any other woman in the world has a husband as understanding and supportive as mine is."

"You keep thinking those good thoughts about

me, honey. We still have a ways to go before the final chapter is over here." Mike held up his last bite of sourdough toast slathered with raspberry jam. "Do they sell this stuff?"

"They have small jars by the cash register."

"I'm taking some home with me."

Mike pushed his emptied plate to the side of the table and stacked his silverware on top. Jo stepped over to their table to clear the dishes and placed a jar of jam on the table next to the check. Obviously she had heard Mike say he wanted to take some home.

"On the house," Jo said. "Glad you like it. I miss Jack coming in and raving about all our jams. He was our biggest fan." She reached for Erin's empty plate. "Do you think Jack is still able to have visitors?"

"Yes, definitely. He's declined quite a bit. But you're welcome, Jo. I can't guarantee my dad will be very aware of what's going on, but he does love to see people when he is awake."

"I've been meaning to come for a few weeks now, but with the end-of-the-season rush I haven't gotten away. It'll be quieter now that autumn is here."

"Feel free to come over any time you want," Erin said. "You can let anyone else who asks know the same thing. All my dad's friends are welcome."

"I'll pass the word around."

Jo walked away, and Erin noticed that Mike left

an especially generous tip for her. "That was nice of you," she said as they walked outside into the brisk air and slipped into the car.

"Well, she gave me the jam. Besides, places like that remind me of my busboy days, and I feel for anyone who is counting on tips as part of their income."

Mike started the engine on his old BMW and patted the dashboard. "I've missed you, girl. Hope you're doing okay up here during the cold nights. I'll have you home and back where you belong soon enough."

"Should I be hurt that you're saying things to your car that I wished you were saying to me?" Erin teased.

Mike gave her a side grin. "I've missed you, too, girl. You know that. And you also know that I can't wait to have you back home and in our warm bed each night where you belong."

"That's more like it."

As Mike drove, he looked straight ahead. "You made the right decision when you chose to stay on here. You've done a great job of walking through this valley of the shadow of death with your dad. You can't do anything more for him than what you're doing. I don't think he will be able to hold on much longer."

She only hoped that moment didn't come before her brother arrived and had a chance to say his good-bye.

18

Wishing you always
Walls for the wind,
A roof for the rain,
And tea beside the fire;
Laughter to cheer you,
Those you love near you,
And all that your heart may desire.

Instead of returning directly to Hidden Cottage, Mike drove to a lookout peninsula area he said he had heard about. The peninsula contained a park run by the state parks system. That fact was quickly evidenced by the well-maintained parking lot and restroom facilities. Only two other cars were parked there. They climbed out of the car and walked across a wide, open grassy area to a point that suddenly dropped off, just as it did at Hidden Cottage. Tumbled, petrified black lava rock formed the side of the lookout that provided a spectacular view of the coast for as far north and as far south as they could see.

"Look." Mike pointed to the water where

gently rolling waves seemed to bob in rhythmic measure to the place where the volcanic rocks met the sea.

"What am I looking at?"

"Keep watching. Down there in the waves. Do you see them?"

Erin shielded the sun with her hand and tried to see what Mike was referring to. When she did, she laughed aloud. Three sleek gray sea lions were frolicking in the easy-rolling waves. Their actions resembled the same sort of playful diving and flopping about that Erin and Mike's three sons did when they were young and would tumble around in the waves at their favorite bay in Laguna.

"Which one should we name Joel?" Mike asked.

"The one who keeps flapping his side fin, of course. Grant is the mellow one who just bobs along in the midst of the other two. And Jordan there is showing off for the other two. Our three sons, right there."

The trio seemed to disappear as a large wave eased its way over them. A moment later they popped up and sounded off with a round of sea lion bellows that made Erin laugh. The joy of life as it is given to every living creature made her feel renewed. For days she had been calculating the measurements of life only in temperature, blood pressure, pulse, and units of saline solution hung from a drip bag. This front-row view of life without any visible limitations just made her happy. Very happy.

She and Mike stood for a long while with their arms around each other, drinking in the immense view, feeling the wild wind in their hair, and watching the carefree sea lions do what they were created to do. The agile creatures made it clear that they were in their zone, and for them, life was a breeze.

An older couple wandered near the edge where Mike and Erin stood. The man had a pair of binoculars and was intent on viewing the horizon.

"Did you see the sea lions?" Mike pointed out the triplets as if he were the proud explorer who had first made the discovery of this place of extreme beauty.

"Oh, Harold, look. He's right. Some sea lions are right there near the rocks."

"Hold your horses, Martha. I'm trying to see those whales."

The woman turned to Erin and Mike. "We were told this was the best place to see the migrating whales."

"Gray whales," the man added without removing the binoculars from in front of his eyes. "They come this way every year and head down to Mexico. All the way from Alaska. How's that for survival of the fittest?"

"Our son is an oceanographer." The woman turned to face Erin, as if she had to explain her husband's recitation of facts. "He goes out on ships and studies the whale pods."

"He's a big flake," the man said, still keeping his eyes pressed to the binoculars. "Good-for-nothing kid who finally managed to find a job. That is, if you call recording whale sounds a real job. He's an idiot."

The woman gave Erin an apologetic look. Erin knew the mother's look all too well. She had seen it for years on her mother's face every time her dad would slam Tony for some reason. Too timid to defend their sons in the presence of their husbands, both of these women carried the burden of loving their husbands and their sons, yet they could be true only to one. The husbands won.

Erin felt as if she had just been handed a revelation. She understood as never before the complicated dynamic that had been at work in her family under her nose. No wonder Tony struggled as he did for so long. He knew he was a disappointment to his father because Tony didn't push hard enough to develop his mediocre athletic abilities. And he never received the full loving support of his mother because Faith was the sort of woman who would always take her husband's side.

The revelation lit a fire in Erin's gut. She stepped around to the other side of the man with the binoculars, and before she had time to lose her courage, she said, "Sir, I hope you'll excuse the way this is going to sound, but do you know how many fathers would love to know their son grew up to be useful to society and not a drug addict? You are blessed more than you know, and you don't want to die an old fool who never took the opportunity to say to his son words that could change his life. Words such as 'I'm proud of you. I think you turned out great.' And most important, 'I love you.'"

The man lowered the binoculars and turned to her, looking angry and stunned.

That didn't stop her. "Let me tell you something. My father is lying in a bed right now, paralyzed on the right side of his body, being fed through a tube in his stomach, and drawing oxygen from a tube in his nose. It happened like that." She snapped her fingers for emphasis.

"My brother, my father's only son, has waited his entire life to hear those simple words from the one man in the world whose opinion of him matters. And you know what? Now that my father has been reduced to a drooling invalid, he's finally ready to say those things to my brother. Finally! But the stroke that took from my father the ability to move also took his ability to speak. He can't form a single word. It's too late."

Erin and the older man locked gazes for a full five seconds before she felt Mike's hand on her arm. She felt her legs shaking and knew the tears would come any minute so she turned and headed back to the car.

"It's been really rough on all of us," Mike said diplomatically before escorting Erin back to the car. The tone in his voice didn't sound as if he were apologizing for Erin's diatribe, nor was he diminishing any of her message.

They drove out of the parking lot without speaking and continued several miles down the winding seacoast highway before Erin felt her gut calming down. She drew in a deep breath, closed her eyes, and leaned her head back.

Mike reached over and covered her hand with his. "I'm proud of you," he said.

She let the affirming tone of his voice wash over her.

"I think you turned out great."

Now she knew he was going down the list she had given the man on the peninsula.

"And I love you."

"I know you do," she said without opening her eyes.

"And I'm going to call all three of our sons today and tell them the same thing."

Erin turned to her husband with a tender expression. "You've already told our boys those things many times."

"It won't hurt them one bit to hear all that again."

Erin gave Mike's hand a squeeze.

"What's keeping Tony from coming over here to see your dad? You said he called back and left you a message."

"He did call me, but that was almost a week ago. I think it might be the money that's holding him back."

"Let's call him right now. Tell him we'll cover his ticket. He needs to come."

Erin placed the call, and both she and Mike persuaded Tony to come. He responded by expressing his gratitude for their assistance and said he would come as soon as he could.

Erin prayed that her dad would hang in there. She didn't want Tony to arrive when it was too late for the two men to look each other in the eye and allow all the unspoken messages that needed to be said pass between them.

Jack appeared to be improving with the help of the medication, painkillers, and perhaps the comfort of being home and in his own bed with continual care. The oxygen was helpful, and the increased fluids Marge faithfully measured out five times a day and forced through his feeding tube also seemed to make a difference.

Erin missed Mike more than ever after he left. She missed the warmth of his body beside her in bed that night. She missed the steady calm he brought to her up-and-down emotions. She missed *him*.

For a long time the next day she sat beside her

dad, staring out the window at the huge white clouds that sailed across the sky and headed out to sea. Her mother used to call puffy cumulus clouds "wish clouds."

She said that when a little girl wishes, she wishes on a dandelion blown to the wind. When a young woman wishes, she wishes on a star. When a grown woman wishes, she wishes on a cloud.

Erin thought of all the wishes that had come true in her life: marrying Mike, three great sons, and a darling daughter-in-law. And now by being with her father for these difficult and yet God-filled weeks, Erin had received the wish she had never dared to wish for on a dandelion, a star, or a cloud. She had received her father's affection.

The next morning Erin noticed how the days had turned warm. The warmest they'd been since she had arrived. A true Northwest Indian summer invited the leaves to turn colors. The sky was filled with cumulus clouds. The sun poured in the front windows.

That evening Erin persuaded Marge to stay a couple of hours after her day shift ended. Together the ambitious two women transferred Jack to his wheelchair. He was of little assistance to them in his weakened state, but he was wide awake as they made the transfer. His left eyebrow remained busy trying to ask Erin what was going on.

"We're taking you out to dinner and a show," she told him.

He made gurgling sounds that were impossible to distinguish. They could have been happy sounds or sounds of protest. It didn't matter. Erin was determined to do this, and she had Marge's support.

Strapping Jack firmly in the wheelchair and making sure all the portable devices such as the oxygen were attached, the two of them opened the persimmon red door and wheeled Jack out into the warm September evening. As soon as they were on the deck, his face lit up.

"Oh, did you think we were trying to trick you into going back to the hospital?"

The desperate look in his glassy eyes told her that was what he had thought.

"Dad, I wouldn't do that to you. Trust me. I wouldn't try to trick you. I said dinner and a show, and I meant it. We're going to take you to the bench. Your bench. And we're going to have some yummy things to eat, and we're going to watch the sunset. So what do you think? Is it a date?"

He appeared to try to raise his left arm, but it wasn't cooperating. With a noble effort he merely lifted his thumb.

Erin laughed. "I see that thumb."

He closed his eyes as if just the effort of lifting his thumb had tuckered him out. Or he might be shutting down to reserve his batteries for what was to come.

"We could just watch the sunset from here on the deck," Marge suggested.

"Let's at least try to wheel him out there. We can always come back if it's not working."

The two women put their backs into maneuvering the wheelchair down the ramp and across the uneven grass. The wheelchair barely fit through the bramble path that was becoming overgrown. But they did it. They reached the bench and set the brake on the wheelchair. The cement slab Jack had poured to support his bench now served as the perfect curb to keep his wheelchair steadied against the updraft.

Erin trotted back to the cottage and carried out the tray she had prepared. For herself and Marge she had put together a plate with cheese, crackers, and slices of pear. For her dad she had several small dots of Jenny Bee's raspberry jam. In a small cup she had some especially dark coffee. With the tastes for her dad she had an assortment of swabs lined up like party skewers.

"Here we go! Dinner and a show!" Erin called out, as she came trotting back on the bramble trail.

Marge was fiddling with the oxygen tube in Jack's nose and finally just took it out. "Is that what you wanted? You want to breathe the sea air?"

He gave an odd quiver and seemed to try to take in a deep breath but was unable to robustly fill his lungs. The women watched him as he quivered and sniffed, quivered and sniffed. He seemed okay, breathing for a while without the oxygen's assistance.

"Well, look at you, Mr. Hotshot. We'll get some of that fresh salt air in you. That'll help clear those lungs." Erin held out the tray to him. She couldn't tell if he noticed. His glazed-over eyes were fixed on the horizon, staring at something far beyond them.

The sun was slipping behind a gathering of clouds.

"God is setting up his easel," Erin said. "He's going to paint a sunset for us tonight."

Marge smiled at Erin and kept her faithful eye on Jack. His cheek flitted slightly at Erin's comment.

"My mom used to say that when we were kids," Erin explained. "We used to go to the beach a lot in the evening and roast hot dogs for dinner, didn't we, Dad?"

His cheek flitted again. He still was breathing unassisted and didn't appear to be having any trouble doing so. His eyes were fixed unblinking on the horizon.

"How about a little coffee to get our dinner party started?"

"Did you want me to make some?" Marge asked.

"No, I meant for my dad. I have some coffee here for him to taste." She dipped the swab in the cup and held it to his lips.

"Do you want to try a taste of coffee, Dad?" She slipped the swab into his mouth, but his gag reflex moved his Adam's apple up, and spittle slid down the side of his face.

Marge wiped his chin and adjusted the back of the wheelchair to give his airway better passage. "I'm going to put the oxygen back in. You'll enjoy this better if you don't have to work so hard to breathe."

This time Jack didn't protest. He wasn't interested in tasting any of the treats. His throat made a variety of odd noises once the oxygen was reattached. They kept fiddling with his straps, the blanket over his legs, and the position of his lifeless arm. Erin hoped this was a good idea.

Jack kept his focus on the magnificent sunset while Erin and Marge kept their focus on Jack.

He began to cough before the sun had set entirely so they turned him around and maneuvered him back through the brambles, across the grass, and up the ramp onto the deck. Once there, the cough ceased. They turned the wheelchair toward the sky, and the three of them watched as God completed his evening painting and turned out the lights on another day.

In an effort to negate her "It's nice" comment about Hidden Cottage from so many months ago,

Erin leaned close and whispered in her daddy's ear, "I love it here, too, Dad. You built a fine home. This is a beautiful place." Then, putting on a contrived Irish accent, she pulled out a line she had heard him say over the years. "Ya' dun good, my man. Ya' dun good."

He made the smallest sort of sound, a sigh. A release. A smile sound that comes with a deep exhale at the end of a good day. Erin believed her father was content. And that gave her a deep peace.

That night Jack snored deeply as he slept. The bit of a field trip must have exhausted him because he didn't rouse easily the next morning when Marge arrived. Her daily routine with him had simplified in that she didn't attempt to get him in the shower anymore.

Erin had done everything she could at this point with all the boxes in the garage. Despite her searching she hadn't found the treasure trove of childhood photos she had hoped to locate. Since the photos weren't with her father's remaining things, she suspected they had been tossed out when he made the move to Oregon.

The thought of such a loss made her sick. She knew she should have taken them the last time she saw them, after her mom's death. A small and ungracious part of her wondered if Delores had come across the photos in her great organizational endeavor and deemed the pictures of no value. She wouldn't deliberately have thrown them away, would she? Erin hoped that wasn't what had happened.

In Erin's trimming down of items in the garage and in the house, she had made sure she had all the insurance papers completed and filed. She also made sure all his bills were paid and went over her father's will once again. Jack had bequeathed all his worldly goods to his wife. Delores had skipped out on him in the moment of his deepest need, but that didn't change that she still was married to him. She would get everything. Including Hidden Cottage.

Jack had written his will when he was "of sound mind," and those were his wishes. Everything was in order. Everything was in readiness. She didn't think it was her place to protest his decisions. It felt as if Erin's most important job was to wait. She was determined to do that reverently and patiently.

19

**May you always walk in sunshine.
May you never want for more.
May Irish angels rest their wings
Right beside your door.**

On the day Tony was scheduled to arrive from Hawaii, Moss Cove was shrouded by a fog so thick Erin couldn't see the ocean out the cottage's front window. She was up early, caring for her dad and starting the fire. She made herself a pot of tea and put on soft music. He was resting comfortably, as he had been ever since the ambitious jaunt in the wheelchair several evenings ago when they had caught the last golden hours of summer sunshine and he seemed to be losing his strength by the day.

One nice improvement was that he wasn't coughing as he had been. He seemed to have little difficulty breathing in and out. That in and of itself was a small mercy.

Erin did notice that her dad seemed to have developed a fixed expression of discomfort. The series of wrinkles in his forehead hadn't been there in the past for an extended length of time. He would pull his face into a frown when a procedure was being carried out that he didn't like or that was uncomfortable. But he hadn't ever looked as if he were in ongoing agony.

She mentioned it to Marge and watched as Marge drew close and spoke to him more loudly than usual. "Do you hurt anywhere, Jack?" Marge kept her face close to his. "Do you have any pain?"

He didn't reply with anything other than a fast exhale. If he were his former self, Erin knew what that sort of exhale would mean. In full strength it would have resembled the snort of a bull with his hoof stomping the ground. That's how her dad acted when he was agitated about something and was ready to charge the first red cape waved in front of him.

This time, though, after the huff of air released from his nonrattling lungs, a wavering tear rolled down his cheek. Erin drew closer to make sure that's what she was seeing. It seemed to her that her father was crying in silence, eyes closed, mouth slack, forehead creviced with lines.

"We're here for you, Dad." Erin slipped her hand into his. "You're not alone." She wondered if the matador now standing arrogantly in front of this old bull was the herald of death. Jack O'Riley was unable to charge forward to fight his foe. All he could do was lie still and wait for death to come to him.

Marge checked his vitals and motioned for Erin to move into the kitchen with her. Lowering her voice, Marge said, "I think it's time for us to call in hospice care."

"Okay. Tell me how that works."

"The agency I work for will provide someone who can be with your father for his final stretch. Hospice nurses are trained to work through the specifics of the last few days or weeks."

"Aren't you able to stay with us?"

"I can stay on as long as you want me to. I just need to inform you that my report for this week will indicate that he's crossed a threshold and that hospice care can be made available if you request it."

"I'd like you to stay, Marge, if you can. If you will."

She nodded in her calm, matter-of-fact way. "Of course. I'd like to stay. I'm trained for hospice care, but you hired me for only day care so I needed to give you the option to change caregivers."

"No, I'd like you. Only you." Erin spontaneously gave Marge a hug and was made aware once again of the strength of this unwavering woman.

Marge stepped farther into the kitchen and spoke to Erin softly. "I think I need to tell you something. There is a possibility that he isn't in pain physically, but he could be bothered emotionally. I've seen this before. Sometimes when a patient realizes he is near to the end and isn't going to improve, he gives space to his regrets."

"I wonder if he's thinking about my brother. The two of them aren't at peace with each other."

"That very well could be it. That's what could be causing the worry lines. He's not at peace. He's not ready to go until he makes peace."

"I didn't tell him that Tony was coming because my brother wanted me to hold off on saying anything. Do you think I should tell my dad?"

"You know the dynamics between the two of them. I can't say what would be best. When does your brother arrive?"

"His flight should have landed in Portland around seven thirty this morning. He was going to rent a car and drive here. I'm guessing he'll be here close to noon."

Marge looked at her watch. "Why don't you check, and when he's about an hour away, let your dad know he's coming."

"Okay." Erin felt a nervous jitter run through her. It seemed she was moving from familiar routine to a vigil. Even the tone in Marge's voice had changed.

She called Mike and gave him the details of her conversation with Marge. He immediately said he would come back up to be with Erin. "Let me cover a few bases here at work today. I'll see if I can catch a flight up in the morning."

Erin knew he had used up all his vacation time and tried to dissuade him from coming right away. "Actually, I think he's okay. My dad will have all the support he needs."

"I'm coming for you, Erin. I want to be there for you while you go through this last stretch."

Her heart felt suddenly young and vulnerable. They talked it through some more, and in the end Mike decided he would wait until Erin called him and said she needed him. Once she made that call, he would come.

Erin went about the rest of the morning as if she were on her usual routine. Fridays were when she changed the linens on the master bed and cleaned the bathroom. She kept up those usual tasks as Marge read a magazine. It felt so strange. When Jack had been struggling he needed constant care. Now that he had ceased fighting for his breath, the air passed in and out of his throat and lungs with an unnerving sort of calm. He appeared to be in a deep, long nap. No noises seemed to affect him.

At one point in her morning round of tasks, Erin went to his side and watched him closely to see if he was breathing. He was. But the rise and fall of his chest was nothing like the great pitches and heaves she had watched over the past month. His eyes were closed as they had been since the sunset viewing. His jaw was slack, his skin was pale, and in his diminished state his cheekbones were unusually pronounced.

Erin smoothed back his white hair. His once snowy mane had thinned and taken on a tint the shade of soft butter.

Marge went to the bathroom. As she stepped away, the song that came on the CD playing softly in the living room was a Mozart piece Erin knew well. Her mother played this piece whenever she was particularly happy. Many glad memories came to Erin of birthday mornings when she woke to hear this piece being played by her mother on the piano in the small living room of her childhood home. To Faith it had been a call to celebration. A prelude to a party.

The poignancy of the music coming on at this particular moment prompted Erin to do something spontaneous. She had been so quick to lecture the stranger at the peninsula about how he should speak words of affirmation to his son. Why couldn't a daughter speak the same words to her father? Especially in such a moment as this.

Slipping her hand into her father's cool left hand, Erin leaned close. "Daddy, I am so proud of you. I think you turned out great."

Her voice quavered, but she kept going. "And I love you very, very much."

His eyes didn't open or move. The deeply embedded fretting lines remained in his forehead. But to Erin's surprise, she felt her father's hand move. The movement was undeniable. He was giving her two firm squeezes: *Love you.*

Erin broke into a grin and bit her lower lip. She had waited so long to feel those two squeezes. Her response was immediate. She gave him three firm but gentle squeezes, and with the squeezes she whispered her echo: "Love you, too."

Just then Erin heard footsteps coming into the living room. Erin tucked her dad in, adjusting his pillows and feeling immensely grateful that she had been given this unexpected moment with her father. She was especially grateful that it had been just the two of them. Marge could return now to her watch, and Erin could go about putting the sheets back on the master bed. When Tony arrived he could have their father all to himself. Erin had said her good-bye.

The footsteps stopped before entering the living room area. Erin turned with a peaceful smile, prepared to let Marge know that all was well.

But it wasn't Marge who stood five feet away from Erin. It was Delores.

Erin had no words. She couldn't move.

The bathroom door opened, and Marge stepped out, coming toward the living room and then stopping. The women formed a triangle, and all three of them were speechless.

Delores looked very different than she had six weeks ago. She wore a paisley pink head scarf tightly wound around her head and knotted in the back. It wasn't a flattering look for her bold face, if that's what she was going for. Although her outfit overall was an improvement over the stocking caps and fleece sweatshirts she had worn every day when she lived at Hidden Cottage.

"How is he?" Delores's voice was soft. The softest Erin had ever heard float from Delores's ample lungs. The usual fierce expression seemed to be rubbed to more rounded corners.

Erin slowly shook her head as a way of indicating her father's condition wasn't good. The gesture also meant *No, you can't do this. You can't just walk in here like this. Not now. No, I don't want you here.*

Delores broke the triangle of tension and walked over to Jack. She looked at him for a long moment and began to cry.

Marge moved closer to Erin and touched her arm. With a tilt of her head, she motioned for Erin to follow her outside. Stunned at the scene unfolding before her, Erin followed Marge. They went outside into the thick fog and sat together on the moisture-dotted bench on the front deck.

"I can't believe she's here." Erin folded her arms across her aching stomach. The damp coldness seemed to permeate her bones.

"She's come just in time, it seems." Marge sighed. "It's their chance to say good-bye."

Erin gave Marge a long look, trying to interpret the passionate expression that softened her face and brought tears to her eyes. Could it be that Marge had read one too many paperback novels and was turning this into a romantic final farewell between Jack and Delores? Erin didn't understand.

"I'm sorry, but I have no compassion for Delores. How dare she do this to him?"

Marge placed her hand on Erin's shoulder. "Erin, you need to look at her closely."

"Why?"

"You'll see. Just look at her, really look at her, when we go back inside. You'll understand."

Erin assumed Marge had gone soft on Delores because she had cried when she saw her husband in his emaciated state. Well, she should cry. She should be very sorry for what she did by walking out on him when he needed her most. She should have lots of regrets. Erin didn't feel ready to brush it all away because Delores found it in her heart to show up and shed some tears. She hated that her heart had turned to stone like this, but at the moment she couldn't find a shred of kindness to use to tie her affection to Delores.

With a shiver, Erin stood. "I'm going inside to get my jacket."

Marge nodded and stayed on the deck bench as Erin marched back into the house.

When Erin entered the living room, she saw that Delores had seated herself on the end of Jack's bed and was stroking his arm and speaking to him in low, tearful tones.

The sight of this woman stepping back into her

intimate role with Jack at this eleventh hour messed with Erin's mind and emotions more than anything else had during this laborious journey. One of them had to go. Erin decided it would be her.

Grabbing her jacket and purse, Erin left without saying a word to Delores. "I have my phone," she said as she strode past Marge. "Call me when my brother arrives."

Erin moved through the thick fog to her car parked by the garage. She was only six feet away from her car when she realized a car was parked behind hers.

Great! Now I have to go inside and ask Delores to move her car so I can get out of here.

At that moment the door opened on the driver's side of the parked car, startling Erin. A man with a full dark beard got out and stood in the fog.

"Do you need me to move my car?" he asked.

"Yes." She didn't ask who he was or why he was there. She barely looked at him. The connection seemed obvious to her. Delores hadn't wasted time finding someone else to be with. The new love interest understood her need to say good-bye and had been sweet enough to drive her here.

The scenario turned Erin's already churning stomach.

The man took his time inching his car back up to the top of the gravel driveway as Erin waited in the BMW with her foot ready to step on the gas pedal. When he honked to indicate that the trail was clear, Erin backed all the way up the gravel driveway in the fog as if she were more familiar with the stretch than she really was.

With a crank of the steering wheel, she ignored the man in the car where he was pulled over to the side of the road, and she headed south. Erin had no idea where to go. It was far too foggy and cold to walk on her favorite stretch of beach at the state park. She didn't want to go to the bookstore that had been a hideout more than once. Jenny Bee's was out of the question. Too many people there now knew her by name, and if any of them were working, they would ask how her father was doing.

For that same reason she knew she couldn't stop by the Shamrock to visit with ever-obliging Sylvia. As much as she enjoyed the small friendship she had developed with kind and faithful Sylvia, she didn't want to spew all her feelings to Sylvia right now.

The only thing she could think to do was to drive inland. She had learned during her time on the coast that even when the fog was thick along the shoreline, after a short drive inland, the fog dissipated, and the temperature warmed as much as ten degrees. Erin liked the thought of finding a spot that was ten degrees warmer, a place where she could buy some coffee, or better yet, a cup of tea with milk and sugar. Then she could sit, think, and listen until she had calmed down enough to return to the cottage.

She was about five miles into the wooded stretch that had been her favorite part of the drive inland from Moss Cove when she called Mike. He didn't pick up the call, and she chose not to leave a message. Then she called Tony. She realized it wouldn't be so great for her brother to show up at the cottage to find Delores there but not Erin.

Tony answered and told her where he was on his drive to Moss Cove. Erin realized they were on the same coastal access road. They might even pass each other.

"Where are you now? Do you see any markers?"

"I just drove past a sign for a turnoff to a town called Glenbrooke."

"Oh, good. I know where that is. We're not too far from each other. Tony, could you turn around, go back to Glenbrooke, and wait for me there? I can be there in about fifteen minutes."

"Okay. Is anything wrong?"

"Sort of. I'll tell you when I get there. Maybe you can find a place where we can have a cup of coffee and talk for a bit."

"Will do. It's beautiful here, by the way."

"It is, isn't it? Is it foggy where you are?"

"No."

"Good. I'm almost out of the fog now. It's really thick at the coast."

"Well, drive carefully."

"I will."

Erin hung up and knew they shouldn't linger in Glenbrooke too long, just the two of them, catching up on all they had missed out on in each other's lives over the past decade and a half. They needed to get back to Moss Cove. They needed to enter Hidden Cottage together and face whatever they found there.

She hoped that once her brother saw their dad all of the old hurts would vanish as they had slowly been melting away for Erin during her time with their father. She had "made peace" with her father, as Marge had called it. All her childhood wounds were faint memories that had evaporated the way the heavy fog had dissipated as she drove inland. The sunlight now slipped its lacy fingers through the towering trees and left faint stripes of amber light across the winding road. She felt those same stripes of golden healing in her heart. All was well between her and her father.

An uncomfortable thought came to Erin in the midst of all the morning beauty. She needed to find a way to make peace with Delores as well. Her father loved Delores. She knew that. He had told her in his own limited way. He shook his finger at her, and she had told him she wouldn't judge Delores. And yet she had. Again and again. With each judgment, a stronger sense of entitlement to her anger and condemnation grew. Each time she added to the list of Delores's failings, the embers of anger in her gut flamed into a fire.

Erin knew that fire could destroy all the good that had been built between her and her father during the past weeks. She also knew that such a flame could burn like a wildfire and sear a continuous path through the rest of her life if it wasn't put out. She had seen what the wildfire of emotional devastation had done between her father and her brother.

With a humbled heart, Erin quieted her spirit. She knew she needed to find a way to release Delores from the prison in her thoughts where she had shackled her. She knew this was what her father wanted. It was also what her Heavenly Father wanted.

Drawing in a deep breath, Erin honored her father one more time. She forgave Delores. With the choice to forgive came another choice to mentally and emotionally destroy the list she had been keeping of all of Delores's wrongs. Erin knew this was the only way to be free.

The whispered words came first. Then the feelings.

20

When the first light of sun—bless you.
When the long day is done—bless you.
In your smiles and your tears—bless you.
Through each day of your years—bless you.

Erin wiped away the tears that flowed silently as she drove into Glenbrooke. Releasing her anger toward Delores had made her feel vulnerable and tenderhearted.

Her brother called just then and said he was in Glenbrooke, too. "I found a place for us to meet. It's called the Wildflower Café. It looks pretty good."

"Sounds perfect. Could you go on in and get us a table?"

"Sure. See you in a bit."

Erin found the Wildflower Café easily and parked across the street. She thought it was the most charming place she had seen since leaving Southern California. The booth where Tony was waiting for her by the window seemed to be a special spot set apart for people who liked private conversation.

He stood when he saw her and came to her, brushing a kiss across her cheek and giving her a warm hug. "Aloha."

"Hi." Erin smiled a weary smile. She could feel the tears still glistening in the corners of her eyes. "It's so good to see you."

Tony looked the best he had in many years. His hair was still long, but he had it pulled back in a ponytail and fastened with a leather strap. He looked more like their mother than Erin did with his dark eyes and broad forehead. She was the one who had inherited all the Irish touches from her dad with her russet-colored hair and his blue eyes.

A young blond woman stepped up to their booth. "Morning. Would you like some coffee?"

"I'll have orange juice," Tony said.

"Do you have hot tea?" Erin asked.

The woman nodded. "We have several different kinds. How about if I bring the basket, and you can choose what you would like?"

"And do you have any pastry you would recommend?" Tony asked.

"Yes, as a matter of fact. We have fresh marionberry coffee cake. It's Genevieve's recipe and really good. I can highly recommend it because I just had some for breakfast."

"How about if we split one?" Tony asked Erin. "Unless you would like something else. Or your own piece."

"No, that's fine." Being with her brother again felt strange and yet familiar. She watched him take the lead in decision-making. She knew he had it in him to be a strong leader like their father. It was so good to be with him.

"So tell me what's going on with Dad. Why didn't you want me to see him yet?"

Erin explained the morning's events and was interrupted by the waitress when she placed a yellow ceramic teapot on the table and presented Erin with a basket full of an assortment of tea bags. Erin reached for the Irish breakfast tea and the waitress asked, "Would you like milk and sugar or honey for your tea?"

"Milk and sugar, please."

The waitress returned a moment later with the milk and sugar as well as a huge piece of warm marionberry coffee cake and two forks.

"Good thing we're splitting this." Tony punctured the corner closest to him and asked, "So do you think Delores is still at the house?"

"I don't know. A man was waiting for her in a car; so I don't know how long she planned to stay."

They ate a few more bites, and then Erin confided in her brother how she had worked through forgiving Delores on her way to meet Tony and how intense and yet rich her time had been with their father.

Tony reached across the table and rubbed the top of her hand. "Thank you."

"For what?"

"For being there with him through all this, for sending the money for the ticket, and for convincing me to come. I should have come sooner." Tony's face changed so that his forehead looked just like their father's did, heavy with anguish lines.

In an effort to comfort her brother, Erin said, "What matters is that you're here now. You can move on from here."

He nodded and put down his fork.

Erin took another two bites of the delicious coffee cake and sipped her tea. She realized that if Delores hadn't left her father, things would be very different right now. Erin had lost her business and had run on empty for weeks, but more than ever she knew her decision to stay was right. Her father had been able to remain at Hidden Cottage to the end. That was his wish fulfilled. And now Tony was here. This was what her mother had hoped and prayed for until the day she died. Erin believed she would soon see the answer to all those prayers for reconciliation.

I will give you the treasures of darkness, riches in secret places, so that you may know that I am the LORD, the God of Israel, who calls you by name.

Erin felt like she was seeing the words of Isaiah 45:3 coming true in front of her. She had experienced treasures of darkness and riches in secret places. Soon the Lord would be calling her dad by name. The line between the eternal and the temporal seemed very thin at this moment in the Wildflower Café.

Tony finished his orange juice but didn't go for any more of the coffee cake. He seemed to have wandered into a deep fog.

"Are you ready to go?" Erin asked.

Tony looked up. "Yes, I would like to get to Dad's place. I've come all this way, I'd hate to be sitting here, this close, and have him turn a corner."

"I'm ready." She dipped her fork into the coffee cake one more time and took a long sip of her cooled tea.

Tony insisted on paying and slipped a generous tip on the table. The two of them left, going to their separate cars. Erin led the way to Moss Cove along the two-lane road that wound through the forest. Some of the deciduous trees were just beginning to take on touches of autumn color. Erin thought about how beautiful this stretch of road would be a month from now on a sunny afternoon when all the fall leaves had changed.

But I won't be here to see it. I'll be back in Irvine by then.

That realization saddened her. Not only because it meant her father would be gone but also because she had come to love the charm of this place. Moss Cove had won her over. How restful it would be to come here one day with their family. Erin could see Sierra and herself slipping off for afternoon tea at the Wildflower Café while the guys tried their hand at fishing. In the evening they would string twinkle lights on the deck and turn up the music as the sun slipped into the sea.

She finally appreciated her father's vision for Hidden Cottage. It was a beautiful vision. But Erin knew she had to stop the dream right there. Delores was the one who would inherit Hidden Cottage. Erin would not have a reason to come back here after her father was gone.

That sharp truth, like a lit match, begged to ignite any mound of kindling Erin could gather. She knew how easily she could tip that flickering match and let it restart a wildfire of anger and resentment against Delores.

Gripping the steering wheel, Erin prayed for strength. That's when she heard her mother's words for the second time since she had started on this journey with her father.

To experience the fullness of love, you must go the distance. Only the strongest and bravest stay on the path. And you, my darling girl, have been given everything you need to be among the strongest and bravest.

Forming a small *O* with her lips, Erin blew into the space between herself and the windshield as if she were physically snuffing out the tempting flame on the freshly lit match.

How could what she had experienced on the way to Glenbrooke be true forgiveness if she let it burn a hole in her spirit when the first opportunity presented itself? Forgiveness was a process. She knew that. Being with her father all these weeks had been a process. Starting over after losing her portion of the business was also going to be a process. But she knew that if she wanted to experience the fullness of love, she had to go the distance with all these difficult relationships. She could do this. God was supplying her with everything she needed—strength, courage, grace, and lots of hope.

The fog had lifted when they arrived at the coast highway. Erin put on her blinker to indicate Tony should follow her, turning right and heading north. To make sure he saw it, she rolled down her window and waved her arm, indicating that he should turn right.

He waved back.

She waited at the stoplight and read the banner that hung between two lampposts across the narrow street.

RACE FOR THE CURE
PORTLAND, OREGON
OCTOBER 9

The light changed, and Erin had driven another few miles when she recalled Delores's face. Not the way she had seen Delores's stern face peering in her side car window during Erin's first visit to Moss Cove. The image in her mind's eye was of Delores's face the way she had appeared that morning, swathed in the pink paisley head scarf. Delores was thin. Her skin was sallow. She wasn't the same robust woman in the Hidden Cottage scrapbook photos wielding a sledge-hammer and taking down the old kitchen wall.

The scarf, her coloring . . .

Erin gasped.

Delores is ill. She has cancer. Delores has cancer.

She thought of how Marge had told Erin to really look at Delores. Marge saw the signs right away. Erin's heart pounded. She had missed it. All the indicators were there.

How long? How long has Delores been fighting this?

Pressing on her brakes and flipping on her blinker, Erin pulled into the nearest parking area and sat in her car with the engine idling.

Tony parked and came over to the passenger's window. He looked in at her the same way Delores had at the grocery store a year and a half ago when she had told Erin that if Jack became an invalid, she couldn't stay with him. She would leave him.

Erin pushed the button to roll down the window.

"You okay?" Tony asked.

"No."

"What is it? What's wrong? Is it Dad?"

"No, it's Delores." Turning to Tony she said, "She has cancer."

Tony opened the passenger's door, slid inside, and sat next to Erin. "Turn off the motor," he said.

She obliged.

"What makes you think Delores has cancer?"

"The way she looked when she walked in this morning. Have you been around many people who are going through chemotherapy?"

"No."

"There's a look. I should have known when I saw the head scarf. And before, when I arrived in August, her hair wasn't right. She was tired all the time. I should have picked up some of the signs."

"Why didn't she tell you?"

"She's an intensely private person. She's aggressive and abrupt. But, Tony, Dad loved her. He really did. I know this must sound strange, but I could read it in his eyes."

"I believe you," Tony said calmly.

"It makes sense now. Don't you see? She couldn't take care of Dad. She needed someone to take care of her."

Erin let out a long, slow breath and looked out the car's front window. "I should have seen it. I should have picked up the clues."

"From what you've said about her, it doesn't sound as if she left many clues."

"She told me something significant right before she left him, only I didn't know what she meant at the time."

"What did she say?"

"She said she married Dad because he was strong and full of life, but now he couldn't do for her what he had promised."

"And you're thinking that he promised to take care of her."

Erin nodded.

"That would explain a lot."

Erin nodded again. "We should go. I just had to pull over for a second when all of that hit me. We're not far away. Hidden Cottage is just down the road."

Tony returned to his car, and Erin led the way. She turned down the long, gravel driveway and was disappointed to see that Marge's car was the only one there. Delores was gone.

Tony edged out of his rental car and stood for a moment, giving the place a full view. "Is this the place Dad fixed up?"

"Yes, this is Hidden Cottage."

"It's amazing."

"Yes, it is. Remind me to show you the before and after photos." Erin paused at the persimmon red door and looked at Tony. "You ready?"

He nodded. His eyes were misted with tears. He

looked every inch the prodigal son at last returning home.

Only it was too late for his father to come running to meet him.

21

**May you live to be a hundred years
With one extra year to repent.**

Opening the door slowly, Erin entered first. Marge looked up from the couch. All was calm. All was airy and light. Soft music floated through the confined space.

"Do you want to be alone with him?" Erin asked Tony. "Marge and I can go outside. Or I'll stay if you want me to."

"Stay," Tony said.

Marge gave Tony a respectful nod and slid out to the front deck.

Shoulder to shoulder, Tony and Erin approached the man who was now a shadow of their father. Erin tried to think of how his state would appear to Tony since he hadn't seen any of the progression.

Tony's lips were pressed together. A hint of horror was in his eyes.

Erin placed her hand on their father's shoulder and leaned close. "Dad, Tony is here. He came from Maui to be with you."

A weak, nearly imperceptible sound echoed in what remained of the great cavity of Jack O'Riley's barrel chest.

"Hi, Dad." Tony reached forward but didn't seem to know if he should touch his dad.

Erin whispered, "It's okay. Here."

She reached for their father's good arm and gently laid it bent across his narrow middle, making it easy for Tony to put his hand in his father's hand.

Tony reached for it as if he were now the one extending the "right hand of fellowship" in a manly handshake. As soon as he grasped his father's hand, though, the energy dissipated. Tony repositioned himself, moving to the other side of the bed to be on the side that wasn't paralyzed. He tenderly stroked his father's weakened hand the way an awestruck parent gentles the hand of a sleeping newborn.

"Dad . . ." Tony cleared his throat. He leaned closer and tried again. "Dad, I want you to know that I'm sorry. In so many ways. I'm really sorry."

Thin, opaque tears slowly edged from the corner of their father's closed eyes and slid over his hollowed cheeks.

Tony looked at Erin with a stunned expression. "Did he hear me? Do you think he heard me?"

"Yes, I'm sure of it. His tears are all he has left with which to communicate." Erin swallowed back her own tears.

Tony let go of his father's hand and crumbled to his knees. He lowered his head, pressing his forehead against the side of the hospital bed. With trembling emotion in his voice, Tony spoke the purifying words. "Please forgive me, Dad. I really messed up."

As Erin watched, her father seemed to draw on every last inch of energy he had. He dragged his hand to the side of the bed and placed his frail fingers on Tony's head, as if in preparation to extend a blessing.

Erin covered her mouth with her hand and blinked back the tears. She was witnessing the answer to her mother's prayers after all those years.

A breathy sound floated from their father's parted lips. It seemed to take all the strength left in him to make the weak reverberation.

It was enough.

Tony's apology had been received and accepted. Erin knew it.

And by the expression on Tony's face, he knew it, too. He rose to his feet and took his father's hand in his. Tony's face was wet with tears, as was their father's.

Erin's heart raced. Like her mother, she had hoped and prayed for this moment but never imagined the sense of beauty that filled the room.

Reaching for a couple of washcloths, she handed one to Tony and used the other to dry her father's tears. His eyes had been closed the whole time, and she imagined he was too weak to open them. What surprised her was that the deep worry lines still were etched into his forehead. She would have thought that after this holy moment he would be at peace.

Erin adjusted his support pillows and did what she had done a number of times during this journey. She tried to imagine what her father was thinking and feeling right now. What did he need that he was unable to express?

She noticed that his lower lip was trembling.

"Dad, is there something you want to say?"

He drew in a long, threadlike breath, but no sound came out. The worry lines deepened.

"Dad, it's okay. Tony knows that you've forgiven him."

Thin tears flowed again. Her father's chin dipped. The veins in his neck quivered.

"What is it, Dad?" Erin felt at a loss. He seemed to be using the few small muscles he had left to communicate, but she couldn't decipher any of the signals.

Then a clear thought came to her. What if her dad wanted to apologize to Tony? What if he wanted to ask Tony to forgive him for the break in their relationship? Erin couldn't imagine how painful it would be to have something like that in your heart and not to be able to speak it when you knew the end was so close and the person you wanted to communicate with was only inches away.

Erin leaned in. She rested her hand on her father's shoulder. "Daddy, do you want to ask Tony to forgive you, too?"

A faint sound like a distant birdcall rose from his throat, and a flood of tears poured over his cheeks.

"Oh, Dad." Tony leaned in and spoke firmly. "You don't even have to ask. It's okay. I forgive you."

Then Tony bent down and held his father's face the way a coach would congratulate an athlete who had run a stellar race and collapsed after crossing the finish line. "You're free, Dad. I hold nothing against you. I know that you hold nothing against me. Be at peace."

Erin stepped back and watched an astounding transformation take place in front of her. It was as if a wave had washed over the shore of her father's face. As it receded, the invisible wave took with it all the anxious, agitated worry lines, carrying them out to the deepest sea and burying them forever.

Tony leaned closer. He pressed a holy kiss on his father's smooth forehead and then drew himself upright. He wiped the last of his tears with the palm of his hand and stood quietly beside the bed as he and Erin held each other's gaze.

The shared moment came to a jarring halt when

Tony's cell phone rang. Erin looked at their father. He had returned to his place of deep sleep. No more worry lines dug into his forehead. His slight and steady breaths eased in and out. The cell phone chime didn't bother him. Nothing seemed to be bothering him.

Tony stepped into the kitchen to take the call. It lasted only a few minutes, and when he returned he took a seat beside his father's bed, waiting, watching, being fully present for the first time in two decades.

Erin went outside where Marge waited on the deck. She looked up from her book. Erin sat beside her and took the corner of the blanket Marge had across her lap and tucked herself under the warmth beside Marge.

"Is everything okay?" Marge asked.

"Yes." Erin didn't have the emotional reserve to try to articulate the moment she and her brother had just experienced.

"And what about you?" Marge asked. "Are you all right?"

Erin crossed her legs. She leaned in a little closer to Marge. "I wish I hadn't left when Delores arrived."

"It was understandable, Erin. You've had a lot to handle for a long time. Delores asked me to tell you a few things. Would you like to hear them now, or do you want to wait?"

"She has cancer, doesn't she?"

Marge nodded. "Ovarian. Stage four."

Erin let out a low breath. "How long?" She meant *How long does Delores still have?* but Marge answered the question differently.

"She told me she had breast cancer five years ago, but it was in remission when she married your father. The ovarian cancer was diagnosed this spring right before they were supposed to go to Ireland. She made several trips to a treatment center in Mexico earlier in the summer. She's in Portland now with her nephew. He's the one who has helped her keep up with the chemo and radiation."

"He's the one who brought her here today, isn't he?" Erin cringed once again at the assumptions she had made about Delores. Wasn't that what Delores had told Clint at the post office when he shipped her boxes to Mexico? That he shouldn't assume things about people.

"I imagine so. I didn't see him. Delores said she didn't want you to know any of this earlier, but since you weren't here when she was ready to leave, she asked me to tell you."

"Did she leave any contact information?"

"No. She seemed to treat this visit with finality. I told her your brother was coming. I hope that's okay with you."

"Of course."

"I thought she might want to meet him, but she was set on leaving when she did."

"How did she even know my dad was here? When she left, we were planning to move him to Irvine."

"I asked her the same thing. She said Sylvia gave her updates whenever she needed them."

Erin nodded. *Of course. Six O'clock News Sylvia.*

"That's why she knew she needed to come right away. I could tell it took a lot out of her. She had a hard time walking to the car when she left."

Erin was beginning to understand more clearly the bond that had formed between her father and Delores. They needed each other. Delores was a strong, unemotional woman who wanted a fresh start, and so did her dad after Faith's death. Moss Cove had provided that. For both of them the move was a chance to dream a new dream.

Erin looked at the properly hung, expertly painted shutters on either side of the kitchen window and thought of how hard both her dad and Delores had worked to rebuild this cottage. With each paintbrush stroke and hammer thump did they feel they were working together to rebuild their own lives? Or maybe they were trying to work together to leave something behind. Delores inherited the cottage. Who would she pass it on to? Her nephew? Maybe this wonderful place would still be a destination for traditional family vacations as her dad dreamed it would. Maybe one day a few young children—

perhaps the children of Delores's nephew—would explore the tide pools and dance with their mother on the deck.

Either way, Hidden Cottage stood strong while neither Jack nor Delores was able to do the same. The bitterness of death's slow sting turned in Erin's stomach like a knife.

"I'm going to try to call her," Erin said quietly. She stood and was three steps away from the door when it opened and Tony stepped outside, his face flushed.

"Everything okay?"

"I just needed some air."

"I'll sit with him," Marge said.

Tony walked over to where Erin and Marge had been and took in the spectacular view. "This is quite a place."

"Yes, it is." Erin smiled when she remembered her dad sitting in his wheelchair in the same spot where Tony now stood surveying the surroundings. "We had a cookout here on the deck when Mike and I first arrived. Jordan and Sierra came on the way home from their honeymoon. Dad was in his wheelchair, right there, where you're standing. All the locals came. They steamed whole crabs for us."

Tony pointed to the embroidered name on her fleece jacket. "Would that happen to be Paddy who steamed the crabs?"

"Yes, from Paddy's Crab Shack. He was here

along with all of Dad's cronies. You would have loved it. This deck turned into a dance floor. We had twinkle lights and music." Erin grinned. "Dad was happy that night. It was right after Delores left. I can't imagine all the feelings he has been going through these past few months."

Erin relayed to Tony all the information Marge had just given her about Delores. She told Tony that she was thinking she would call Delores. "I really wish I hadn't run out this morning."

"Well, I wish I hadn't run out so many years ago."

Erin gave her brother a sympathetic nod. "All we can do is take it from here and run a good race to the finish."

"Sounds like what we grew up hearing Dad say."

"True, but now we're finally at the place to take it to heart, I guess."

Tony drew in the sea air, his chin lifted toward the sky the same way their dad drew in the air. "This feels so much like Kipahulu," he said.

"And what is Kipp—a—whatever you said?"

"It's the place where I was camping last month on the backside of Maui. It's pristine like this with rugged coastline and black volcanic rock. Only on Maui it's about thirty degrees warmer."

"That would be nice. Believe me, I've sat out on this deck many times when I wished it were thirty degrees warmer." Erin plunged her hands into the pockets of her green fleece and discovered she had put her phone in her pocket. Pulling it out, she checked her directory, clicking through the list until she found what she was looking for.

She held up her cell phone. "I'm going to call Delores."

"I'll have a look around while you make your call."

"If you take that trail through the brambles, you'll come out at a bench Dad installed at the cliff's edge. The path through the woods takes you down to some tide pools."

"Thanks. I won't be gone long."

Before dialing Delores's phone number saved in her cell, Erin rolled back her shoulders and drew in a deep breath. As she exhaled, she closed her eyes and formed a prayer, once again releasing the anger she had felt toward Delores since the beginning. She pressed the Send button, feeling her heart pound. Delores's voice mail answered.

Erin chose her words carefully. "Delores, this is Erin. If you would like to call me back, that would be great. If you don't want to call me back, I understand that as well. I want there to be peace between us. I'm sorry I didn't understand the whole picture of what was going on with you. I know it was your choice to keep your condition private. I want to honor that even though, to be honest, I don't understand it."

She took a quick breath and knew she needed to talk fast if she was going to get everything out in one message. "The point is, I know that my father loved you. That should be a good enough reason for me to love you, too, but I don't think I did a very good job of that. I wish I'd opened my arms and my heart to you. Marge gave me the information you left with her. I'm so sorry you're going through all this. I'd like to keep in touch, if you would. Mostly I just wanted to say that I'm sorry."

When Erin hung up, she had a strong sense that she never would hear from Delores. Yet she felt free. She felt as if she had cleared her own angry thoughts toward Delores and was at peace. Tony and Jack weren't the only O'Rileys who experienced the mending of a torn relationship that day.

The emotional peaks and valleys had worn her out. Erin went inside and sat beside her father. The marathon wasn't over but it felt as if a new pace had been set for this race. Best of all, Erin now had Tony with her. Together they would go the final distance.

Later that afternoon Sylvia came by to visit. She brought four other townies with her, including Jo from Jenny Bee's Fish House. Jo hadn't seen her favorite breakfast customer for some time, and when she noted how weak and unresponsive he was, she cried.

Erin wondered how much all of this was getting through to her dad. Was he aware of what was going on, or had he used up his last bit of strength in communicating with Tony earlier that afternoon?

After everyone left, Tony brought in his bag and settled into the upstairs bedroom. Erin held her father's limp hand and hummed softly. More than once she thought her father had slipped away quietly because his chest looked so still. Each time she would lean closer and could tell that he still was breathing in and out like the ocean tide.

Tony volunteered to make dinner after Marge left. Erin didn't protest one bit. As she sat beside her dad, she kept up a one-sided conversation, recounting memories of childhood, remembering holidays and other happy moments when they were all together.

At one point she felt so engaged with him that she expected to see her father open his eyes and give her the wink of the Irish. But he didn't move. He didn't blink. He didn't squeeze her hand back. He just breathed.

Tony set the tiny kitchen table and placed two bowls of steaming chicken soup in front of each place along with toasted garlic bread and a small plate with apple and cheese wedges. When they sat down together, Tony reached across the table and offered his hand to Erin as had been the habit around the table when they were growing up.

They held hands, and Tony prayed. This was a moment Erin hadn't expected to experience again in her life, and yet there they were, as natural as could be, just the two of them, holding hands and praying, thanking God for his generous provisions to them.

Erin took a sip of the soup from her large spoon, and her taste buds woke up. "Wow! What did you find to put in this? All I had left in there was some rotisserie chicken and a bag of minicarrots."

"I made use of a few things I found in the cupboard. Do you like it?"

"Yes, it's delicious." She took several more sips, savoring the wild rice and slight taste of basil. "I would go so far as to say that aside from the omelets at Jenny Bee's, this is the best food I've eaten since I arrived."

"You really didn't inherit Mom's cleverness for cooking, did you?"

"No, not at all. I'm glad you did."

Tony seemed to appreciate that praise from his big sister. She wondered if he was beginning to experience the same sort of liberation she had felt when she realized that her father's 100 percent approval didn't matter the way it used to. It was more important that she knew within her own spirit that she was becoming the person God had created her to be. Tony seemed to be more his true self than she ever had seen him in the past.

She hoped her father had picked that up as well. She hoped part of his being at peace now was in knowing that both his children were doing well.

Erin offered to clean up after dinner so Tony could sit with their dad. He brought a pillow down from the bedroom and said he wanted to keep vigil that night by sleeping on the couch. His offer was a sweet relief for Erin after so many nights of interrupted sleep. She felt exhausted mentally, physically, and emotionally.

When she entered the master bedroom, she found two wrapped gifts on the end of the bed. Had Marge placed them there? One was marked for Tony, and the other was for her. Erin sat down and unwrapped her gift. Inside was a beautiful, handcrafted photo album with her name on the cover. She opened to the first page and a bittersweet smile rose.

This was where her childhood photos had ended up. Delores had found that shoe box of her mother's and had created a beautiful memento. All Erin's memories were lovingly preserved. Delores had expressed her kindness to Erin in the only way she seemed to know how: she did a project—a beautiful project. As Erin turned each page, she realized this was Delores's way of showing Jack's two children that she cared about them.

Erin took her time looking at each photo, remembering the moment the photo represented.

Delores seemed to have known, in an uncanny way, the order to put the photos in. Perhaps Erin's father had helped with the project months ago, separating out the hundreds of pictures.

The last photo in Erin's album was a picture of her wrapped up in a blanket, sitting beside her father on the tailgate of their old station wagon. Her nine-year-old grin was a great big tangle of teeth, and she was sleepy-eyed in the hints of first light. Erin remembered the morning that shot was taken. Her father had gotten them up to watch the sun rise at the beach on Easter. Her mom was the one taking the picture. By Erin's calculations her mom would have been very pregnant with her brother and not eager to have her picture taken.

Erin's dad was sitting beside her on the car's tailgate with his chin up, shoulders back, and his face to the fresh ocean breeze. She could almost hear his roaring voice. "Top of the morning, Glory!"

She stared at the photo for some time. The man beside her on that tailgate was the father she would hold foremost in her memory. That image of him when he was in the prime of his life, fit and happy, and with his blue eyes twinkling with mischief. That was the Jack O'Riley who would soon be escorted into eternity, the Jack O'Riley who would bow before the Maker of heaven and earth and with his resurrected tongue confess, as he had his entire life, that Jesus Christ was Lord of all.

All would be revealed. All would be made right. The rancid sting of death would be swallowed up in victory.

Soon.

22

May the good earth be soft under you
When you rest upon it,
And may it rest easy over you
When at the last you lay out under it,
And may it rest so lightly over you
That your soul may be out from under it
Quickly and up and off
And be on its way to God.

For the next three days Jack O'Riley lingered, barely breathing, bobbing between heaven and earth the way the mountain range of white clouds hovered on the horizon each night at the edge of the deep, wide ocean out the front window.

On Tuesday morning Erin woke just before dawn. Instead of rolling over and trying to capture a few more hours of sleep, she felt compelled to get up. Wrapping her robe around her and pulling on a pair of her dad's socks that she had been using in lieu of slippers, she padded into the living room.

Tony was asleep on the couch. Their father was

in the same position he had been in for days. Nothing had changed.

She tiptoed closer and placed her finger under his nostrils as she had done a dozen times over the last week or so, being careful not to touch his upper lip.

His breath peacefully ruffled against the skin on her finger. He was still here. She gazed at his emaciated frame in the glow of the morning light that came through the front window like a silver mist. The hollowed-out places where thick jowls had once been made him look delicate and frail. Reaching over, she gently stroked his snowy white crown.

His jaw went slack. The motion surprised her. He had been so still for so long. Then she heard a sound rise up from the depth of his chest. It was a faint gasp followed by a tone that was closer to a musical note than a sigh. The sound was barely audible. If she hadn't been only inches away from him she would have missed it.

He made no motion and seemed to have no breath.

Erin held her finger under his nose. She placed the palm of her hand in front of his open mouth. Leaning over, she placed her ear against his chest.

No sound. No movement. No breath.

He was gone.

Erin drew back, feeling as if a surge of ice water were running through her veins. For weeks she had known this moment was at hand. For days she had checked him, thinking he was gone, and then checked again only to find that the shadow of life still clung to him.

No more.

God had called his name.

Erin lingered in the awful holiness of the moment.

Her father was dead. Jack O'Riley was no longer earthbound. His soul had soared across the sea. The absence of his presence became vivid as daylight filled the room, making his features clearer. It was evident that the essence of her father no longer was there. His body was empty. She couldn't explain it any other way but to say that she was looking at a shell. A human shell. The eternal soul that had used that shell was gone.

Erin felt an unexpected sense of relief. In a way her father had been released from prison, the prison of his broken body. He could walk again and run and lift both arms. And he could sing. That thought comforted her the most. He could sing to the One who called him by name.

Erin stepped over to the couch. "Tony. Tony, wake up. He's gone."

Tony sprang off the couch and repeated the same checks that Erin had. He looked at her, distraught. "When? Just now?"

"Yes." She told him how she had gotten up and was with him at the last breath.

They stood for a long moment with their arms around each other. Orphans together. Reunited by means of a severe mercy.

"I'll call Marge," Tony said in a low voice.

Erin went into the kitchen, put on the kettle for a morning cup of tea. She was very matter-of-fact. Not emotional. For a moment she wondered if something was wrong with her. Maybe she was dreaming all this.

No, she wasn't dreaming. This was real. Her father was gone.

She realized she hadn't cried. She thought it was because she had no more tears. They all had been squeezed out of her over the past two months. That was why this wasn't a shock. Her father had inched his way to glory with one small breath followed by another until there were no more. She had journeyed beside him, shedding one tear followed by another until at this final moment, when he reached the destination, there were no more.

Not until Jack's memorial service on Saturday did Erin cry. Her sons were all there. Sierra sat on one side of her, Mike on the other. Tony took on the role of greeter, extending the "right hand of fellowship" to every one of the eighty-five folks from Moss Cove who came to the service. Erin knew their father would have liked seeing his son take over the role of the church usher that way.

Her father also would have liked the way everyone drove through the afternoon mist and packed into Hidden Cottage, where they ate and talked about Jack. Paddy and some of his pals stayed on the deck under a tarp covering that Tony had rigged for the occasion to keep the autumn rain off them. Every time Erin looked out the kitchen window, the boys on the deck raised their bottles to her and gave her a nod.

Sylvia kept herself busy in the kitchen. At one point she slipped her arm around Erin and gave her a hug. "How are you holding up?"

"I'm doing okay. Thanks. I know my dad appreciated all your visits, Sylvia."

"Least I could do. He was one of a kind, that's for sure. I half expected Delores to show up at the memorial service. It would have been honoring to him if she had come. Did I tell you she called me to check in on him a couple of times? Up until a week ago, then she stopped calling."

Erin debated how much she should divulge to Sylvia. Anything Erin said would be spread all around; so she resisted providing any further details. Then she realized that what she had to say about Delores needed to be spread around.

"She came to see my dad last week." Erin selected her words carefully. "Her nephew brought her because she was too weak to drive."

Sylvia lifted her reading glasses from the beaded chain around her neck and placed them on the bridge of her nose, as if trying to read the fine print in Erin's expression.

"Delores has cancer. Stage four. I called her when Dad died and left a message with the details of the service. Her nephew called me back and said she would be with us today in her thoughts and prayers."

Sylvia looked stunned. No one out newsed her on any topic.

"Delores stayed with my dad as long as she could. She made her peace with him, and I've made my peace with her. And, you know, Delores was right. We shouldn't assume things about people."

"I had no idea." Sylvia shook her head and mumbled, "Well, shut my mouth and call me a crow."

Erin had a feeling that would never happen.

Sylvia turned, to go spread the word, no doubt. But she stopped and asked, "Then who gets this place? Not Delores."

Erin nodded that, yes, the cottage was to go to Delores.

"Then if you don't mind my asking, who is Delores going to leave it to?"

"I don't know."

Sylvia looked Erin up and down once more. "You certainly are a calm sea over all this. Do you know what this land is worth? This ocean-front property covers more than three acres."

"I've seen the real estate report."

"And you and your brother aren't going to fight for it?"

Mike, Tony, and Erin had talked several hours about the possible scenarios. In the end, all three of them agreed that they wouldn't contest whatever Delores listed in her will. She had put equal sweat and tears into the place while she lived there with their father. As his wife, it was her choice.

"No, we're not going to fight about anything."

Sylvia cocked her head. "You're not?"

"No."

"You know, I will say this for you O'Rileys. You make it seem like God could be real. You know what I'm saying? There's a lot of strength and integrity in all of you. As for your father, he was something special, wasn't he?"

All Erin could do was nod and offer a small smile.

Over the next week, more silent smiles came to her lips. On Sunday she hugged her brother good-bye and promised to visit him one day on Maui. On Monday she and Mike had their final breakfast at Jenny Bee's Fish House and said good-bye to Jo and the rest of the crew.

Erin especially smiled when she closed the persimmon red door for the final time and took one last stroll out to the bench. The world was gray and shrouded in clouds. She couldn't distinguish where the ocean ended on the horizon and where the sky began.

She stuck her hands into the pockets of her green fleece jacket because she knew her season here was ending as it had begun. In silence.

As Mike backed the car up the gravel driveway, she listened to the sound of the tiny pebbles under the tires. The car seemed to know its way along the two-lane winding road through the Narnia-like forest where brilliant touches of yellows and reds made it clear that autumn was on its way.

During the long drive home, Erin mostly slept. She was bone weary.

When she and Mike arrived home at dusk on a warm Southern California October evening, Erin noticed three things. First, the flower beds in the front of their home were a disaster. Second, none of the windows in her home looked out at the ocean. She knew she was going to miss the view of the changing sea. Third, she had an extraordinarily vast assortment of clothes hanging in her closet. She had forgotten how many outfits she owned.

Their first morning back home, Erin made eggs for breakfast. She walked out to the driveway and kissed her husband good-bye. He gave her an affectionate pat on her narrow backside.

"Big day for you."

Erin gave him a brave smile. "Yes. Yes it is."

Mike pulled out of the driveway. His old BMW that had stayed in Oregon with Erin was in dire need of a run through the car wash. Erin ignored the withering flowers along the front walk. She made her way back inside and closed the door. The house felt very still. She heard a dull, steady tick from the clock and a low hum from the dryer. Erin missed the ocean with its dependable rhythm and varying shades and shapes. She missed the gulls' cries and the small creak the persimmon red door made every time anyone came or went. Most of all, Erin missed her father.

A small chill went up her bare arms. Padding her way to the laundry room, she pulled the green fleece from the dryer and put it on. It smelled like lavender fabric softener and not like salt and fish. She walked through the house, touching the back of her sofa, straightening the chairs around the dining room table, reacquainting herself with her surroundings and reminding herself this was her home.

In the same way that she had entered the uncharted stretch of time at the Hidden Cottage and accepted that being there was the new normal, she now returned home and accepted this as the new normal. Picking up the phone, Erin dialed the number.

"The Happiest Day. This is Sharlene."

"Hi, it's Erin."

"Erin, how are you? I got your message about

your dad passing. I sent flowers. Did you get them?"

"Yes. They were beautiful. Thank you."

"I hoped you would understand that I couldn't make it up there for the memorial service."

"Of course. I didn't expect you to come. I just wanted you to know the details."

"How are you doing?"

"I'm tired, but I'm okay. I thought I better call and let you know that I never received the papers I needed to sign to turn over my half of the business."

Sharlene paused just a moment before saying, "Didn't you get my e-mail?"

"Which e-mail?"

"Oh, Erin! I feel awful. Are you saying you didn't see it?"

"I don't know. I haven't had any e-mails come from you for quite a few weeks."

"Oh, no, this isn't good."

"Do you want to resend it?"

"No. Let's meet. Can you be at Café Kate in ten minutes?"

"Okay." Erin scrambled to put on something other than her green fleece jacket and sweatpants.

Sharlene was already at the outdoor table where they used to always sit. She popped up and gave Erin one of her tiptoe hugs as Erin leaned over trying to compensate for the variance in their heights.

Erin hadn't expected this sort of reception. For weeks she had anticipated that the next time she and Sharlene met face-to-face it would be in front of a lawyer as they signed final papers.

"It's so good to see you." Sharlene sat down and pushed one of the two lattes over to Erin's side of the table. "Hope you don't mind. I went ahead and ordered."

"No, that's fine. Thanks."

"I should have called you," Sharlene said. "I knew I should have called you when you didn't respond to my e-mail. I just guessed that you were in agreement with what I'd said and were busy with your dad."

"In agreement?" Erin asked. "About what?"

"Erin, I withdrew my offer to buy your half of the business."

Erin leaned back. This was significant news. How did she miss that e-mail?

Sharlene leaned forward. Her eyes expressed sincerity. "I wish I'd never suggested that we split up our partnership. I panicked. I was an insensitive idiot. There are stronger terms than that, but I'll stick with *idiot* for the moment. Honestly, Erin, I couldn't sleep at night after I realized what I was trying to do."

Erin felt numb. She had come to accept the loss of the business over the last few weeks and never expected Sharlene to change her mind. Sharlene was a determined woman. When she had said she was meeting with an attorney, Erin was certain their partnership was being resolved.

"What I told you in the e-mail was that I wouldn't bother you. I said that if you wanted to call me, then by all means I wanted to talk to you anytime. But I figured that you were taking as long as you needed with your dad, and when you came back, we would figure out how to pick up where we left off." Sharlene paused, waiting for Erin to respond.

"I don't know what to say."

Sharlene's eyebrows rose. "You're not thinking about pulling out, are you? I mean, I finally got some full-time help, but I don't want to go it alone. I want us to work together. We're such a great team. What are you thinking?"

"I'm not sure what to think. I mean, you were right about being stuck with all the responsibility and needing to make a decision to keep the company going. I understand why you did what you did. I felt like I was the insensitive one who was too caught up in my emergency to recognize the sort of emergency situation I'd put *you* in. I'm sorry, Sharlene. I'm really sorry."

"Oh, Erin, I'm sorry, too."

The two friends reached across the table and gave each other's hand a squeeze. Erin felt her eyes well with tears. After so many weeks of dealing with loss, she didn't know how to receive this turnaround.

"I'll tell you the most difficult part in all this." Sharlene pulled her hand back and dabbed under each eye with a napkin. "I couldn't bear the thought of losing your friendship."

Erin nodded. "I know. I felt the same way."

Sharlene drew in a deep breath. She fanned her eyes with her hand. "I can't stop crying. Erin, this is our shared dream. We're going to go the distance together on this. Agreed?"

"Agreed."

They shook hands just as they had done at this same table several years ago when they first met and decided to start their business together.

"To new beginnings." Sharlene lifted her latte.

"To new beginnings," Erin echoed, giving the edge of Sharlene's paper cup a dull *fwap*.

Sharlene stopped with her cup suspended in midair. "Oh! I heard an Irish blessing. I was trying to remember it. I know you're the one who likes to bring out one of your mom's verses or your dad's sayings at moments like this. But I found one, and I've been saving it for such a moment as this. Here it is. 'May the strength of three be in our journey.'"

"Ah, the Blessing of the Trinity. Yes, and may it be so."

"You already know it?"

Erin wished she hadn't blurted out that it was the Blessing of the Trinity. She loved that Sharlene was thinking of how to keep some of their small traditions going. In an effort to move ahead with a new tradition, Erin said, "How about if we meet like this every week? For the first hour we have to agree not to talk about business at all."

"Sounds good to me. Sounds very good, actually."

Every week for the next few months Erin and Sharlene met at Café Kate at three o'clock on Thursday afternoons. The time together was like medicine. Sharlene listened as Erin processed some of the lingering experiences from her time at Hidden Cottage. Then Erin listened as Sharlene talked through the frustrations she had encountered during Erin's absence. By the third time they met they were back in sync and ready to be done with talking about themselves. They were excited to get going with a restructuring plan for the future of The Happiest Day.

The plan they came up with was that they would continue to work out of their homes and both take on a full-time assistant. It was a brilliant solution, and as a result the business continued to grow. In December they hired another part-time assistant, and when February rolled around, they gathered everyone at Sharlene's house to celebrate the two-year anniversary of their business.

Mike and Erin pulled up in front of Sharlene's a few minutes before the party was scheduled to start. Erin's cell phone rang. She pulled it from her shoulder bag and checked the number. She didn't recognize the 503 area code and number, but she went ahead and answered, planning to tell the caller that she would return the call in the morning.

To her surprise, Delores's nephew was the person phoning.

After leaving several unanswered messages on Delores's cell phone last fall, Erin had given up hope that she would hear anything more from Delores or her nephew. Then the week after Christmas, Delores's nephew had left a message for Erin, letting her know that Delores had passed away that afternoon. Erin sent a card and flowers, even though the message indicated there would be no memorial service. Only a small graveside benediction with immediate family. It was clear that Erin and Mike weren't considered immediate family.

"I'm calling to let you know you'll be receiving a letter from Delores's attorney," the nephew told Erin as she sat in the car next to Mike.

Erin looked at Mike and felt her heart pounding. "Why, may I ask?"

"My aunt left her estate to you." His announcement was weighted with disappointment.

"Her estate?"

Mike's eyebrows went up.

"Yes. The cabin on the coast. The place your dad left to her in his will. She signed it over to you."

For a moment Erin couldn't speak.

"Hello? Are you still there?"

"Yes, I'm here. Are you sure she left Hidden Cottage to me?"

Mike reached over and gave Erin's leg a squeeze.

"Of course I'm sure." The nephew sounded sullen.

"But I . . . I assumed she would pass it on to you."

"So did I. But that's how it was with my aunt. She never liked it when people assumed anything. Especially if they assumed things about her."

"Yes, I know," Erin said quietly.

"As the executor of her will, I'm calling as a courtesy for the attorney. He needs to know if your address has changed."

Erin repeated her address, and he hung up.

"Thank you," Erin said to the sound of a dial tone. She put down her phone and turned to Mike.

"Well?" he asked.

All she could do was nod.

"Delores left Hidden Cottage to you? Really?"

"Yes," she said in barely a whisper. "Yes!"

In her mind's eye, Erin could see the view out the front windows of Hidden Cottage. She saw the mysterious, magnificent, vast stretch of the wild Pacific. Above the blustery blue rose an especially charming fleet of clouds, all tumbling together and skittering out across the horizon. She saw herself dancing on the deck with Mike and their children and their grandchildren. She saw the persimmon red door, and she smiled.

Turning to her stunned husband, Erin playfully said,

> Her smile is as wide as the ocean,
> She lives in the cottage by the sea,
> She's the daughter of Jack O'Riley,
> So give her a kiss for me.

And so Mike kissed her. And she kissed him back. They looked at each other and started laughing, laughing as neither of them had laughed in a very long time.

FROM THE AUTHOR'S NOTES

There is a real Hidden Cottage by the Sea and here it is—red door and everything! Friends of ours owned this wonderful hideaway for many years. During the sixteen years our family lived in Portland, Oregon, we enjoyed a number of getaways to Hidden Cottage. When I started writing this book, my husband and I stayed here for three days and listened to the sounds of the ocean along the wild Oregon coast.

Here I am at the red door. It was easy for my imagination to picture Erin standing at this door in her many states of mind and emotions. I could also imagine how a busy woman from the suburbs could easily develop a strong affection for a special place like this.

I love the way this picture gives a sense of the smallness of Hidden Cottage and the ruggedness of the ocean at low tide. There is a distinct beauty to the Northwest and a memorable fragrance that lingers in the air. It's a blend of Douglas fir and salty sea breezes.

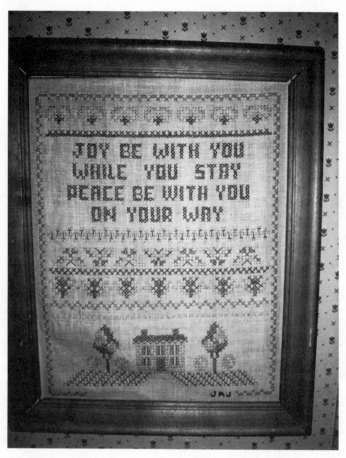

This sampler hangs in the upstairs bedroom at the real Hidden Cottage. When I went there to start working on this book, the sampler gave me the idea of including Irish blessings at the beginning of each chapter. What makes this hand-stitched sampler even more special is that it was lovingly made by my sister Julie, who gave it to our mutual friends, the owners of Hidden Cottage. She stitched it more than thirty-five years ago, and the blessing has remained in that little hideaway all these years.

Tiny kitchen with a view. Here's what we could see from the kitchen window and what I imagined Erin looking out at as she made her morning Irish breakfast cuppa.

Living room with a view. It was clear as I was writing that if this was Jack's daily view from his front window, there was no way he wanted to give that up.

Robin
Jones Gunn

Robin would love to keep in touch with you via her Robin's Nest Newsletter. You can sign up on her website, www.robingunn.com. While you're there, visit her Online Shop to find out more about her other books with Howard Books. You can also keep up with Robin on her Facebook Public Figure Page, listed as Robin Jones Gunn Author (https://www.facebook.com/pages/Robin-Jones-Gunn/110691292261) or on Twitter (@RobinGunn).

COTTAGE BY THE SEA
Reading Group Guide
Discussion Questions

1. A theme throughout the book was the idea of hidden things. What were some things you noticed that were hidden in the beginning of the story and then later revealed? How did those revelations change Erin and the other characters in the story?

2. Looking at each of the key women in this story, what three or four words would you use to describe her life: Erin? Sharlene? Delores? Sierra? Which woman can you most relate to at this point in your journey?

3. How did Erin's heart toward her father change throughout the book? What do you think led to that growth? Do you think her father's heart changed? How?

4. Both Erin and Tony received words of healing from their dad. What did he say that impacted them so much? What is the one thing you wish you could hear from your

father? Your mother? What is the one thing you would like to say to them? What is the one thing you would like to say to your children? If it is still possible, would you be willing to tell them?

5. Throughout the book Erin's stress was evidenced by the way she was torn in two directions: caring for her father and investing in her new business venture with Sharlene. Have you ever had a season of life where you felt torn in two directions? What was pulling you, and what was the end result? What and who helped you to make it through that time in life?

6. Looking at the key men in the story, can you describe how each of them changed/grew as the story unfolded: Mike? Jack? Tony? Jordan?

7. How did the "cottage by the sea" tie into the story's development? How did Jack and Delores describe the cottage before they renovated? In what ways did the cottage's transformation parallel Erin's?

8. What role did Erin's mother play in this story? What older woman has shaped your life? How?

9. "There are no shortcuts in committed love. This is your path. No matter how long or lonely it may be right now, to experience the fullness of love, you must go the distance. Only the strongest and bravest stay on the path. And you, my darling girl, have been given everything you need to be among the strongest and bravest."

Erin's mother gave her this advice at a crucial time in life. What thoughts come to mind as you read it? What do you think she means when she says that Erin has been given everything she needs?

10. "It's not always about what I think it's about. The older I get, the more convinced I am that God has a hidden objective tucked into every disagreeable situation I encounter. If only I would collect those sparkling gems of truth while I'm in the midst of each difficult relationship or experience, I'd leave this earth a wise and spiritually wealthy woman."

What were the hidden objectives the Lord had in store for Erin through this story? Looking at this season of your life, what do you think is the hidden objective that God has tucked away for you to glean?

A Conversation with Robin Jones Gunn

1. On several occasions in the story Erin had a perfect scripture or blessing to apply to what is going on in her life, such as when she reads Psalm 90:17 to mark the first day of business for The Happiest Day. How does your own personal faith influence your everyday life? Do you have a favorite passage of scripture?

I am continually seeing God's hand at work in everyday situations and I'm always amazed at how his care for us is so deliberate. My faith grows every time I trust God in a new situation and see how he works out all the details. My grandmother kept several journals where she wrote favorite verses and sayings. I inherited those wee books and have learned a lot from what she jotted down. I keep a journal as well and frequently add a new passage of scripture or a memorable moment.

Psalm 139 is my favorite chapter in the Bible and has been since I was in high school. Over the past few years Acts 20:24 has meant a lot to me. "But my life is worth nothing unless I use it for finishing the work assigned me by the LORD Jesus—the work of telling others the Good News about God's wonderful kindness and love."

This is exactly what I long to do with every book I write—to tell others about God's wonderful kindness and love because there is so much to tell!

2. *Cottage by the Sea* **is a novel built on the intricacies of family relationships and friendships. How have your experiences influenced the way that you create these fictional relationships?**

This story draws from what I went through emotionally when my father had a stroke more than fifteen years ago and how he was partially paralyzed and unable to speak. He found ways to express that he loved us and those memories are still vivid and powerful. The stroke brought his emotional responses to the surface and that caused him to be more expressive than he'd ever been. A lot of healing took place during those last five and a half years of his life. My mom cared for him at home in California the entire time and she did an excellent job. This story needed more conflict than what my real-life experience had been. So when I overheard a woman on a long flight talking about her difficult stepmother situation I knew I had the imaginary tangle I was looking for and created the character of Delores.

3. **On your website, you say that teenagers at your church first challenged you to try writing fiction. How has your role as a mentor to other young women influenced the way you live your life? How has it influenced your career?**

The girls in our youth group were reading books that were way too evocative for their thirteen-year-old hearts. I tried to find other books that would be more nurturing and they suggested I write a story for them. They'd even tell me what to write. That first Christy Miller novel took two years to write and received ten rejections. Each week the girls in the youth group critiqued my chapters and often told me they wanted better role models than the characters in the stories they were reading. They wanted to be shown how to make good choices. They wanted the main character to be a girl they would want to be friends with in real life. It all worked because I learned how to write through the mentoring of those teen girls and now, twenty-five years later, those books are still in print and are mentoring young readers around the world.

I've had a very God-blessed life. So many young women have not. I love having the opportunity to speak truth to young hearts and affirm who they are and how God has dreams for their lives that are beyond any sort of dream they could imagine.

Along with our own daughter, who is now twenty-five and recently married, there has been a stream of young women who have lived with us or spent a lot of time in our home throughout our thirty-five years of marriage. The influence of these women has profoundly impacted what I write about, how the characters develop in the story, and even the outcome of the books. I know from all the reader mail I receive that the stories I write influence women of all ages. What the readers don't know is how much the women in my small circles have inspired and motivated me as I've been busy crafting a new tale. I do believe that the mentoring influence women have with other women is life-giving and essential. This overall theme of friendships between women is what I wrote about in the eight Sisterchicks novels.

4. **You have often said that you love traveling. How have your worldwide travels inspired your writing? Where would you like to go next?**

God made such an amazing world with such fascinating people. I'd love to see it all!

In *Under a Maui Moon* I drew from many of the experiences we've had on Maui and the deep love I have for Hawaii. *Canary Island Song* is set in the Canary Islands, an exotic locale I've visited three times and would love to visit again. The flamenco lessons, camel rides, and fabulous foods I was introduced to there all became part of the novel.

While I was writing the Sisterchicks novels the publisher asked for them to be set in places like Paris, Venice, and Australia. I was given a travel budget so I could visit each locale before writing about it. Talk about a writer's dream come true!

I'm on the board of directors for Media Associates International, an international organization that provides training for writers and publishers in difficult places around the world. As a result of that position I've taught workshops in Brazil, Kenya, England, and Bulgaria. Every place I've visited has ended up in a book somehow. Interacting with so many people in various cultures has given me valuable insights into human nature and given me deeper understanding of political and social complexities.

5. **Erin makes a lot of sacrifices to be with her father during his last months. How have you made sacrifices for your loved ones? Looking back, would you make the same decisions knowing what you know today?**

Nothing heroic. Over the years I have made sacrifices for my loved ones and my loved ones have made sacrifices for me. But nothing to the extent of what Erin gave up in the story. I would make all the same decisions again knowing what I know today. However, I would hope that I would be less fearful of what the outcome was going to be and less fretful about trying to recoup time, energy, or resources that were given up or given away. God always seems to faithfully return a double portion of all that we give if we do it with pure motives and out of genuine love for the other person.

6. **Although the primary audience for *Cottage by the Sea* is adult readers, it could be an appropriate story for younger readers as well. As you are writing, do you picture your audience?**

I agree that readers of all ages will be able to relate to this story. Readers who have followed me for a while will undoubtedly be eager to have a peek at Jordan and Sierra's wedding since this is the same Sierra as in all the Sierra Jensen books. The story of how Jordan and Sierra met is in *Love Finds You in Sunset Beach, Hawaii.*

It has gotten easier to picture my audience with all the photos viewable when readers contact me on my Robin Jones Gunn Facebook page or via Twitter at Robin Gunn. When I first started writing I had a bulletin board in my office and whenever I received a photo from a reader I added it to the board. I soon had a gorgeous collage of expectant faces looking down on me as I typed my little heart out. Images and comments from readers are ever in the forefront of my thoughts as I write.

7. **Between your work with your church, keeping up with your family, your tour schedule, and your writing, how do you find time for yourself?**

My agent and I have worked together for twenty-five years. She was here visiting me last year and the two of us took some time away from our meetings to go to the beach, nestle our feet in the sand, and just sit together in great contentment and listen to the ocean as the sun set. "How often do you do this?" she asked. My answer was, "Counting this time? Twice." She gave me one of her best agent looks and said, "That's going to change." And it has.

She and I also made ourselves promise that just like the women in *Canary Island Song* we would show ourselves a kindness once a month. I've done things I'd never allowed my busy little self to do before, such as getting a facial and going to the movies in the middle of a perfectly good workday. My friend Jill calls this "mental health improvement" moments.

It makes me think of how Jesus told his disciples to "come apart and rest a while." My husband is a counselor and he reminds me every now and then that if we don't "come apart" we may soon find our lives are about to "come apart." The interesting thing to me is that I love what I do. All of it. Writing, speaking, traveling, and entertaining in our home. That makes it even more essential to learn how to set an internal timer that goes off and says, "Stop what you're doing and go put your feet in the sand and just listen."

8. **On your website (robingunn.com), you write that you never "set out to be a**

writer," but at this point in your life, with more than seventy-five books published, is there anything else that you could see yourself doing with your life if you weren't a writer?

No.
Well, maybe. I love to speak to women's groups and to groups of teen girls. I've been doing more of that lately so maybe that's part of what's next. I send out a Robin's Nest Newsletter and give updates of new book releases and speaking event locations. The sign-up link is on my website and my Facebook page.

9. What is your favorite part about living in Hawaii?

I love the mornings. I love watching the sunrise and listening to the doves when they give their canticle of praise through the open bedroom windows at first light. My favorite time to go swimming is before 7:00 a.m. I walk down to the water, about a mile away, and stride directly into the ocean without pausing. It makes me feel so alive. I bob and splash around for about half an hour, watching the fishermen and paddle boarders and joggers on the beach. Then I grab my towel and walk home, glistening as the salt drops dry on my arms.

I also love the people we hang out with. We have lots of kindred spirits in our church community.

10. What are you working on now?

I just finished the fourth book in the Katie Weldon series. It's titled *Finally and Forever* and is set in Kenya. The whole time I was writing that story I felt as if I were vividly reliving all the experiences I had in Nairobi three years ago. My desk was covered with photos and excerpts from my journal. When I turned the book in I literally felt as if I had been to Africa and back.

What's next? Good stuff! I'll be revealing details when I can in the upcoming Robin's Nest Newsletters, so please sign up, dear readers! Flit on over to www.robingunn.com or go to my Facebook page, Robin Jones Gunn, public figure.

And one more thought. For any of you who are in a situation like Erin in this story and are giving and giving at a great sacrifice to yourself, your family, or perhaps your career, keep doing what you're doing with an uncluttered heart. Give generously and with much love. God will give back to you even more. And make sure you take time to "come apart" and show yourself a kindness so that you can rest a while and be renewed.

Aloha, Robin

Center Point Large Print
600 Brooks Road / PO Box 1
Thorndike ME 04986-0001 USA

(207) 568-3717

US & Canada:
1 800 929-9108
www.centerpointlargeprint.com